PER

MW01686443

PERMUTED PRESS

NEEDS **YOU** TO HELP

SPREAD THE INFECTION

FOLLOW US!

FACEBOOK.COM/PERMUTEDPRESS

TWITTER.COM/PERMUTEDPRESS

REVIEW US!

amazon.com | BARNES&NOBLE | goodreads | YOUR BLOG

GET INFECTED!

SIGN UP FOR OUR MAILING LIST AT **PERMUTEDPRESS.COM**

PERMUTED PRESS

THE TILIAN VIRUS

THE PANDEMIC SEQUENCE BOOK 1

TOM CALEN

A PERMUTED PRESS book

ISBN (trade paperback): 978-1-61868-090-7
ISBN (eBook): 978-1-61868-091-4

Cover art by Roy Migabon.

This book is a work of fiction. People, places, events, and situations are the product of the author's imagination. Any resemblance to actual persons, living or dead, or historical events, is purely coincidental.

PERMUTED PRESS

For my sister,
Who has encouraged all my crazy dreams.

Disease is the retribution of outraged Nature.
-Hosea Ballou

CHAPTER ONE

The achingly soulful voice of Jeff Buckley roused him from sleep. Eyes barely open, the faint light of the dawn illuminated the small room enough for him locate the half-empty pack of Marlboro Lights on the nightstand. A grunt and the flick of a lighter later, Mike Allard sat up in bed. The snooze button was not an option this morning as he had scheduled a parent conference at seven. With one hand towards the ashtray and the other petting his equally tired gray terrier, the second-year teacher listened as "I Want Someone Badly," drew to a close.

After the final note, Mike stubbed out the cigarette and tossed the covers aside to shuffle towards the bathroom for the morning ritual of a hot shower and shave. As the water quickly turned cold, he shut it off and toweled dry. Frequent trips to the gym had kept the twenty-three year old in better shape than most of the guys with whom he had graduated college. Leaning closer to the fogged mirror, Mike checked the barely-there brown stubble and opted to leave the scruff for the day. The high school had a "casual" policy allowing the staff to wear jeans, so in a way, he felt the scruff went not only with his attire but also his mood.

Gazelle, now fully awake, stood at the back door waiting for her morning walk. He could not help but laugh when the dog danced in a chaotic circle once he attached her collar. The morning was crisp as the two stepped out into the backyard, the leash extending to its full sixteen feet. Gazelle dashed to her area and did her business and within minutes, Mike had given the dog a treat, locked up the house, and revved the engine in his truck.

Tennessee spring was beginning and the temperature was forgiving if one did not have time to warm up his vehicle. The drive to work was a short one through a few back country roads. He parked, taking one last drag on another cigarette, popped two pieces of gum into his mouth and headed into the building.

The rural high school looked rather uninviting to most outsiders. With its gray pod structures, the facility bore more of a resemblance to a nuclear fallout shelter than an institution of education. And a rather rundown shelter, at that. The roofs had several areas of rust, which provided the only splash of color. The growth of any flowers and grass still lagged behind the calendar. Mike hustled past the gray columns with their chipping paint and entered the main office.

"Morning, Mike, you're here early," greeted the school's aging receptionist. Much like the school, Mrs. Holigan had seen better days. But, also like the high school, she was an institution not only in the building, but in the small farming community as well.

"Yeah, parent conference this morning."

"The conference room should be unlocked. Are y'all going to want some bottles of water?"

Mrs. Holigan, whose children and grandchildren had long since graduated from John Moore High School, had essentially adopted not only the students, but also the staff as her own. As Mike was about to reply that he would grab them, Mrs. Holigan answered the ringing phone.

"Good morning, John Moore High School. How can I help you?"

Mike went to the rear of the office to check his mailbox and pour himself a cup of the receptionist's famous coffee. Most faculty members went through several cups of it by the time the dismissal bell sounded at 3:00 PM. Not wanting to take away from the flavor, Mike skipped the milk and sugar and returned to the front desk where Mrs. Holigan was wrapping up the call.

"Okay, darling, you tell him to feel better and don't worry about a thing. You just take care of that boy. Something sure is going around. I had to use up my entire substitute list to cover teachers today. If you need us to send work home, let us know. Okay. Take care now. God bless."

Mike smiled behind his coffee mug. In an overly politically correct field like education, a school official ending a call with a blessing would have been frowned upon. But with Mrs. Holigan it came out as natural as one says "hello" and "goodbye" and everyone ignored her little rule breaking.

As she hung up the phone, she turned to him saying, "Well, darling, looks like you got in early for nothing. That was Maybelline Turner, Stacy's momma, and she says that Stacy came down with an awful high fever last night and they won't be able to make it in for your meeting."

Actually, it was not *his* meeting at all. Stacy's mother had asked for the meeting to discuss one of her daughter's test grades. Normally, Mike would have been able to take care of that over the phone, but Maybelline Turner was one of those "helicopter" parents - a bit too involved in her child's education. A week did not go by that there was not an email or voicemail from her. Still, in an age of declining parental involvement, Mike Allard indulged her.

With an unspoken expletive for the unnecessary early arrival, he thanked Mrs. Holigan for the message and headed to his classroom in the history pod.

The interior of the school was only a slight improvement from its exterior. Most of the lockers bore the dents and scratches that came from decades of overuse. The ceiling tiles were stained with water from the leaking roofs. At the beginning of each school year, many teachers pooled money together to buy paint for the walls of their respective pods. It was perhaps the only improvement the school had seen in over thirty years. Many petitioned the school board to improve or even repair the school. Yet, whenever the time came to pass a tax increase to cover the costs, the initiative always received a resounding defeat.

Mike's room, Room 15A (though there was no 15B) was one of five classrooms in the pod. He flipped on the lights, walked over to his desk and sat down. The room was not large, but likewise did not feel cramped. With the pod structure, classrooms were shaped like a Trivial Pursuit wedge, with one end significantly wider than its opposite side. Thanks to the night custodians, the thirty-five desks were arranged in seven neat rows. Mike kept his desk off to one side, as he preferred to lecture from a podium and stool.

With an hour to kill before first period European History, Mike decided to get ahead on lesson plans and catch up on grading. He enjoyed teaching. He enjoyed working with students and sharing his expertise in history. However, he hated grading papers, exams, and quizzes, etc. To that end, he planned as few of them each semester as his principal would allow. The old guard of teachers frowned upon his grading methods. But he was fresh out of college and only in his second year of teaching. He preferred to employ new tactics, which to him seemed to capture the interests of his students more than the dusty methods of previous years.

The hour slipped by quickly and he could hear the steady increase of teen voices roaming the halls, lockers opening and closing, cell phones ringing, and the other usual sounds of the school coming to life.

"Mr. Allard," came the soft voice of Michelle Lafkin, a junior from his fifth period American History II class. She was the type of student every teacher dreamed of: studious, engaging, genuinely interested in learning, and not the least bit pretentious. She came from an impoverished home where the mom had long since run out, leaving Michelle's father to raise her and her two younger brothers. She had the intelligence that all but guaranteed a full-ride scholarship to college, which would be the only way she could afford a post-secondary degree.

"Good morning, Michelle. What's up?" Mike replied, happy to turn away from the barely decreased stack of ungraded work.

"Well, I was wondering if there was any way you could give me the assignments for the next few days? My brothers have the flu, and my dad can't afford to take any more time off work, so I'm going to have to stay home with them for a bit."

It was a very unusual request from Michelle. Since Mike had been teaching at John Moore, she was known to have one of the best attendance records. He normally was not a fan of the "take-out" style of education for absentees, but Mike knew that if this particular student made the request, the need must be genuine.

"Sure. Let me run and make copies of my notes and the worksheets for the next few days. It should only take a minute."

"Thanks. My dad's waiting in the car. I'll just tell him I'll be out in a bit."

As the petite blonde hurried out of the room and towards the exit, Mike gathered his notes binder and made his way to the copy room.

As he approached the room, Mike thought he was in luck as the usual line of teachers making last-minute copies was nowhere to be seen. The spreading smile just as quickly faded when he saw why there were no teachers waiting for the copier.

Copier Out of Order stated the hand-written sign taped to the top of the ancient machine. Unlike some teachers, Mike had not gotten in the habit of making copies at local office stores due to the copier's fickle operational status.

"Son of a bitch," he exhaled through gritted teeth, and returned to his room to find Michelle waiting.

"Bad news…the copier's out again. But, how about this? After school I'll make some copies at the library and drop them off at your house?" Mike offered.

Either out of embarrassment of her low-income home, or not wanting to have her teacher go out of his way, Michelle politely refused.

"No, you don't have to do that, Mr. Allard. I can just catch up when I get back to school."

"Nonsense. I pass your neighborhood on the way home. Besides, I owe your dad for the work he did on my truck. I'll be there around five this evening."

One of the benefits of teaching in a small, blue-collar town is the willingness of parents to offer their trade skills at ridiculously low prices. In this instance, Mr. Lafkin had repaired Mike's muffler free of charge. Dropping off school work was the least he could do to return the mechanic's kindness.

Beaming with gratitude, Michelle thanked her history teacher and rushed back out to her waiting father. As he turned back to his desk, the five-minute bell sounded through the halls.

Students began shuffling in, chattering about whatever Monday night television they had watched the evening before. The majority of the girls in this sophomore class were all too serious in their discussion of which woman had been given a rose and which had been sent away by the reality star du jour.

Though not much older than his students, Mike shook his head and smiled with amusement. *If only they could get into World War II the same way,* he thought. With a knack of tying popular culture into his lessons, his amusement grew as he began picturing a scenario in which Chamberlain hands a rose to Hitler to explain appeasement.

The late bell rang and the students took their seats. It always amazed Mike that students chose to sit it the same seats day after day, yet they would have balked if he assigned them seats. He greeted the class and began to take roll.

After sending the office his list of absentees—four in

total—Mike continued his lecture notes on the Treaty of Versailles from the day before. For the next forty-five minutes, the class scribbled away in their notebooks. All too soon the bell rang and the students dispersed, quickly replaced by his second period World History class. The day rolled on, and the end of fourth period came quickly, which meant Mike had a lunch period to recharge before the final two classes of the day.

Opting not to trust his luck with the cafeteria's culinary creations, Mike instead raided the vending machine in the teachers lounge. Today, unlike most days, the faces in the room belonged mostly to strangers. Mrs. Holigan had indeed had to call in back-up substitute teachers. Easing into one of the cushioned chairs around the conference-style table, he took in the lunchtime conversation.

"I just hope my kids don't end up catching it. My husband just got over the flu. Last thing we need is another round of it."

"Oh, I know! I heard at the middle school there was one class with only five kids."

"I haven't had a full class all day. Of course, all the delinquents managed to show up."

This from the security guard turned substitute, who clearly disliked most teenagers, yet eagerly accepted any call to sub. As the conversation dragged on with teachers comparing class absences, Mike nodded and mumbled agreements in between bites of his strawberry Pop Tart and thought about his own classes. Yes, there were kids out sick, or claiming they were sick, but he usually had a few out each day. Third period was the only class that really stood out with eight kids absent. From the Northeast originally, Mike noticed that when the flu struck down South, it struck hard.

Spring break was next week, and he hoped he would not get sick. He had not been home to see his family since Christmas and was eagerly looking forward to the mini-vacation. With lunch almost at an end, Mike headed back to his classroom for the last two periods of the day.

* * *

Making the copies of his notes took less time than expected, and Mike was in his truck heading to the Lafkins. Michelle's home was in a small, make-shift trailer park on a back road off the main thoroughfare. The five or six trailers that made up the park were placed close together and were connected by clothes lines. On most days, the view out of the brown-stained windows of the trailers was the dripping laundry of a neighbor.

Mike pulled into the gravel lot and parked in front of Michelle's home. A minute or so after tapping on the screen door, a tearful Michelle appeared.

"Hi, Mr. Allard," she said with a muffled voice.

"Michelle, what's wrong?"

Stepping out onto the small landing at the top of the steps, the tired looking girl explained that her dad had taken one of her brothers, the younger one, to the hospital because his fever was quite high. She was home watching her other brother, who also seemed to be getting worse. A voice behind him interrupted Mike as he was about to offer help.

"Excuse me, can I help you?" asked a graying woman, in what looked to be her mid-fifties.

"Grandma, this is my teacher, Mr. Allard. He's dropping off some work for me since I missed school today."

With a kind smile, she said, "Not enough teachers like you these days…making house calls."

"It's on my way home, and Michelle is one of my star students. She told me about her brother. Is everything all right?" Mike asked.

The older woman's face faltered slightly with the question, the concern was clear in her eyes, and he could hear the lie behind her words. "Ryan should be fine. They just had to get that fever down."

After another minute or two of small talk, and an offer of

help should they need it, he was back in his truck on his way home. He felt sorry for Michelle and her family. They had so little and he knew that a hospital visit was going to be very costly for them. The girl had all the potential in the world, but it seemed like the world was working against her. He smoked another cigarette while the truck sat in his driveway.

Gazelle was, as always, bouncing with excitement when he walked in the door. After feeding and walking her, Mike sat on the couch and began to flip through the channels. His appetite had waned during the ride home from the Lafkins. With nothing else of interest on, Mike settled for the local evening news.

...to Vanessa Mitchell with more. Good evening, Vanessa.

Good evening, Chris. I'm here at Vanderbilt Hospital in Nashville, where administrators say they saw a surge in emergency room visits today from people complaining of the same flu-like symptoms. One doctor I spoke with said it is unusual for the flu to strike this widely, this late in the season. Across town at Methodist Hospital, the staff says they are facing the same crisis.

Vanessa, we have information coming in from our affiliates across the country with similar reports. Are you able to confirm that a flu outbreak is occurring in the middle Tennessee area?

Yes, Chris. A source at the Tennessee Department of Health confirmed to me that several cities across the country are scrambling to accommodate a veritable flood of emergency room patients.

All due to the flu?

Yes, patients are reporting symptoms which are concurrent with the flu. This is Vanessa Mitchell live from Vanderbilt Hospital. Back to you, Chris.

Thank you, Vanessa. That is certainly a story we will be keeping an eye on. Up next, how to protect your family from germs.

As a commercial began to play, Mike flipped over to one of the cable news channels:

...from London and Rome with similar increases in flu cases.

To another:

...has said it is rare for the flu to spread globally with such speed.

And to another:

...already with more cases than the avian and swine flu combined.

Mike's appetite did not return that night, nor in the early hours of Wednesday, as he sat glued to the television screen. Each hour passed with less and less actual new news. Most reports just repeated another; cities across the globe reported massive cases of the flu. It was during the 3:00 AM newscast, however, that something new was announced. The flu now had a name:

The Tilian Virus.

CHAPTER TWO

"Number fourteen's dead. Mike? Umm…Mike?" came the voice from the shadowed figure in the doorway.

"Yeah."

"Did you hear me?"

"Yeah."

"Okay, number fourteen's dead."

"Yeah, I heard you, Paul," Mike Allard replied with frustration, finally lifting his head from the mound of maps and lists that covered the small work table. Like the table, the room was cramped, worn down, and too small for his needs. The camp was compact, as it needed to be for security, and therefore afforded very little privacy.

"Well, I'm just saying, the doc is gonna want a new one."

"Well, maybe the doc should get off his fat ass and get the next one himself," Mike exclaimed as his fist slammed on the desk, his eyes angry and glaring, locked with those of Paul Jenson's.

Paul stood silent for a moment, letting Allard's anger fill the space between them.

"Can I *please* tell him that?" Paul eventually asked, the sarcasm evident.

With the bark of an unexpected laugh, Mike chuckled, "Yeah, how well do you think that will go over?"

Immediately the tension that had occupied the room

seconds before was replaced with humor. That was Paul Jenson's gift. In his late-twenties, older now than Mike had been at the start of the outbreak, Paul served as his second-in-command in the small refugee camp. Mike had bonded quickly with the former park ranger when they met on the road four years ago. With an aptitude for knowing the land, the young man had proven his worth early. Now, years later, Mike had grown to rely on Paul more than any other in the camp, and considered him not only his chief advisor, but also a friend. It was only due to his experience with mountain farming and land development that the refugees were able to set-up the high altitude camp.

Paul took the open seat by the work table and proceeded to brief Mike on any potential questions or situations that might be brought up in the council meeting. Each week, the core leadership team met to discuss and plan for the camp community. Paul had taken it upon himself to make sure Mike knew as much as he could before going into those meetings.

Shortly, the two men exited the scant warmth offered by the small room and headed into the chill wind of the Appalachian Mountains of Eastern Tennessee. The camp, which sat on the western face of the ridge, was composed of closely situated wooden structures and the occasional tent. Nestled in a small valley a third of the way to the peaks, the height offered a clear view of any approaching threat from below and ensured no risk from above.

The refugees had established the mountain camp some three years ago, at the end of a mild winter. Paul Jenson had helped them select the secure location, create small pockets of arable land, and build structures that would survive the strong winds of the mountains. The ragged community had survived its first winters in the mountains and was now preparing for a fourth.

Crossing the short distance, Mike and Paul entered the community room, the largest structure in the camp, accommodating the small gathering with general ease. The former history teacher took his seat at the head of the uneven meeting table. Paul assumed his usual place standing to the right side of the rear of Mike's seat. The ranger's 6'3" frame forced him to slouch slightly in the low ceilinged structure. Mike had long ago stopped offering him a seat, knowing that Paul would continue his refusal and opt to take up his preferred position behind Mike. Secretly, he admitted to himself that Paul was right; the arrangement lent an air of authority to Mike's leadership.

"All right," he began. "Let's get started.

As usual, Allen Marena, the camp's doctor, immediately listed his supply needs. Syringes, vials, penicillin, bandages, more lab equipment, and—as Paul predicted—a new test subject.

"Doc, it's been a year and you've gotten nowhere with the first fourteen Tils," interjected Steven Olinder, the head of the camp's security. The scarred, barreled-chested lieutenant had seen action in both Iraq wars and the responsibility would fall to him and his team to capture another infected for the doctor to run his tests on. Olinder greatly disliked the idea of having a Til, their name for the infected, in the camp.

With his innate disdain for the head of security, the doctor countered, "And without other subjects, I certainly *won't* get anywhere."

"Here we go." This from Michelle Lafkin, who managed the food supply of the refugees.

Mike sighed inwardly. He could already foresee the arguing that consistently occupied these weekly meetings. The group assembled handled their respective duties with a rigorous attention to detail, but often failed to see the needs of the others as important as his/her own.

"You're not the one out there putting lives at risk to get your little pets," the veteran said through a clenched jaw. Olinder had lost one of his men three months ago in a failed capture attempt. Like most military commanders, he had not forgiven himself for the loss, nor had he forgiven the doctor for the request.

The short, pale-faced doctor answered, "No, I'm just the one trying to find a cure for the damned thing." He spat the words with hostile superiority. In the early days of the outbreak, Allen Marena had watched helplessly as patient after patient succumbed to the virus. Much like Olinder, the physician saw each loss as personal attack on his ability as a doctor.

"There is another option." It was a request the war hero had issued repeatedly in past meetings.

"No."

For the first time in the meeting, Derrick Chancer spoke. Once a student of Mike's, the twenty-four year old was one of the original refugees that had survived the attack on the high school six years earlier. Since then, Derrick had survived the hard life of those first years on the road, and now served as the camp's manager of day to day operations. A deputy-mayor of sorts, if such a thing existed anymore.

The last six months had aged the young man greatly. Mike had worried that the loss of Jenni had shattered him. In many ways, it had. Derrick no longer had the optimism that had encouraged the others to keep going, even in those harsh early days. The darkness under his eyes had deepened these last few months from too many sleepless nights fraught with nightmares and care-giving. Once clean-shaven, the former running back now sported a full blonde beard, matching his hair in its lack of maintenance. The sparkle of life in his blue eyes may have dimmed, yet he still performed his job ably, and Mike could not bring himself to replace him. *Not yet,* Mike always told himself, *not yet. I can't take this from him, too.*

"All right. Enough." Mike attempted to break the tension mounting in the room. There was still business to conduct, and he would not waste any more time on old arguments. "Add it to the list."

With a satisfied grunt from the doctor, and a curt nod from the veteran, Mike moved the meeting along to other topics. As always, food was a chief concern. Michelle informed the gathering that while supplies currently remained steady, the approaching winter would require an increase in hunting and foraging. Even with Paul's knowledge, hunting had still proven more difficult than expected. The camp had once employed the use of traps, but they quickly discovered that the cries of the animals drew the attention of the Tils, forcing the hunting team to rely only on instant kill and collect measures. Foraging had proven equally as challenging, not unexpectedly, as any excursion out of the mountains to a more populated area risked an attack from the infected.

"Lieutenant, how long will it take to prepare a security detail to take Michelle and her people off the mountain to forage for food supplies?" Mike asked.

"Barring weather, I can get the boys ready and a route scouted in three days," replied the security officer. The camp had learned the hard way that repeating the same routes too often piqued the curiosity of the infected; the virus having increased their predatory skills. Mike knew that over the next days, Olinder and his men would scout possible paths off the mountain to ensure minimal contact with the Tils.

"Three days then."

Michelle and the lieutenant both nodded in affirmation. Mike still marveled at how a battle-hardened man far superior in age accepted Mike's command of the camp. Once, when alcohol was still readily available, he asked Olinder that very question. The man replied simply, *I'm a soldier. I don't make the plans, I execute them.*

The meeting continued with an arms update from the lieutenant. The excursion two months earlier to a military base some twenty miles south of the camp had proven worth the risk. The refugees had enough weapons and ammunition to fend off a large scale attack if needed. Of the seventy-six people in the camp, more than half were able to handle a firearm with some amount of skill. Mike hoped that the camp's mountain location meant that such an attack would ne.

rrick was the last to update the assemblage. Some of the refugees had begun complaining of items missing from their shelters—small jars of food, water containers, and such. The items were not cause for much attention, though the idea of a thief in the camp was unsettling. Not willing to move men from perimeter security to patrol the camp, Mike told the young man to tell the refugees to be more vigilant. In the back of his mind he knew, though, that if the thefts continued, stronger action would be required, and he felt uneasy about the result of such action. The community had lived together relatively without incident since the last group of refugees joined them a year ago.

As the group was about to disperse, Dr. Marena spoke again.

"Before we adjourn, there is something I think the council needs to be aware of. I don't know if the old rules apply anymore," the doctor said with obvious hesitation.

"What rules?" Mike asked.

"Doctor-patient rules. But I think, well, for security…Abby Jarvis is pregnant."

The word hung in the room with a deadening silence, all eyes turning to the doctor.

"I thought the council should know."

"Are you sure?" Mike inquired with open shock.

"Well, without the proper tests, no. Pregnancy kits were not top of the list. But, the signs and symptoms are there. My best guess is that she's four months along…" The doctor's voice trailed off.

"Dammit," uttered the lieutenant under his breath.

Michelle looked to Mike, seeing the concern clearly etched across his face. "I don't understand. Why is it a security issue?"

From behind him, Mike heard his second in command's voice, his tone a mix of pity and compassion.

"Because, we don't know if the virus is still airborne. Or if the baby would be immune to it."

CHAPTER THREE

Sometime in the early hours of Wednesday, the glare of the television had lulled Mike into a brief, dreamless sleep. As the haze of slumber slid off him, he stretched his arms and legs, and was surprised to find himself still on the couch. Mike's senses began to process his surroundings—the stiffness in his neck, the color images and the low hum of voices from the flat screen. The serenity of those first wakeful seconds was shattered as the previous day's events came flooding back.

Reaching for the remote, Mike raised the volume as he sat upright on the sagging couch. Gazelle dashed from her dog bed on the side of the couch and leapt into his lap, covering his face with licks.

"Hey girl, good morning," Mike laughed as he scratched her ears and neck. He moved her to his side as his focus drifted back to the broadcast. The anchor, a blonde woman in her mid-thirties, had clearly not found any rest of her own since he had last seen her, hours earlier. Normally a fresh-faced evening newsreader, this morning the strain of round-the-clock reporting was evident.

Scientists now believed that the flu was a mutated strain of a virus called Inclusion Body Disease virus found in snakes. It was, however, still too early to discern how transmission to humans occurred. *Great*, Mike thought, *first birds, then pigs, now snakes.*

A doctor was introduced by the anchor and he proceeded to list the early signs of infection. They were the standard symptoms of any flu. Elevated temperature, nausea, body aches and chills. His advice at this time was to seek treatment at the first onset of the symptoms.

"No shit, ya think?" Mike said to no one. As if in response, his cell phone began to ring.

"Hello?"

"Mike, it's Jim Ashcroft," came the voice on the line. Jim was the principal at the high school. An affable man, he was well-liked by both staff and students. He had been head of the school for well over ten years, one of the longest serving principals in the district.

"Hey, Jim. What's up?" Mike asked.

"I'm sure you have seen the news by now. Are you okay?"

"Yeah, I feel fine. How about you?"

There was a slight crack in Jim's voice as he informed Mike that both his wife and her mother, who lived with them, had taken ill with the flu.

"I'm sorry, Jim. Is there anything I can do?"

"Well, the county has made the decision for schools to be open today."

Mike was rather surprised to hear that.

"With so many parents either in the hospital themselves or caring for loved ones, the superintendent felt that the schools could help out the families by staying open so that the kids that aren't sick have a place to go and at least two meals to eat," the principal explained. "If you're able, we could really use you today. If you have family to care for I totally understand."

With all of Mike's family in the Northeast, he agreed to the request. After ending the call with his boss, he went to his home phone and dialed his parents' house. No answer. He next tried calling his brother and sister-in-law. Again, no answer. Finally, he was able to reach his aunt on his mother's side. She informed him that his father had taken his mother to the hospital late the night before. Likewise, his sister-in-law was at the hospital with both his brother and their young daughter. As she continued to update him, Mike pulled out his laptop and began searching for flights home. Most airlines were showing cancellations across the board. The earliest flight was at 4:25 that afternoon.

"Okay, I just booked a flight up for this afternoon. I'll be at work until 3:00, so you can reach me on my cell until then, and I'll call you when I get to the airport. Keep me posted."

As Mike prepared to head into work, the anxiety he felt for his family had turned his stomach sour. Forcing himself to eat, he grabbed a bagel from the bag on the counter and got in his truck.

* * *

The cafeteria crew was serving breakfast to the hundred or so students that were in attendance. Mike, along with seven other teachers, divided up class lists of the teachers not present and headed to their respective rooms as Mrs. Holigan announced the room changes over the PA system.

As the students in his room passed around a sign-in sheet, Mike noticed that it was not just a few hundred students absent that day. The teenage energy that filled the halls on a typical school day was also missing, replaced by a somber unease. Soon, conversations of the illness dotted the room. Students began discussing who they knew that had fallen ill. They compared the text messages they had received through the night from friends and family. Several students found themselves crying in the arms of their peers, fearing what might become of their loved ones.

Mike understood that hours of this type of speculation was not going to be healthy. He turned the old classroom television to the local news channel. Though the picture was fuzzy, the students started to cut off their conversations and watch.

The estimates had grown since the night before, with the

World Health Organization now putting the number of infected at approximately twenty-three percent of the global population. The scale of the outbreak was unprecedented. Minutes later the broadcast was interrupted by a breaking news alert; the image of the presidential seal filled the screen. As the emblem faded, it was replaced by the image of the Vice-President standing behind the podium in the White House Press Briefing Room.

Good morning.

My fellow Americans, today is a day of struggle and uncertainty. Early this morning, President Obama was taken to Georgetown University Hospital with what appears to be symptoms of the recently discovered Tilian Virus. Before leaving, the President invoked the 25th Amendment of the United States Constitution, temporarily passing executive powers to me until he is able to return to office.

Mike was stunned. As a history major, he knew that the 25th amendment had never before been invoked. Even when Ronald Reagan was shot in 1981, he passed his powers to his vice-president yet did not actually invoke the 25th.

It is with grave respect that I accept this temporary role to maintain the safety and security of our democracy, the Vice-President continued. *This flu outbreak has shown how we truly are a global community. Doctors and scientists from around the world are working in a concerted effort to address the needs of those fallen ill and to rapidly develop a vaccine to prevent further infection. I have directed the Center for Disease Control, the National Institutes of Health and the Department of Health and Human Services to make this their top priority.*

In a minute, Regina Benjamin, the Surgeon General, will provide the most recent information regarding the Tilian Virus.

I ask, in what seems like a dark time, that we remain resilient in the face of adversity, as have generations of Americans before us. Thank you. May God bless you and may God bless America.

As the Vice-President, now Acting-President, stepped aside, an African-American woman in what looked to be her mid-fifties and dressed in a military uniform, began to speak. Mike was unable to focus as he digested what had just been announced. By invoking the 25th, the president had made history, but it also made Mike understand that the severity of this flu, this Tilian Virus, must be greater than even the news was letting on. *And why was the Surgeon General briefing the country and not the Secretary of Health and Human Services? Was it to put a military face to the situation, to show the government was still in control? Or was the Secretary unable to brief?* As the questions multiplied in his head, Mike caught snippets of the briefing.

Apparently, the virus had only targeted those with blood type O, both positive and negative. Due to a car accident in his youth, which required a transfusion, Mike knew he had A-positive blood type. Relief quickly spread over him as it seemed, at least according to the Surgeon General, that he was immune to the virus.

The first sign of infection was the typical elevated fever, followed by nausea. More advanced cases were displaying hemorrhaging from the ears and nose, hives over the body, and ruptured blood vessels in the eyes. The Surgeon General stressed repeatedly that there were no reported cases of fatalities, and there was no indication of permanent damage once the flu ran its course.

The briefing continued for another thirty minutes before returning to the local affiliates. The remaining time provided tips to prevent a spread (washing hands frequently, and the like), as well as phone numbers to call in case of a possible infection.

As the morning wore on, the class continued to watch the news. Little information had changed since the White House briefing three hours ago. When the students returned to the cafeteria to eat lunch, Mike tried reaching his aunt. After several attempts resulted in no response, he headed in to join the students and perhaps grab something to eat. The cafeteria was subdued as the students quietly ate pork riblets or peanut butter and jelly sandwiches. Mike chose one of the latter and sat at a table with the other faculty members that made it in to work. The conversation among them was no different than the students' own discussions.

Lost in thought, Mike did not hear at first when one of the other second year teachers asked him if he had been able to reach his family. He told her what he had learned that morning about his mother, brother and niece. Using his Blackberry, he then checked to see that his afternoon flight was still scheduled. With the flight confirmed and lunch concluded, Mike walked back to his class with the students. Michelle Lafkin passed him in the hall and asked if she could spend the rest of the day in his room. Mike said it would be fine, but told her to make sure her other teacher knew she was switching rooms.

Once again in the room, the class returned to its rapturous watching of the local news. Michelle came into the room and handed her history teacher a note. She then took a seat with her friends, Derrick Chancer and Jenni Calente. Before her mom left, forcing her father to downsize the family home, Michelle had been Jenni's neighbor. Though Jenni was a year ahead, the two had remained friends through middle school and into high school.

Jenni, one of the school's star soccer players, came from a middle class family. Her father worked in the city at a mortgage company and her mother worked part time as a teacher's aide at the elementary school. It was not a shock that her delicate features had attracted the attention of Derrick at the beginning of their freshman year. The two quickly paired off and had been dating ever since. Not wanting to be separated by graduation, both had applied and been accepted to the University of Tennessee at Knoxville. Jenni hoped to pursue a career in nursing, while Derrick was hoping his football scholarship would lead to a chance in the NFL.

As time passed, the reports coming in from around the world increased the number of infected significantly. Twenty-three percent became twenty-eight, which was soon replaced with thirty-two. By 2:00 PM, the world's leading health experts placed the number at forty-three percent of the world's population with confirmed cases of the Tilian Virus. As far they could tell every country across the globe had been exposed. There was still no clear consensus as to how the virus had spread so quickly. The talking heads on the news speculated on everything from global warming to solar flares and, of course, terrorism. These speculations were always followed with: *There is no reason to suspect a terrorist plot.*

Then why say it? Mike thought angrily. He could see how just the mention of terrorism had magnified the fear in the room. Mike knew that throughout history fear-mongers could topple a government just as easily as a war. It was only when cooler heads prevailed that stability was maintained. All too often, though, those cooler heads were shouted down, or in more severe cases removed from the rest of the body. As he was about to get up to turn the television off, the anchor interrupted the pundits and turned the broadcast over to a reporter at the hospital.

With umbrella in hand, the reporter was talking about some type of disturbance at the hospital. In all the chaos of the day, Mike had failed to notice the rain outside his classroom windows. As he peered out a wet window, he saw the tell-tale flashing blue lights of the sheriff's patrol car parked in front of the building. Upon closer inspection, Mike counted two additional patrol cars. Before the question even formed in his head, there was a knock on the classroom door. As he approached, Mike could see through the small window that Valerie Mulligan, the assistant principal, waited on the other side.

Closing the door behind him, Mike found that she was not alone—the sheriff and one of his deputies were with her as well.

"Hey, Mike," her soft voice cracked. Only in her third year as AP, she had already won over the students with her dry wit and enthusiasm, neither of which she expressed now.

Anxiously looking from her to the officers, he said, "Val, what's wrong?"

Bo Cartwright, the sheriff of the county for the past thirty-five years, answered for her.

"We just received word from the governor that he has issued a lockdown. We're gonna have to ask that you and your students stay in the school until it has been lifted."

"A lockdown? I don't und–I mean, for what? What's happened?"

"We're not quite sure, son. Details are pretty sketchy right now. Apparently, some of the people that are sick…well, they're actin' strangely," the graying man replied.

"Strangely?" repeated Mike. "What does that mean?"

Fumbling with the broad-brimmed sheriff's hat he held in both hands, Bo Cartwright was struggling for words. Mike had only known the man two years, but he was a community favorite. Seeming to know the names of each citizen in the small rural county, Sheriff Cartwright was famous for greeting everyone and making time to talk. Now, incredibly, it seemed words failed him.

"Sheriff, what do you mean, strangely?" Mike asked again, the frayed nerves sharpening his tone more than he intended.

"Violently."

Mike's head pulled back slightly at the utterance. It was then that his eyes were drawn down to the white shirt the sheriff wore. The left sleeve, pristinely clean down to the elbow was splattered with blood from elbow to wrist.

The sheriff, seeing the understanding in Mike's face, continued. "We got a call about a domestic disturbance down at the Lafkin place. When we got there…it was like something out of a movie. I mean there was blood everywhere. We found Jerry Lafkin in one of the back rooms. He was standing over his mother's body, and he was covered in..." he paused. "It looked like she'd been torn apart by an animal. When he saw us, he lunged at me and my deputy. He wasn't himself. His eyes were…they were like a wolf going in for the kill. It took five shots to bring him down. We've gotten almost a dozen other calls since then."

The sheriff was clearly rattled as he concluded. His tone made him sound as if he were in a confessional, regret and pain dripping on every word. Mike's head spun with the news, then he quickly understood why the sheriff had told him of the incident.

"Michelle...his daughter, she's in my room," his voice hoarse and small.

Through muffled tears, Valerie Mulligan, spoke. "We have the counselor waiting for her in guidance. Can you ask her to step out here with us?"

With a paralyzing numbness, Mike had to force his body to turn and open the door. Each movement seemed distant from him. The body was his, but he felt disconnected from it. Each step inside the room was agony, knowing that in moments a young girl's life would be shattered.

While the world outside came crashing down, nothing had changed inside the room. The students still were glued to the television. The same reporter was still talking about the unknown disturbance within the hospital, though now his voice was tinged with panic. The camera panned across to the front doors as dozens, maybe hundreds, of people came running out, voices pitched in frantic screams. Students gasped as they watched people trampled in the frenzy. The camera began to falter, and Mike could hear the reporter's voice, "Keep filming! Keep filming!" The camera once again focused on the reporter, a human mass of movement behind him. His mouth moved, but his words were drowned out by the screams. As he tried to shout over the din, a stumbling figure broke away from the sea of bodies in the foreground. As it drew nearer to the camera, Mike could make out the distinct shape of a red hospital gown haphazardly tied around the man's body.

Horrified, Mike realized that, like the sheriff's shirt, the gown had not always been red. He knew he should turn off the television, that these images were only going to get worse. But his body no longer responded.

Within seconds, the figure had closed the distance. The cameraman screamed out a warning, but it was too late. The gowned man leapt at the reporter, his face a mess of hives and gore. They watched in horrified silence as the attacker bit the man's throat, and he screamed in pain. Blood sprayed onto the glass lens of the camera. Before the screen went black, Mike saw the eyes of the gowned man. They were like a wolf's eyes…going in for the kill.

CHAPTER FOUR

With frightening familiarity, Mike placed the magazines into his custom leg harnesses. The years had proven him to be rather adept with firearms, though prior to the outbreak he had never even held a gun. The two semi-automatic Glock 17Cs strapped to him now were quite different than Sheriff Cartwright's service revolver. His mind sometimes drifted back to that moment when he first felt the cold steel in his hands, the stiffness of the trigger, the smell of the gun powder that stung his nose after he fired.

The man that stared back at him from the mirror was almost unrecognizable. His face was leaner, harder, than it had once been. The brown hair he once kept neatly trimmed now reached well past his ears. Haircuts just didn't seem as important in this new world. He kept his face clean-shaven though, having learned quickly that an itching beard was more aggravating than shaving with soap. The clothes he wore, black military-issue shirt and pants, fit him well. While he failed to see the importance of regular haircuts, Mike fully understood the necessity of staying in peak physical form. Where once it was a point of vanity, his athletic build was now maintained for survival.

With a knock, Paul ducked into the cabin. He was outfitted in a similar fashion as Mike Allard. "Ready, chief?" he asked.

"You're not going," Mike said flatly, for what felt like the hundredth time in the last two days. It had been a hotly debated point of contention between the two. With Mike heading the search team, he had instructed Paul to remain behind to keep the camp secure. Paul had strongly, and loudly, disagreed.

"Like hell I'm not. Our best security went out with Michelle and the others. The camp can't afford to have you run off to play hero without protection," the ranger replied. "And don't give me that bullshit that the guys going with you are protection. You and I both know they're green. They haven't seen action beyond securing the camp."

Mike knew he was right, though he hated to admit it. With the lieutenant and his men gone, what security force remained was compromised of refugees that, while skilled with firearms, had not seen the same kind of fighting that seasoned the camp's main security.

"I need someone to run the camp," Mike said, quickly turning to his second reason for Paul to stay behind.

"I thought that was Derrick's job."

After the loss of Jenni, Mike and his second in command had likewise disagreed with Derrick's ability to perform his duties. Paul had seen the toll the loss had taken on the boy just as Mike had. Stubbornly, and perhaps incorrectly, Mike refused to ask him to step down. In truth, his own doubts about Derrick had played a part in his telling Paul to stay behind.

Mike knew Paul well enough to understand that once the ranger's mind was set on a course of action it would take a herculean effort to deter him. In many ways, he knew that the ongoing debate of the last two days was fruitless and that Paul would win out in the end. Mike gave him credit though; Paul had never debated him on the point in public. He believed too strongly in the chain of command to question Mike's leadership where other ears could be listening. With a nod of consent, the two made their way to the center of camp and joined the four others that waited to begin the journey.

The security and foraging teams had begun their own journey eleven days earlier. They were now four days overdue from their scheduled return. The buzz of worry swept through the camp quickly. Mike did his best to avert the obvious tension that was building among the refugees. But, like dust on the wind, the anxiety had spread beyond the point of containment. Two days ago he addressed the camp, informing them of his plans to lead a search party. The intervening time was spent gathering food, water, and medical supplies. Mike had been tempted to have the doctor join them in case one of the missing was injured, but had quickly rejected the idea. The doctor's lack of fitness would only serve as a hindrance, and his skills might be needed in the camp.

Following the same trail the others had used, it would take two days to get off the mountain, and, if they could find a working vehicle, a third to reach their destination. It was just after dawn as the group set out. With somber goodwill, several of the refugees wished the party safety on their journey. Mike had hoped that Derrick would see them off, but as his eyes drifted to the isolated tent at the other end of the camp he knew those hopes were empty.

The trails leading down the mountain had been cleared by the lieutenant's scouts, thus making the journey for his team less perilous. By the time they stopped for lunch, he was pleased to see that they had covered more ground than expected. As with the first hours of the hike, the group remained in relative silence as they ate. He knew the thoughts of his companions without asking, for Mike's mind raced with the same concerns. The team that the lieutenant and Michelle had led totaled thirteen refugees, eight of which were skilled fighters. What could they have encountered to delay such a large group?

Andrew Weyland, the youngest of his team at eighteen years old, was the first to notice the dark storm clouds pushing in from the West. Not wanting to squander the ground they had gained, Mike ordered the party to pack up and resume the hike. They managed to buy four more hours before the first of the rain began to sting their faces. Though the trail rapidly began to turn to mud, they trudged on until the sucking at their boots forced them to make camp for the night. With tents pitched and a low fire burning, Mike and his men ate the chicken and rice one of the women from the camp had packed for them. After the meal and the cooking gear was cleaned and packed away, Paul and Andrew opted to take first watch. Sleep was elusive as Mike listened to the two outside his tent.

"What do you think happened to them?" Andrew questioned.

"Don't know, kid," was Paul gruff reply. He did not have the answer and any speculation would just fuel the teen's anxiety.

Andrew and his mother had been some of the first people Mike and the survivors of the school had met on the road. Just twelve at the time of the outbreak, the boy had grown up in a world that, to him, had now become the standard. A lanky youth with dark blonde hair and green eyes, his family had been farmers two counties over from the school. The virus had taken his father and three siblings, leaving Andrew and his mother, Sarah, to survive the aftermath on their own. Understandably, he had been withdrawn and nearly mute from the shock of what he had witnessed when Mike and the others found them stranded together on the road. Lost in the world, Sarah eagerly accepted the help of the strangers, and she and her son had joined them.

When their second camp was overrun by the infected, Andrew's mother stumbled as she and her son attempted to flee with the others. Clubbing the infected that immediately pounced on her, Andrew was able to drag her to safety. Unfortunately, in the attack, Sarah had been bitten by one of the Tils that swarmed through the campsite. Andrew was forced to watch in horror as the virus took hold of his mother and she began the "change." When her predatory eyes fell on the boy before her—prey now and no longer a son—he scrambled backwards on the ground with tearful screaming. Her mouth curled into a vicious snarl as she advanced on the stricken child. As he stumbled in a panicked escape, his hand brushed across the gun of a fallen refugee. His arms shook as he pointed the weapon and fired, his mother falling dead at his feet as sobs ripped from his body. It was three days later, in a make-shift camp that the escaped refugees had constructed, before Andrew spoke of the incident. His voice through the retelling was hollow and empty.

Mike had lost six people the night the camp was attacked. Andrew, like so many others, had become an orphan to the Tilian Virus. Refusing to let his mind create scenarios of a similar fate befalling Michelle and the others, he forced his attention back to the present.

"He's working on it. Sooner or later he's bound to have some luck," Paul replied to a question Mike had missed.

"I know, but those people…they scream so much when he's…you know," the teen said falteringly.

"You gotta stop looking at them as people, kid. Unless the doc studies them, they're gonna be infected like that forever."

"But, Derrick…I mean, he still sees them as people," Andrew said.

Mike could not see him through the tent, but he knew Paul's face reflected the sorrow in his voice when he replied, "It's different for him."

The conversation trailed off and the silence of the wooded camp allowed Mike to drift into a brief slumber.

* * *

Morning saw the group of six continuing their trek down the mountain; the storm of the night before had left the trail muddy, but not impassable. However, the rain had washed away the boot impressions left by Michelle and the others that his team had been tracking. Whatever happened to them had happened in the city, as the footprints thus far had only led down the mountainside.

The roads, more distinct as they made their way, were filled with abandoned cars. When the infected began displaying the end results of the virus, motorists stuck in the evening rush hour commute had abandoned their vehicles in an attempt to escape the onslaught. Even from this height, Mike could see skeletal remains—bones picked clean by the infected and wildlife and sun-bleached—that littered the pavement.

The closer they got to the road, the more his team lost the relative protection of the trees that covered the mountain. Even with the storm, they had reached the base of the mountain a few hours before nightfall. Now, any watching eyes would easily be able to see the six hiking figures.

"All right, keep alert guys," he instructed the men. He motioned Paul to one side and conferred with him about their options.

"What do you think? We have about four hours of daylight left. Do we make camp? Or find a truck?" he asked the ranger.

Paul's eyes scanned the surrounding area, as he replied. "Once we start an engine, we have to keep going."

In the stillness of the post-infection world, any sound, especially that of a truck's engine, would rouse the Tils from docility. If there were any in the area, the noise would have them swarming down on the team immediately. Mike disliked the idea of traveling at night, even by truck, but he loathed to lose any usable hours, and he was anxious to find the others.

"There are three trucks that could work if you wanted to keep going," Paul said as he pointed down the road. Mike saw the SUV and two extended cab pickups. If they were going to travel at night, he was not going to risk having anyone ride in the bed of a truck.

"Okay, let's do it." Mike rejoined the others and laid out

his plans. Within minutes, the group had reached the SUV, a dark red, '08 Chevy Blazer.

Tim Cornell, a part-time mechanic prior to the outbreak, lifted the hood and began to inspect the truck's condition, as the others took point around the vehicle.

Several minutes later, Tim made his diagnosis.

"The battery looks good, the oil is not great but it will get us where we need to go. The engine looks like it should crank up. I need ten minutes to siphon gas from these cars and fill the tank," he informed Mike, wiping sweat from his shaven head. With Mike's go-ahead, the mechanic got to work.

Time ticked by slowly as the team waited, eyes glued to the area, scanning for any sign of movement.

"Mike, we got company," Paul hissed. Mike turned to follow the ranger's stare. In the distance, about a quarter mile north of their position, he saw it. A lone figure walked among the abandoned cars and trucks. Still too far to see much else, it was clear that whoever it was, it was headed towards Mike and his men.

"Tim, how we doing?" Mike asked over his shoulder.

"The tank was dry, if we're gonna make it without having to stop I need to get it at least half full," he replied while quickening his pace.

Instinctively, Mike reached to his chest holsters and removed his twin Glocks, disengaging the safeties. Loaded with extended magazines, each pistol held thirty-three rounds a piece. With an additional twenty magazines on his person, and more in his pack, Mike knew he had enough firepower, but discharging a weapon would attract much unwanted attention from any Tils nearby. If the truck was not ready, that could mean an extended firefight, and that was something Mike hoped to avoid. Tils tended to remain in an area once they spotted prey, and he planned on returning to the mountain via the way they had come.

As the figure ambled closer, Mike could now easily make out the tell-tale sign of an infected: the side-cocked head.

"How much longer?" he asked, forcing the concern to remain hidden from his voice.

"Five minutes."

"You have two," Mike instructed.

As the mechanic finished siphoning from a nearby car, he made his way back to the SUV, titling the gas can into truck's tank and mumbling, "Then why'd ya ask?"

Ignoring the comment, Mike kept his eyes on the infected, now only a hundred yards away.

"Andrew, Erik, and Shane get in the truck…*slowly*," he ordered. As the three men eased their way to the rear passenger doors, the infected stopped its approach.

"Mike…" Paul began, but was cut off by a bestial growl that erupted from the Til. The infected then sprang into a full sprint, bearing down on the SUV. As the creature raced towards them, other forms began appearing from the road, howling in predatory rage.

"Dammit," Mike shouted as he and Paul began opening fire. The first Til fell after six rounds, but it was quickly replaced by several dozen others. Mike heard shots being blasted from the SUV behind him. With a glance, he saw that Tils had sprung up on all sides, and the men in the truck were firing on them.

The silence that had previously blanketed the afternoon was split apart by the screams of infected and the gunfire from the men. In his periphery, Mike saw a Til jump onto the hood of the car to his left. Three shots took it down, but the swarm was too close now to hold them off with any real assurance. He quickly expelled the spent magazines and slammed his weapons down onto a pair of full ones strapped to his thighs. Without surrendering more than two seconds, he was once again unloading into the seething crowd.

Paul, armed with an assault rifle, held off the Tils on the front passenger side as best he could. With the virus destroying all pain receptors in the body, the infected were undaunted in their approach. Head and heart shots were the only immediate way to bring them down. Andrew and the others inside the truck had their doors ajar and were firing shotguns at the attackers, keeping them away from the mechanic as he worked. Finally, Tim's voice rose above the chaotic din, announcing that he was finished.

"Get in the truck, NOW," Mike shouted to Tim and Paul. Racing backwards and firing at the Tils closest to them, the three men jumped into the front seat of the truck.

In the driver's seat, Tim turned the key to start the Chevy's engine, but the effort was met with only a brief rev.

"Shit," Tim exclaimed as he pumped the gas pedal and kept turning the key. The Tils were at the truck now, and they banged relentlessly on the glass, their bodies covered in blood and sores.

"Let's get the heck out of here," came a frantic scream from the rear, the voice indistinct among the screams and howls of the Tils. As if in reply, the engine roared to life.

Glass shattered beside him as Tim put the truck into drive. Mangled arms grabbed at him, nails scoring his face and chest. As he screamed, Mike began firing at the ravenous infected that were attempting to rip the mechanic from the driver's seat. The truck moved steadily forward, then, in his struggle, Tim's foot slammed into the gas pedal sending the SUV crashing into the Tils, pinning them against the car in front of the truck.

Blood splattered the interior, as the mechanic slowly lost his struggle with the horde of grasping hands. With a final scream, he was pulled through the driver's window, neck snapping as his head struck the doorframe.

"NO!" Mike screamed as he lunged towards the door.

Paul held him back shouting, "He's gone, Mike, he's gone! We gotta get out of here!"

In a daze, Mike saw the pinned Tils before him, other infected climbing over them. He heard the screams and gunshots from the backseat, shotguns ripping apart the bodies of the Tils surrounding the truck. Hands shaking, Mike gripped the blood-slick steering wheel. He shifted the truck into reverse and slammed on the gas. With a tight cut of the wheel, he angled the truck free of the other vehicles and plowed through the dense mass of infected. The Blazer bounced heavily as it veered off the paved road and onto the grass.

CHAPTER FIVE

Mike Allard's voice strained as he tried to shout over the hysterics that filled the room. He had been unable to get a signal from the television since the screen went blank ten minutes earlier. Understandably the students in the room had reacted with screams, tears, and panicked confusion. *You're not doing much better*, he thought to himself. He tried his cell phone again, but like others in the room, he could not get a signal. Sheriff Cartwright had gone out to his cruiser to radio the station, as his two-way was also dead. As each student reported an inability to get a cell signal, Mike at first assumed the towers were overloaded, but a voice inside him was beginning to suspect that the cells, radio, television and internet were perhaps intentionally shut down. For what purpose, he did not know. As he tried again to calm the students, the familiar squeal of the emergency broadcast system blasted from the television's speakers. The tone was quickly followed by a mechanical voice.

This is not a test. The federal government has issued a warning for the country. Please remain indoors at this time. Structures with minimal windows and doors will provide the best security. The National Guard has been activated to address the situation. Again, this is not a test.

The message repeated several times before the screen returned to static.

"Mr. Allard, what do we do?" asked Derrick Chancer,

worry cracking his normally steady voice.

In response, Mike moved over to the windows. The courtyard beyond the glass was dotted with slow moving figures. Their shambling movements were identical to the man from the news report; as he tried to digest the situation, three gun shots ripped through the late afternoon air. The sound caused him to jump back as he saw two of the figures in the courtyard fall to the ground. The people still standing began to rush towards the police cruisers. Five officers, with guns drawn, stood behind their patrol cars. Mike could see the flares of gunfire as more shots rang out.

"Guys," he said urgently, "help me get these bookcases in front of the windows."

Four students, Derrick among them, joined Mike in his effort to slide the bookcases to the windows. The wood made a screeching sound as it slid along the linoleum flooring. In the distance, he could hear glass shattering, followed by screams. *The front office,* he thought. With the windows secured, Mike quickly made his way into the hall. The gun shots had now moved indoors, and he could hear the commanding shouts of the officers. With steady back-stepping, the officers came into view.

"Get those kids out of there!" one shouted over his shoulder to Mike. With instincts and adrenaline racing, he raced back into the room.

"Everyone, follow me. We're going upstairs."

The students ran out of the room and made their way to the stairwell at the other end of the hall. As the last few exited the class, Mike saw one of the officers get tackled by a frenzied woman. Her hands and mouth were ripping into the officer. With several shots of his sidearm, the officer killed his attacker and dragged himself clear of the others now pouring into the building. Mike ran to the stricken man and pulled him towards the stairs. He could hear the windows of his classroom smash, followed by the crashing sound of the bookcases crumbling to the floor.

We're going to die, his voice screamed in his head.

Reaching the stairs, Mike reached down to lift the officer, whom he now recognized as Sheriff Cartwright. The man had large gashes in his chest and face. The blood that before was only splattered on his sleeve was now indistinguishable from the red that stained the shirt entirely. Struggling to lift the large sheriff, he grunted with exertion. Barely lifting him to his shoulder, the sheriff began to convulse wildly. With the strain too great, both men crashed to the floor and Mike's head smacked loudly on the tile. While still trying to assist the sheriff, he looked back down the hall and saw the remaining officers falling back quickly as they were overrun by the crazed attackers.

As suddenly as it began, the convulsions that overtook the sheriff ceased. During another attempt to lift him, the sheriff's hands grabbed at Mike's shirt. Struggling to fend off the attack, he stumbled backwards as the sheriff rose to his feet. The man towered before him, eyes wild and primal growls ripping from his mouth. The sheriff crouched into what could only have been called a pouncing position.

Mike looked to his sides as he continued to slide himself away from the sheriff. His eyes locked onto the man's service revolver that had fallen a few feet to his left. Grunting, he dove for the gun just as the sheriff launched himself. With a crash, the big man met empty floor, and Mike turned quickly, revolver in hand, and squeezed the trigger. One round smashed into the sheriff's shoulder. The shot staggered the man, but he steadied himself and again began to move towards Mike. The revolver felt heavy in his shaking hands as he cocked and aimed again. The second shot ripped through the sheriff's chest and he crumpled to the floor.

His hearing now dulled from the shots, Mike stood slowly, the world a fuzzy haze around him. With a start, his vision cleared as he heard another shot fired. Looking towards the far end of the hall, he realized that the remaining officers had fallen and had been enveloped by the mass of blood-drenched attackers. One, a male in what appeared to be his early teens, looked up from his feeding and his eyes locked onto Mike. The creature howled in rage and soon the others that filled the hall raised their heads, spotting him standing alone some fifty feet way.

He turned quickly as the attackers leapt into action. The blood that covered their clothes and shoes caused them to stumble on the slick surface of the floor. He reached the top of the stairs just as the others began their climb. The frantic gesturing of the students signaled to him.

The faculty room, he thought to himself as he sprinted the length of the hall. The children screamed warnings as the crazed creatures breached the second floor behind him. With a grunt, he smashed into the arms of the students who pulled him inside. Michelle slammed the door behind them, while others strained to slide a vending machine in front of it.

Exhaustion overcame him as the adrenaline left his body. His vision again began to blur as he slipped into unconsciousness. He could hear the worried students in the distance, their voices seemed miles away. As his eyes closed, he heard the crashing sound of bodies slamming against the barricaded door.

* * *

His body ached. That was the first sensation he became aware of as Mike slowly stirred from his sleep. The surface under him was hard and cold. He soon could make out the faint sounds of weeping.

"Mr. Allard?"

The voice caused him to jump and he immediately brought himself to a seated position. His eyes took in the familiar surroundings. Students huddling together in the corners of the faculty room.

"Mr. Allard, it's Derrick. Are you ok?"

Turning to the voice at his left, Mike asked urgently, "What happened? Is everyone okay?" he asked the student urgently.

"We're fine. You've been out for an hour or so," Derrick informed him.

Rising to his feet, Mike remembered the last sounds he had heard before blacking out. He quickly turned to the door. The crashing and growling were absent.

"Are they gone?"

"We don't know. They kept trying to get in but twenty minutes ago they stopped," replied Jenni Calente, offering him a bottle of water. Michelle Lafkin stepped forward. "No one has been able to get a signal on their phones."

Mike looked around the room and saw the fear in the eyes of those before him. Natural risk takers and self-believing immortals, the teens in the room now cowered like mice before a snake, and they were looking to him for answers. Trying his best to assess their situation, he made another visual sweep of the room. The twenty by thirty foot, second floor faculty lounge had a small bathroom in the right rear corner, no windows and one door to the hallway. That door was now blocked by a large snack food vending machine. To his left, Mike saw the beverage machine, its glass front smashed open. *Smart move, kids,* he thought, *at least we have food and water.*

"Okay, this room is good," he said.

"Derrick picked it," Jenni replied, her voice holding a bit of pride for her boyfriend.

"Always thinking with your stomach, eh, Derrick?" Mike laughed.

"Yea, he usually thinks with something else," called out one of his buddies from the football team.

At first nervously and perhaps a bit forced, the room soon filled with laughter.

It wasn't long before more jokes were told, more comments made, and the survivors found themselves holding their sides from the mirth. The stress of the day's events had been channeled into a new emotion.

It was Jenni, however, that brought them back to harsh

reality, asking, "Mr. Allard, what do we do?"

Pensive for a moment, Mike turned to the barricaded door and replied, "We need to see what's out there." As he spoke he picked up the revolver from the large table that sat in the middle of the room and discovered there were two bullets remaining.

"Give me a hand with the vending machine," he directed as he shifted his weight against it.

"Mr. Allard, no way. You're not going alone. Those things could still be out there," Derrick stated with a hint of authority.

Mike appreciated his concern—he was not fully keen on the idea of investigating the hall alone—but he knew that with just the one weapon, any that followed him would be unarmed and vulnerable.

"We only have the one gun, Derrick," Mike began to explain, but was interrupted by Jenni.

"The table," she said simply.

Everyone turned to the table, then back to her inquisitively.

"The table legs. Take them off and use them as clubs."

Before Mike had a chance to object, the students flipped the table and used a pocket knife multi-tool to unscrew the table's legs from its top.

"You have a knife at school?" the history teacher said to the tool's owner, Blaine Grimson. Mike realized the absurdity of the comment, having slipped easily into school official mode.

With his usual sarcasm, the senior with the military crew cut looked towards Mike Allard and replied, "Big picture, Mr. Allard, big picture."

Within minutes, the table was disassembled and Derrick, Blaine, Jenni, and another student with whom Mike was unfamiliar, stood armed with their makeshift clubs. Secretly feeling guilty, he relented and agreed to accept their assistance. Three other students cautiously moved the vending machine from its spot in front of the door, careful to make as little noise as possible.

"As soon as we are out, I want you guys to block the door again," he instructed those that were remaining behind. Taking a deep breath in a failing effort to still his nerves, Mike motioned for one of the students to slowly open the door.

Fearing the same onslaught he had so narrowly escaped, the five stepped out into the hall. The doors to the other classrooms in the pod were closed, and no lights shone from the rooms. The circular hallway was deserted, walls and floor covered in blood were the only evidence of the things that had chased him. Placing a finger to his lips to instruct silence, Mike began to lead them towards the staircase at the opposite end of the pod. The halls in the school were not long, but crossing them now seemed an eternity. The four students were fanned out behind him, with Blaine and Derrick diligently watching behind them.

Upon reaching the top of the stairs, an unfamiliar stench quickly overwhelmed them. As they made their way down, the group recognized the lifeless form of Sheriff Cartwright at the foot of the steps.

"Oh, my God," came the whispering voice of Jenni. The others followed her gaze and saw the horror at the end of the long hall leading to the front office. Mutilated and dismembered corpses of students, faculty, neighbors and officers filled the space before them. The stench was attributed to the disembowelment that coated the once-gleaming floors.

Before continuing onward, Mike reached down to the sheriff's body and quickly searched it for more rounds, finding them in a small pouch secured to the man's belt. Unfamiliar with guns, having fired his first shots that very day, he had to rely on the skills of the teens with him that regularly hunted with their families. He cringed slightly when Blaine snapped the action back into place and returned the fully loaded gun to him.

Scanning their surroundings, Mike was relieved that the

sound had not attracted unwanted attention. Further down the hall, they found the remains of the three officers that had tried in vain to hold back the crushing wave of attackers. Two of the boys, Blaine and Derrick, retrieved the firearms from among the bodies as well as four full magazines of ammo.

Forcing himself not to get sick, and seeing the others fight the same internal battle, Mike carefully maneuvered his way through the carnage to the main office. As expected, the phone lines were down, thus eliminating the easiest route to a rescue. Through the large glass-less window that faced the parking lot, he saw the three patrol cars that sat idly outside the building's front doors.

"Blaine, your dad's a reserve deputy, right?" Mike asked the boy.

"Yeah, why?" replied the tall, well-built eighteen year old who intended to enlist in the Marines immediately after graduation.

"Those patrol cars have shotguns and shells in them, don't they?" Mike continued his questioning, an idea taking shape in his mind.

Understanding his point, Blaine confirmed the assumption and informed them that there were usually a few rifles and shotguns in each cruiser. The weapons, however, could only be unlocked from their storage with a key—a key that Blaine would recognize easily.

As he and Derrick made their way back to the slain officers to search for the keys, Mike went to the front doors and surveyed the front courtyard. Before him, the lawn was littered with the corpses of the infected the officers had managed to kill before being forced to retreat inside. Walking aimlessly among them were several bloodied figures, heads severely cocked to one side. He counted seven within sight, but worried how many others remained unseen. *It might be too risky to go out with guns blazing,* he thought.

The two youths returned, their smiles signifying a

successful search of the bodies. Mike quickly detailed the plan he had formed. Blaine, Jenni, and the other boy—who he learned was a freshman named Josh Sorenson—would make for the cruisers and retrieve the weapons, while Mike and Derrick would provide cover fire.

Now armed with two guns apiece, they kept a vigilant eye on the infected, as the others crouched low to the ground and headed for the cruisers. Mike could feel the nervous beads of sweat falling down his face. The sun hung low amidst the clouds, coloring the sky with faint tones of pink and red. Each of the three students had reached their respective targets, and he could see them unlocking the weapons from the center consoles of the cruisers. With a hesitant sigh, he hoped that the mission could continue without raising the interests of the infected that milled about in the courtyard.

As the three scavengers made their way back, arms heavy with the stolen weaponry, they struggled to remain crouched and hidden from view. The broken glass that scattered across the pavement caused Josh to misstep and fall to the ground with a loud clatter. Almost in unison, the creatures turned towards the break in the late afternoon silence. The same growls and screams that had chilled Mike's bones preceding his barely survived attack now echoed off the brick walls of the school.

Derrick wasted no time in firing at the infected that now bore down on them. An experienced hunter, his shots hit their intended targets with much greater success than Mike's own inexperienced aim. Within seconds, Derrick had brought down three of the figures.

When Blaine and the others reached the relative safety of the school, the future Marine quickly began blasting the pump-action shotgun he had retrieved from the cruiser. Eventually all seven of the infected had fallen to their wounds, and Mike hurried the students back through the hall. As feared, the gunfire had alerted the infected that still remained in the building. The stairs leading to their safety were blocked by a dozen infected that had begun making their way to the sound of the shooting. Without pause, the quintet met their attackers with the full force of the arsenal they now carried. Blood and bone ripped away from the bodies of the infected as bullets tore through them.

Mike was no longer in control of his movements as instinct and the primal urge to survive took over. The revolver was spent, but the semi-automatic from one of the officers still responded to his trigger finger. Aiming ahead and behind, he whirled about with the determination of a warrior. The others with him appeared caught in the same frenzy as they cleared a path up the stairs. Reaching the top step, they turned and began aiming downwards at the infected that followed. Shot after shot felled those that pursued them.

As the proverbial smoke cleared, so too did the adrenaline-induced haze of their fight-or-flight reactions. They quickly made their way back to the shelter of the faculty room, its door already opened when those inside heard the shots in the hall.

Safe, they dropped their weapons to the ground. With the ecstatic relief known only by soldiers in war, they began to hug and congratulate each other. Their victory was small, but it was amplified by the horrors that had defeated them in the last twenty-four hours. The teens regaled their peers with details of the endeavor.

Only Mike remained apart from the celebration of survival. He did not interrupt them, nor admonish them in anyway; he watched them, a crush of pity and sadness swept through him. He knew that, unlike soldiers in a foreign war, those before him would soon realize that the enemies of which they now spoke were friends and neighbors. He worried that their youthful minds would be unable to reconcile what they had been forced to do that day, that their youthful minds would be unable to reconcile what they would be forced to do in the days ahead.

For now, though, he thought, *let them be kids one last time.*

CHAPTER SIX

They drove through the night in silence, no man in the truck willing to put voice to the loss of Tim Cornell. The suddenness and brutality of the attack left them each in a stunned stupor, those crazed moments endlessly replaying in their minds.

The truck lights lit the abandoned road before them, and they kept their eyes alert for any signs left by their missing companions. As dawn crept over the mountains behind them, Mike forced himself to compartmentalize Tim's violent death and focus on the task ahead. There had been a time, in those first days of the outbreak, that such a loss would have crippled his emotional control. He had learned to accept his role as leader of the camp; by force of the world that now existed, he had grown hard. With each death, with each attack, Mike Allard drifted further from the man he had been in his youth. What remained was a war-weary, reluctant soldier that sacrificed his own emotions for the sake of those that followed him.

As the sky brightened, the passengers could see the darkened outline of the powerless city some miles in the distance. The original plan had been for the lieutenant to escort Michelle and her team to the southern outskirts of the city to scavenge for canned goods and medical supplies. Having seen no sign of them thus far, Mike knew that whatever had caused their delay in returning occurred somewhere in the next twenty miles. He issued curt commands to recheck weapons and prepare to search on foot once they reached their destination.

Over time, it had become clear that urban environments proved to be the most hazardous to the uninfected. There were too many buildings, abandoned cars, and alleys in which the Tils could build their dens. Mike recalled with a shudder the first den he and the refugees had stumbled into. Less than half of the twenty-two with him then had survived to see the following day. It had been a costly mistake, a mistake he had ordered and one that still brought him screaming out of his sleep most nights.

The truck rolled to a stop in an intersection of what was once a booming business district. Guns at the ready, the five men stepped onto the cracked macadam of the street. They quickly formed a passable military diamond formation that, at least in theory, would protect them in all directions. A small grocery store, their intended target, lay a block north of their current position. Proceeding with caution, the team made steady progress towards the store. The street was littered with bones, the only graves the fallen would ever know. Though the scene was gruesome, Mike was relieved that there were no fresh bodies to indicate a Til presence.

The glass door entrance to the market was shattered and Mike stepped gently on the fragments as he led the others into the store. The shelves were mostly bare, having been scavenged by other survivors many times over the past six years. He had learned some errant cans usually remained if one looked diligently enough. Aisle by aisle, the team found no sign of their fellow refugees. They did, however, find the rotting remains of infected. Paul made a quick inspection of the corpses and surmised that they had been killed within the past few days. The casings on the floor matched the ammo that supplied the camp's arsenal.

"Best I can tell," Paul said, "they made it this far, which means they probably headed over to the hospital."

Mike agreed with Paul's conclusions and ordered the

team back to the truck. The hospital was four blocks to their east and should have been the last destination of the scavenging mission. The drive took longer than it would have before the outbreak, as he was now forced to weave the truck through a maze of haphazardly abandoned vehicles.

A block from the hospital Mike eased the truck to a stop.

"Jeez," Paul said, fear and awe clear in the tone.

The front entrance to the hospital was surrounded by a seething mass of infected. Some threw themselves at the thick glass doors, while others howled with rage, pacing like caged lions.

"There's gotta be two hundred of 'em," Andrew spoke from the back seat.

"Our guys must be pinned down inside. No way those Tils are that worked up unless they know there's a meal in there," said Shane.

"We have to assume those are our people in there. Any suggestions on getting them out?" Mike asked.

A few moments later the sound of gunfire tore through the air, accompanied by the blaring of the truck's horn. The Tils, already in a hunting frenzy, abandoned their attack on the hospital and charged down the street towards the truck. When the distance between the infected and the vehicles was less than one hundred yards the truck reversed its direction and began to cruise back the way it had come. The Pavlovian Tils, snarling as their new prey attempted to escape, hounded behind the rear of the Chevy, and within minutes, the entrance to the hospital was cleared of infected.

The truck, driven by Shane with Erik in shotgun, was receding from view with the Tils still in pursuit. Mike, Paul, and Andrew crept from the sanctuary of one of the many abandoned store fronts and hastily ran to the hospital entrance. The glass doors were locked, but shattered easily with shots from Mike's side-arms. Once inside, the three risked detection by calling out for the missing. They crossed the lobby, its floor covered with papers and files long since discarded, and pushed through the double doors into the first of many long corridors. With nothing but their own echoes as a response, Mike signaled for a stop.

"Shane and Erik will be back in twelve minutes. We need to find our people and get the hell out of here. Once they pull up, we won't have much time to load in. Andrew, you search the first three floors. Paul, you'll take the next three. I'll head up to the tenth and work my way down. Whether you find them or not, I want your asses back down here in ten minutes. Clear?"

Paul was clearly against the idea of splitting up, but, as expected, he took the orders without question and the trio headed to their assigned detail. As Mike climbed the stairs to the top floor, the exhaustion of no sleep in over twenty-four hours warred with the adrenaline needed to reach the top. His legs burned with pain and his breaths came in short gasps by the time he reached the door to the tenth floor.

The corridor was a sea of upturned gurneys and wheelchairs. Deep red flakes of dried blood splotched the walls. Mike ranged his arms before him, the twin Glocks in his hands having long since become a natural extension of his own body. He called for his fellow refugees knowing that in doing so he risked attracting more Tils. With minutes fleeting by, the usual caution with which he operated had to be temporarily suspended. As with the lobby, his calls were met with no reply from the missing. He raced through the halls relying on what little they had learned about those infected with the virus. In most cases, Tils shied away from the upper floors of buildings, preferring the lower places where prey was plentiful. No sign of the others, Mike looped back to the stairs and began his search of the floor below.

The ninth yielded the same result and within minutes he headed to the eighth. The digital watch strapped to his wrist indicated that he only had five more minutes before he needed to return to the lobby. Despair began a slow but steady march in his heart as the minutes rolled by without a sign of Michelle and the others. As he reached for the door to the eighth floor, Mike heard Paul call to him from the stairs below.

"Mike, we got 'em!"

Pivoting swiftly, the refugee leader took the steps two at a time as he made his downward retreat to his companions. Over the railing Mike could see six or seven heads racing down the stairs. A half minute passed in a blur before he reached the lobby. Immediately, he took stock of those gathered. Michelle Lafkin leaned against the lobby desk, her arm in a splint. With her were two others from her team of foragers. On the floor before them rested the prone body of the lieutenant. His side was wrapped in thick layers of blood-soaked gauze. The visible skin of his face and hands were sallow from obvious blood loss. Tending to him was Lisa Velazquez, one of the handful of female members of the camp's security team.

Paul was midway through briefing Mike on the situation when Andrew joined them from his search of the hospital.

"Lisa was able to take down the Til before it bit him, but the glass from the window went in deep. They've done what they could here, but, Mike, if we don't get him to the doc soon, he's not going to make it."

"And the others?" Mike asked.

Shaking his head, Paul replied, "The team got separated during the attack. Michelle and the others managed to get inside the hospital, but no one has seen the others since."

Still missing were two from security and one from the foraging team. Glancing at his watch, Mike cursed silently realizing that he would be forced to make the decision to abandon the three unaccounted for in order to save the lives of the ones now under his protection. Three blasts of a car horn indicated that Shane and Erik had returned.

"Load up!" Mike commanded.

As the group exited the hospital, they found the Chevy waiting outside, doors ajar. Further down the street was the seemingly tireless horde that had followed it. Quickly placing the backboard carrying Lieutenant Olinder into the rear hatch, the others piled into the now cramped SUV.

When Mike gave the all-clear, Shane threw the car into drive and sped down the street, once again weaving his way through the obstacles.

The Tils had been able to keep pace with the deliberately slow moving truck before, but now at top speed, those that chased the refugees vanished in the distance. Two miles into the drive, Mike ordered a halt.

"How are we on gas?" he asked Shane.

Checking the gauge, he informed Mike that the truck now held slightly less than a quarter of a tank. Even without the added excursion to distract the Tils, the truck had been unlikely to make it back to the mountain without a refill.

"Okay," Mike said as he stepped out of the truck and gave Shane his instructions. "When you get outside of the city siphon what you can with the kit. You should only need another quarter of a tank to make it back; more if the Tils occupy the trail we used and you need to use an alternate route. When you get to the base of the mountain, send up a flare so the others know you need them to meet you."

"And where will you be during all this?" Paul asked.

Looking his second-in-command eye to eye, he replied flatly, "I still have three more men out there somewhere. I'm going back to get them."

Without pause, Paul gathered his pack and exited the truck, saying, "And I'm going with you."

"So am I," both Lisa and Andrew spoke in unison.

Mike did not argue. He knew that spending a night in the city was dangerous at best. While he would not order them to accompany him, he was willing to accept their volunteering for the mission. *Besides,* he thought with a smile, *if I said no the three would have just gotten dropped off further down and doubled back to me anyway.*

The four took whatever food, water, and weapons the others could spare and filled their packs. Mike then went to the driver's side window for a word with Shane. The young man, recently turned twenty-four, looked nervously towards Mike.

"You can do this. I wouldn't leave you guys if I didn't think you could," he spoke softly, his words measured and filled with authority. "You're in charge of them now. Get them back safely."

As he nodded his head, Shane seemed to relax. "Yes, sir," he replied, his voice was strong, saturated in pride and a desire to serve his leader well.

Mike stepped back from the truck and watched them drive away. Taking a deep breath, he turned to the others. They stood before him, these soldiers of the new world, awaiting instructions.

"Let's secure a location, then we'll discuss the plan," he announced, hoping that in the interim he could come up with a plan to discuss.

In their scouting of the surrounding streets, thankfully empty of any infected, they found several locations that would serve as a secure shelter for the night. Mike settled on a bank two avenues over from where they were dropped off. Between the vault and the tellers' cage, the bank afforded them reasonable protection in the event of a Til attack. As Lisa and Andrew cleared the cage of discarded debris, Mike and his second-in-command began barricading the front door.

He was deep in contemplation when Paul, his voiced hushed so the others could not hear, said, "So, no plan, yet?"

Mike huffed a laugh and replied, "That obvious, huh?"

Lifting one end of a desk, while he hefted the other, Paul reduced some of Mike's concern by saying, "To me, yes. To them, probably not, but I can tell when you're turning things over in your mind."

In the time that Paul had been with the camp, Mike had sought his counsel on numerous occasions. While he begrudgingly accepted the role of leader, he was self-aware enough to know when he needed the input of others. Even when he was a teacher, in what seemed a lifetime ago, he had sought advice from the veteran educators regarding lesson plans, classroom management, and various teaching techniques. One of his best skills had been taking what others told him and adapting it to fit his needs. When the virus broke out, he had been but one year away from tenure, and perhaps another two from chairing the history department. In the intervening years, he had laughed at his former self and the concerns that once plagued him.

"If they got separated at the hospital, they would have holed up within the vicinity," he said as the two placed the desk atop its twin in front of the doors.

"If they survived," Paul countered.

"Until we see proof that they didn't, we're operating under the assumption that they're still alive." The tone in Mike's voice clearly indicated he would hear no argument on the subject.

"That still leaves a lot of buildings for them to hide in."

Mike nodded, "So you agree that they would have stayed in the area?"

"Jon was with Lisa under the lieutenant. There's no way he'd leave them behind. Especially not with all those Tils surrounding the hospital." Paul's sense of loyalty made any deviation from his statement inconceivable to him.

Sliding a four-drawer filing cabinet across the green marble floor, Mike, his voice strained from the physical effort, replied. "I saw three buildings near the hospital with enough height to offer some security."

"So we start there tomorrow?" Paul asked.

"Tonight." After he spoke the word, Mike waited for the coming debate.

"Tonight? So that's it, huh, you're just trying to get killed?" Paul's voice quickly rose from its previously hushed tone. "It's suicide to go out there at night and you know it! Why the hell are we barricading the damn door if we're just gonna give ourselves to the bastards anyway?"

Mike knew his second meant well in his frustration, so he did his best to keep his voice level. "Because in here at least the four of us can get some rest without having to keep watch. It's just after noon now. That'll give us six or seven hours to sleep before the sun goes down. We know Tils are less active at night unless agitated. If we stay…"

Paul cut him off saying, "And the four of us traipsing blindly through the streets isn't going to agitate them?"

"If we stay alert," Mike continued, "we can slip past them. If the others are in those buildings they know to keep a light shining in the window for rescue. You and I both saw what this place is like during the day. And after our rescue stunt, those Tils aren't going anywhere for a while."

Jaw clenched in frustration, Paul remained silent.

"Look, I'm not saying it's the best plan, and I'm open to suggestions. But come sunrise tomorrow, those streets are going to fill up with hundreds of hungry Tils hell-bent on finding the meal that got away."

"You've always said travelling at night is too risky," Paul reminded him, his voice lower, but still gravelly. Lisa and Andrew continued clearing the debris in the cage feigned disinterest, but his previous volume and body language had already caught their attention.

"I know. And it is. But, this time I don't see any way around it," Mike conceded. He did not continue, having laid out his argument as fully as he could.

A moment of silence passed between them.

Paul raised his eyes slightly to the ceiling, his head shaking side to side as he took a deep breath. "You're a crazy son of a bitch. You know that right?" Paul responded, the slightest of smiles breaking across his face, signifying the end to the debate.

CHAPTER SEVEN

Sleep claimed its mastery over the huddled mass of students that filled the faculty room floor. Though not an overly large room it did, however, provide adequate space for the sixteen students Mike Allard watched over. Unlike the others, sleep did not enslave the teacher that night. Propped in one of the soft leather chairs that once encircled the conference table, he stretched his legs out in front of him. The relaxed manner of his body failed to accurately represent the tense thoughts that held much needed sleep at bay. His left hand fiddled with a pen he had fished from the pocket of his jeans some hours earlier. Turning the pen over and over again with his fingers was the only thing that satisfied his craving.

I need a cigarette, he thought to himself. The concept of thinking of such an insignificant need during the situation he and the others faced amused him. There were moments when he imagined himself fighting off a horde of those creatures below to reach the half-full pack of Marlboros in his truck.

You've watched the Die Hard movies too many times, the voice in his head mocked, *and you're no John McClane yipee-kaying through the airport.*

Forcing his mind away from the nicotine-induced hero delusions, he began to wonder what the coming sunrise would bring. He thought about the chance of a rescue from some unknown source. Recalling how quickly the virus had spread, the number of infected announced by the world's governments, and the result of the sheriff's bite wound, Mike was beginning to think that any rescue was unlikely. Four armed men had been overrun in mere minutes.

The realization left him with one thought.

"We're on our own," he whispered softly in the dark room.

That was difficult to accept. Before the attack, almost one hundred students had been in the building. Were he and the others all that remained? Or did others now hide in rooms around the school feeling the same sense of defeat and isolation?

Tomorrow, we have to check for other survivors in the school, he silently decided.

Mike knew that the school would not be able to support a prolonged stay. There were too many entrances, either through windows or doors, to offer long-term protection. Even if they could raid the cafeteria kitchen for food more substantial than chips and candy, the faculty room was not going to be able to serve their needs indefinitely. He turned escape scenarios over in his thoughts. If more infected blocked the courtyard, the group would have to devise a way past them. *Then what?* Mike questioned himself. *Where do we go?*

Some thirty miles north was a large military base. To Mike, it seemed like the best option. The sheriff had said dozens of calls had come in from the town before the school had been attacked. Reluctantly, he had to assume the small rural community had been overrun just like the school. With their numbers, and if more survivors were found in the school, Mike estimated that at least three or four vehicles would be required to make the trek north to the base. The military and its defenses would be the best protection, and hopefully a source of information as to what was happening.

Before his next thought took shape, Mike heard a shuffle from the floor to his right. The sound startled him, and he was surprised to see how instinctively his hand had moved to the gun in his lap.

"It's Derrick, Mr. Allard," the running back whispered.

Relaxing, Mike said, "You should be sleeping, bud."

"I can't. Every time I try all I see are those…those people. It's like…I don't know, man, I mean, is this happening?"

Mike could hear the frustration and fear in the young man's voice. The first hours of the night had found him ruminating over the same question. Growing up, he had been a fan of horror movies and the zombie, werewolf, and vampire villains terrorizing the foolish characters that inevitably made ridiculously bad attempts at escape. More humorous than frightful, those movies were indulgent breaks from the real world. If he wanted to be really scared, Mike had watched films with psychotic serial killers that hunted unsuspecting victims. To him, the fear was real because the villain could be real.

Now, though, it was not a serial killer that stalked them, but rather something closer to one of those creatures from horror movies. His mind struggled between acceptance of the situation he and the others faced, and rejection of the heretofore implausibility of such a situation.

"It's crazy, right? Things like this aren't supposed to happen," Mike responded.

"Is it everyone? Do you think everyone that got sick turned into…" Derrick's voice trailed off.

"I don't know. My mom, my brother and his daughter were all in the hospital with it this morning." Mike felt a pang of guilt as he realized that he had not been able to reach any of them after he had talked to his aunt.

"I'm sorry, Mr. Allard. Jenni's folks were both sick this morning, too."

Mike wondered how many dead would need to be mourned by the people surrounding him.

"How about your parents?" Mike asked.

"They were fine. My mom didn't want me to come to school today, but I wanted to be here for Jenni."

"How's that working out for you?" Mike laughed, the

comment slipping from his lips before he could catch himself.

Taking no offense to the offhand remark, the teen jokingly retorted, "It's right up there with when I decided to jump off the barn with a sheet for a parachute."

In the stillness of the night, Mike heard a familiar click followed by a soft, red glow.

"You guys are gonna wake everyone up if you keep laughing," came a voice from the darkness.

The faint burning ember of a cigarette tip moved closer to Mike and Derrick. As the cigarette's owner took a drag, the face of Erik Lasdale was illuminated. The second-time senior had spent the last four and a half years at John Moore High School creating a very large reputation, matched only by the equally large discipline file bearing his name. If there had been a fight in school, most assumed Erik had been involved. He had grown up in a challenging home; his mother spent more time with a bottle than her five children, and a revolving door of men that moved in and out of her room. His father was long gone. Whereas most could easily write him off as a prison-bound delinquent, Mike—who had taught Erik since beginning his career at John Moore—had come to see a different side.

Erik, though he tried hard to hide it, was actually rather intelligent. Clearly not a student that studied, he did possess an impressive skill to hear details and catalog them for future need. Of course, that assumed he saw passing a test as a need. He performed well in Mike's classes, it was most of his other subjects that he blew off with casual ease.

Taking a seat in one of the empty chairs, he tossed both lighter and cigarette pack into Mike's lap.

"Go ahead, Mr. A.," Erik teased. "You've been fiending for one all day."

Quickly rejecting the notion of not only smoking in school, but smoking in school with a student, Mike began to hand the pack back to the long-haired nineteen year old.

"You're kidding, right?" the young man said through

one side of his mouth while a cigarette dangled from his lips. "You shot up how many people today? And a cigarette's breaking the rules? You think anyone's gonna care that you smoked a butt while keeping all these kids safe?"

Either hearing sense in the words, or willing to give into his craving, Mike felt a small amount of guilt as he inhaled from a newly-lit cigarette. That guilt left with the smoke he exhaled.

The few remaining hours of the night passed as the three discussed Mike's plans for the coming day. He felt relieved when both agreed with his decisions. Derrick, however, suggested a small detour before heading north to the military base.

"My dad has a bunch of guns. He collects 'em. Our house is only a minute off the main road outta town. If my parents are there they can come with us, and if not, I know the combination to his gun safes."

Mike understood Derrick's true motive for suggesting the excursion, but he worried that each student would then ask to check their homes for loved ones. Travelling to sixteen different houses was a risk he was unsure about taking. He was cautious in rejecting the idea. Since he had no family in the area, he did not want to ignore the needs of the others. Agreeing to discuss it further in the morning, the three let the conversation drift to an end. Soon, he could hear the steady shallow breathing of Derrick and Erik as they slept.

* * *

Michelle was the first to wake, with the others quickly following suit. Though the room held no sunlight, the natural rhythm of the body brought them all out of their slumber. Mike informed the group of the plan of action he had devised during the night's isolation.

No sounds from the hall beyond the barricaded door were detected. Within half an hour the team to search the school—Mike, Derrick, Blaine, Erik, Josh, and Jenni—were loading weapons and ammunition onto their bodies. The others watched with worry, knowing how deadly dangerous yesterday afternoon's excursion had been. Though sharing some of their concern, the six prepared themselves with greater confidence due to their previous success in collecting the guns from the patrol cars.

Jenni Calente had insisted on being part of the group. With stereotypical minds, the males of the group at first balked at the demand. Derrick especially had wanted to keep her out of harm's way. But the lean and agile senior would not be dissuaded. As the youngest of five, all brothers before her, she had grown up hunting, fishing, and camping. She was as adept with a firearm as she was with her hair straightener. Jenni often joked that she was an "Ah ha" baby, as the youngest of her brothers was seven years her senior. They had long since graduated from the high school and had moved to various parts of the state, with one establishing a residence in California. Though her 5′5″ frame was diminutive in comparison to the others of the search party, her years playing soccer had conditioned and strengthened her body well. Her athletic prowess was matched by her intellect. At the last grading period, Jenni had been ranked fifth in her class. The combination of brains and brawn had secured her a full scholarship at the state school. Sensing a no-win argument, the others soon relented and she took her spot among the search party.

Mike's watch showed him that it was a little after 7:00 AM, as four students pushed aside the vending machine. Though a night had passed, he felt like his last two adventures in the hall had occurred only moments before. As much as he wished to remain in the relative safety of the faculty room, he knew that answers and help could only be attained beyond the door he now opened.

Having passed on the revolver, which Erik now carried, the history teacher had armed himself with two semi-automatic handguns. Derrick had informed him that they were Beretta 92FSs, though the classification held no meaning to him. During the night, he had practiced loading and unloading the weapons to prevent any fumbling that could change the outcome from life to death. Checking that the hall was indeed free of infected, he motioned for the others to file out after him.

Travelling down the stairs was more difficult than the day before as the bodies of their attackers lay in a congested mass on each step. As they passed the front office, Mike made note that while they might not have encountered any hostility thus far, the front courtyard was once again filled with roaming figures.

A corridor to their left led to the Math pod, and was the first of the seven pods the group planned to search. The hall was lined with trophy cases displaying past glories of the school's athletic teams. Their reflections in the glass startled Mike as he saw himself fully for the first time since this nightmare had begun. His clothes were stained with blood, one shirt sleeve torn where the sheriff had grabbed him. The back pockets of his jeans bulged heavily with the magazines he had stuffed into them. His face was drawn and haggard, which was perhaps the biggest shock to him. Twenty-four hours earlier he had looked similar to those his age. Now, though, it seemed he had aged greatly overnight. His jaw was held tight, the scruff covering it thicker now with two days of not shaving.

The mathematics pod had its walls covered with displays and posters students had made earlier in the semester. Some explained the quadratic formula, while others showed the various geometric computations for height, width, and volume. Silently, he opened each of the five doors, quickly scanning the rooms for signs of life. The classrooms appeared to have been untouched by the attack of the infected. *Can they not open doors?* Mike wondered to himself. Within minutes, he concluded that no one had sought refuge in the pod.

"Alright, guys. One down, six more to go. Let's hit the English pod next," he instructed. With remarkable bravery and determination, the others nodded their silent assent and followed him back out of the pod.

An hour had passed, and the search of the English and foreign language pods had yielded no positive results. The rooms in each showed no sign of survivors or infected. Mike began to allow himself to hope that all the others had managed to escape to safety. That hope mingled with a selfish disappointment that there would be no one else in the school to help him and the students in his care.

Immediately upon entering the hallway leading to the science pod, the signs of the infected were apparent. White walls were splashed with blood and gore and the floor grew increasingly slick beneath their feet. The now familiar stench of death and decay wafted towards them with each step nearing the classrooms. Mike could feel the building tension in his muscles as he gripped the guns he held out in front of him. Of the five rooms in the pod, one had its door open. The threshold into the class was blocked with an unrecognizable torso. Feeling the bile rise in his throat, he swallowed hard and willed himself forward.

The scene in the room was far worse than that which he had prepared himself. Desks and chairs were carelessly tossed around the room. The walls, floor, and ceiling were almost completely drenched in crimson, but his eyes focused solely on the carnage that filled the room. The dismembered limbs of the occupants, arms and legs gnawed down to the bone, lay scattered amidst the debris. Behind him, Mike could hear the sound of Josh Sorenson emptying the contents of his stomach. Easing his way into the room, it was clear that the infected had not left one body intact.

Anger welled up inside him as he stood silently among the devastation. As best as he could tell, some thirty to forty victims had lost their lives within the walls of the classroom. With a sickening irony, he felt grateful that none of the faces were recognizable after the savagery. Turning towards the door, he saw Jenni comforting the trembling freshman while the other three young men were struck still with shocked horror, the tears evident in their eyes. He could offer them no solace, for what comfort could be found in such a thing? Rather, he just stood before them as their stares eventually met his own. No words were spoken; any utterance would have fallen far short of its intent. As their eyes locked with his, Mike willed them what little strength he had left, through the gaze he offered them the resolve he now felt. *We will not become them,* he said to them silently. *We will live.*

A slight shuffling noise behind him caused Mike to whirl around, his feet barely maintaining a grip on the slippery floor. Derrick and Blaine were immediately to his sides, their weapons once again raised. The room was silent again and had the two teenagers not rushed forward, Mike would have thought he had imagined the sound. A tense moment passed as three sets of ears strained to locate the source of the noise. Finally, after a seeming eternity, the shuffling sound came again. Prepared for it, the three armed males quickly directed their sight to a small cabinet in the far right corner of the room. With steady, deliberate steps they approached the cabinet. Signaling for Blaine to open the door, Mike and Derrick took aim. Nodding slightly, Mike braced himself for whatever lurked unseen as the door was pulled open.

Within the cabinet huddled a small figure, arms wrapped around tightly drawn legs. Long, brown hair framed green eyes that were filled wide with pure terror. Taking a shuddering breath, Mike lowered his weapon, the two boys following his action, and rushed to the girl. Amanda Piper, a recent transfer student from Kentucky, threw her arms around him with desperation. Uncontrollable tears and gasping breaths poured from the sophomore as he held her. Turning her quickly so that her eyes were not directed to the room, he tried his best to calm the frightened child.

"Shh, it's okay. Everything's going to be okay," he told her, hoping his words rang with a truth in which he did not believe.

Lifting her gently, Mike brought her out of the room as the others took point around the pod. In hurried, broken sentences, the young girl explained that some time yesterday Mrs. Holigan from the front office had come running in screaming about the devil. Before she had a chance to speak further, boys from the class were shouting and trying to push the door closed as people covered in blood forced their way in. Someone had pushed her towards the cabinet and closed the door. Amanda told Mike of the horror she had witnessed through the small crack of the door as dozens of people streamed in and attacked the class. Her tears flowed anew as she recounted hiding in the small space as the infected tore bodies apart and consumed flesh and muscle.

Knowing that the girl was in no state to continue the search with them, Mike declared an end to the task. Jenni helped the shaking girl to her feet and the group made a somber retreat. He was reluctant to skip the search of the kitchen, but he told himself that he could not risk the further blow to sanity that another gruesome scene might deliver. Upon reaching the secure confines of the faculty room, those that had remained behind sighed with relief and scrambled to embrace them.

Mike entered the bathroom and turned on the hot water tap. He quickly knelt before the toilet, no longer able to fight the bile that had threatened him earlier. With the heaving subsided, he steadied himself as he stood and cupped his hands beneath the faucet and brought the warm water to his face. Lowering his hands to grip the sides of the sink, he raised his head and stared into the small mirror. Several moments passed before he heard a knock at the door.

"Mr. Allard, are you all right?" asked Michelle, voiced muffled through the door.

Turning off the water, he dried his face with the small hand towel that hung damply on a bar next to him. He stepped out into the faculty room, closing the bathroom door behind him. His eyes took in the entire room as he opened his mouth to speak.

"We're leaving tomorrow morning."

CHAPTER EIGHT

Having lost power years earlier, the city street was lit only by the faint illumination of the waning moon. When clouds obscured the silver sliver, vision was limited to but a few feet. The four refugees carefully picked their way down the wide avenue; a task increasing in difficulty as they drew closer to the hospital building. The black macadam was covered in the skeletal remnants of the city's former populace. Bags stuffed with clothing and personal belongings, now tattered from several years of weather exposure, lay scattered about. These obstacles paled in comparison to the other, far more deadly, hazards of the street.

Sprawled sporadically across the refugee's path were the still forms of slumbering Tils. Each step the four members of the search team took risked waking one of the infected and stirring them all into ravenous frenzy. With bated breath, Paul led the others, weaving his way through arms and legs. Mimicking each placement of his foot, Mike, Lisa, and Andrew followed closely behind the ranger. Their destination was still some five hundred yards in the distance, and over two hundred unconscious Tils made the trek painstakingly slow.

Mike was beginning to feel the first signs of self-doubt as beads of sweat rolled down his face in the cool night air. Back in the bank, Paul had tried to dissuade him, knowing that walking among sleeping infected was wildly imprudent even in the best of circumstances. Being outnumbered fifty to one, making the journey in almost complete darkness, and having no means of a quick escape made it idiotically suicidal. All this, he knew, but he continued to remind himself that the alternative was even worse. *Who am I trying to convince?* he thought and laughed internally.

An hour had passed since the group set out from the bank.

Lisa Velazquez, a daughter of Mexican immigrants, had spent two years in the military before the Tilian Virus outbreak. Like Paul, she had initially objected to the night mission on the grounds that the potential for deadly failure was too immense. Andrew, however, had remained quiet and once Lisa agreed, he willingly followed the others into the darkness.

It felt odd to Mike to walk among the Tils. He had spent so many years shooting, burning, and killing them, that to be silently creeping through a Til-congested avenue forced his mind into an unfamiliar paradox. Instinct burned in his trigger fingers, but rationality forced him to hold that instinct at bay. The stench of disease and defecation that clung to living infected further increased the desire to remove their threat. Now that the four new world soldiers walked among the sleeping bodies, he knew that any such action would be met with assured death. *Or worse,* he thought, *we could survive to become like them.*

There existed an unspoken pact among the survivors. They had seen too many of their companions fall victim to the poisoned blood of the infected. Through his experiments, Dr. Marena had discovered that while many had seemingly been immune to the airborne outbreak, the virus quickly mutated inside a host. While not only altering the infected, turning them into vicious predators, the same occurred to any that were bitten by a Til. Those that now survived had silently agreed to do whatever was necessary to spare others from the horrifying change. On several occasions, Mike himself had to deliver a killing blow to those who only moments before had been friends and allies. He had hesitated only once—six months ago—and the decision had proven more costly than he dared to admit. He often wondered, during those long nights as he lay awake in his cot, if the price had yet been fully exacted.

The night wore on and after two anxiety-riddled hours, the team noticed that the number of infected that rested on the pavement was beginning to thin. It came as a shock to Mike that the hospital was now behind them, and the first building he believed the missing might have sought shelter in, stood only feet from their present location.

The twelve-story edifice, an office building that once bustled with the hectic pace of business, towered before them. Its dark windows, most still unbroken, showed no sign of the missing. Mike felt uneasy operating under assumption, but he signaled for the others to move on to the next building. If the others had survived, their training would have demanded that they light a signal. The three sides of the building that the team could easily inspect had no such illumination, so they pressed onward.

It was the third building, about a half mile from the hospital, which allowed hope of success to plant its seed. On the top floor, in a window on the eastern face of the structure, a dim glow emanated. A cautious but hurried climb up eight flights of stairs brought Mike and the others to a typical office space. Cubicles filled with desks, chairs, and computers formed a maze at the center of the floor; while the sides were lined with doors leading to executive offices. Quickly getting their bearings, the four fanned out and proceeded to the east side of the floor. The urge to call out to the three missing refugees had to be forced down with some effort. While the light they had seen in the powerless building was clearly man-made, they could not be sure that it was set by their fellow refugees.

In the wake of the viral devastation, bands of marauders with no ties to civility or morality, had installed themselves throughout the country. Much like the British boys surviving on a deserted island in the *Lord of the Flies*, after the outbreak societal norms eroded with a speed that surprised Mike. His education in history, studying ancestral mistakes that destroyed civilizations, had not prepared him for such a rapid decay in his own time. He had learned quickly, though, just six days after the virus first took hold, that once driven to the extremes, some did not recover.

The door they sought was easily found. Desks had been stacked in front of it before the door had been shut. Paul extended his left hand cautiously, his right hand gripping his firearm, and rapped gently against the hard wood of the door. Though muffled, the sound of shuffling could be heard from within the room. A brief moment passed, and again Paul repeated the soft tap.

"Who's there? State your name," a strong voice demanded.

"Paul Jenson."

Once Paul offered his name, the sound of shuffling grew louder and it was clear that objects were being dragged away from the interior of the door. When it finally opened, Mike could see the weary face of Joe Connelly. Within minutes, both barricades had been disassembled and relieved greetings were exchanged.

"Where are Sara and Pete?" Mike asked, breaking into the joviality.

Joe explained that after the initial attack days earlier, the three had sought refuge in the building. They had made several attempts to return to the hospital, but the Tils had prevented that action. Running low on ammo, they were forced to make the strategic decision to wait for a rescue. The tone in his voice made it clear that their hopes of a rescue had dwindled greatly over the ensuing days. Upon exploring the building for food and water, the trio had made a remarkable discovery in the basement floors of the complex. Like many such buildings in the state, a tornado shelter had been installed below ground. What made this one unique, Jon declined to say. He offered no further details as he led them down, saying only, "You have to see it to believe it."

* * *

"Nearest we can tell they left a little over a year ago, most likely right after the winter." Pete Marshall spoke from a small desk which was surrounded by stack of maps and other miscellaneous documents. The seven refugees now occupied a large room five levels below the main lobby. Unlike the rest of the building, Sub-Level 5—as it was marked on the thick steel doors that guarded the entrance—was well lit from solar panels on the roof, feeding it power. A cursory tour of the complex revealed a massive room lined with dozens of cots, a few smaller rooms that had clearly served as storage and cooking areas, and a working bathroom facility complete with hot water showers.

"They had to be pretty sure about it to leave," Paul commented. He was referring to the papers the three had discovered during their wait for rescue. The well-organized notes detailed the years of survival since the outbreak, the names of those who sought shelter, and lastly, the radio message that had inspired the former occupants to leave. It was the last notations upon which Mike focused his thoughts.

November 18, 2015: Ken L. discovered radio broadcast. Coordinates in broadcast indicate the island of Cuba. Message claims island is secure and free of infection. Instructions to rendezvous at a port in Miami, FL for transport to island.

Further entries detailed the repetition of the broadcast through late December and the preparations undertaken to prepare for the journey south. The last entry was dated February 23, 2016 and simply stated: *Waiting for weather conditions to improve before leaving.*

The group discussed the broadcast and the notes at length. In days past, the assumption had always been that an island, isolated from any mainland, would be the best place to eradicate any infected and attempt to rebuild a society. The refugees had spent the years since the outbreak searching for radio broadcasts, though as battery resources dwindled, that task soon became impossible. The camp had decided that flashlights and other battery-powered necessities were more essential to survival than vainly listening to static.

Mike and the others talked for hours before their stomachs and physical weariness got the best of them. After hot showers—the first the four members of the rescue team had had in years—and a meal prepared with left-behind provisions, everyone soon settled into cots and drifted off into a relaxed sleep. Everyone, that was, except for Mike Allard. His mind raced with the implications of the log entries. *Could it be possible? Could the broadcast be true? Could salvation be so close?* The questions danced through his thoughts.

"You were pretty quiet before," Paul spoke from the neighboring cot.

"What do you mean?" Mike replied, knowing full well to what the ranger referred.

"Cuba. What's your take on it?"

Mike searched for words to express the doubts that filled his mind.

"I don't know, to be honest. It's a helluva risk. Miami is, what, like a thousand miles away? And the broadcast, if it is genuine, is over a year old. A lot could have happened between then and now," he finally answered.

"You don't think we should go?" Paul asked the question Mike had dreaded.

"I'm not saying that. It's just that right now the camp is relatively safe. We have food and water. To risk all of that on something unknown…I just don't know."

"That's because you've given up." Paul's voice was flat, yet the words held meaning and cut Mike deeply.

"How have I given up? I've spent the last six years making sure we all survive this thing," anger tinged Mike's words as he replied.

"We've survived in large part thanks to you and the decisions you've made, there's no denying that. But, somewhere along the way you got stuck on survival mode. Maybe it's because you've had to focus on day by day, but what about a year from now? Five years? Do you really see us all still in a camp somewhere in the mountains?"

Mike remained silent. Since the first days of the outbreak he had been forced to make decisions that not only meant the difference between life and death for him, but also the life and death of those in his care. Each month, each year, had seen the number of those that depended on him grow significantly. There had been no formal vote, no spoken declarations, but the role of leader had been eased onto him, evolving into a de facto position. Yes, the burden was like the weight of a buoy at sea; keeping it upright, keeping it from sinking, always at the mercy of the ever changing tides. But he refused to believe that he had given up.

The awkward silence stretched on until Paul spoke again.

"There's something that comes after surviving. It's living. It's rebuilding some sort of a future. And that can't happen when we're hidden away in the mountains." His voice cracked as he softly continued. "I lost my wife and baby to this damned virus. I hated myself for being the one to survive. But, I did. And now it's time to live…otherwise what's the point?"

Mike had no answer to the question. Paul rarely spoke of the wife and child he lost six years ago. After a year of marriage, the couple had welcomed a baby girl into the world. Amy, his wife, had given birth just one day before the outbreak. He was to bring them both home from the hospital when mother and child spiked high fevers. Only once did he tell Mike how he had been holding the yet-unnamed infant when she had changed, the angelic features turning into a grotesque, snarling face. The doctors had rushed the child away and quickly ushered Paul out of his wife's room. It was the last time he saw either of them.

The two spoke no further that night, the ranger leaving Mike to his tortured thoughts. He did not know what type of future he saw five years hence. His mind had been so preoccupied with surviving a day, and the one that followed. For the first time, Mike began to realize that while he had worked towards daily survival, to meeting the immediate needs of the refugees, that six years had slipped by. He began to wonder if perhaps Paul was right. *Have I traded living for surviving?*

* * *

The underground sanctuary offered no indication as to whether night or day ruled the world outside. Blearily, Mike sat up in the cot and glanced at his watch. He was shocked when he read the digitized numbers, stating that it was 8:17 AM. Fatigue had kept him asleep for almost ten hours. The other cots in the room were empty, and he could make out faint voices coming from the kitchen.

Not wanting to jump back into the discussion now being held about the broadcast, he headed for the showers. He let the water scald him, the intense heat relaxing muscles that seemed to constantly ache with tension. He felt slightly guilty for enjoying a second shower while those back at the camp were forced to bathe with cold mountain water. The soothing steam rose around him in the stall, as he placed his head under the steady flow of hot water. He breathed deeply as his nose absorbed the light aroma of the scented-soap with which he cleansed his body. Even with the shower the afternoon before, the water that circled the drain ran dark with dirt and grime.

As he stepped out and dried himself with a large, soft bath towel, he noticed a small shelf stocked with shaving cream and disposable razors. Wiping the steam-covered mirror, he began to lather his face with the mentholated cream and shaved away the scruff that had accumulated over the past several days. Rinsing his face, Mike soon discovered that the clothes he had worn yesterday lay folded in a neat pile on a chair in the bathroom, the fresh scent of detergent and dryer sheets evident as he dressed.

Surprisingly rejuvenated, Mike stepped into the kitchen as he adjusted the straps of the holsters buckled to his waist and torso. The others were seated around the large wooden table, eating a breakfast of oatmeal and canned fruit. Taking an empty chair, he joined them and quickly poured himself a cup of coffee.

"A washer and dryer, too, huh?" he asked with a smile.

Sara Marshall, Pete's wife of over twenty years, acknowledged that she had discovered the machines in a back room of the complex and had taken it upon herself to clean the garments of the four new arrivals.

The group spoke amicably as they reminisced over the last time each had enjoyed a mug of fresh brewed coffee, or the hearty warmth of a bowl of oatmeal. For most, the memories lived in better times, before the outbreak. Mike took note of how quickly these people, who had spent years in make-shift camps, slid back into the normal pace of an era he thought lost for good.

Paul turned the conversation back to the immediate present when he asked Mike, "So, what's the plan, chief?"

Savoring the last sip of the coffee, Mike placed his cup on the table as he addressed the room.

"First off, we need to get a vehicle since there is no way we're going to make it back to camp on foot."

"I've been scouting from the roof over the past couple of days, and it looks like there is a used car lot a few blocks over. With enough fire power we should be able to reach it easily enough," Jon Connelly informed Mike.

"How long will it take to reach?" Paul asked.

Jon responded as he scratched his chin, calculating the distance and obstacles, "If we head north and circle back around down one of the other streets, we can avoid the Til by the hospital. If it goes smoothly, we could make it in thirty minutes."

Mike absorbed the information. "Okay. Paul, Lisa, Andrew, and Jon, I want you guys to head out within the hour. We're going to need two cars, preferably SUVs. I assume the loading dock to this building is on the west side, Jon?"

"Yes, sir."

"Good, when you get the transportation, head there. Sara and Pete, that leaves us a little over an hour to get as many of these supplies up there and ready to load in when they return."

The middle-aged couple both nodded in agreement.

"You're probably going to stir up a good number of Tils along the way, so as soon as you four get back, you're to lay down as much cover fire as we have left while the three of us load up. After that, we pile in and plow through anything that's still standing. I want us back at camp in forty-eight hours."

As he finished, the others dispersed and set about their tasks. Paul was the last to rise from his chair.

"Listen, Mike, about what I said last night—" he began slowly.

"What you said last night was what needed to be said," Mike interrupted, rising to meet the ranger eye to eye. "Now, I have supplies to haul up five flights and you have a couple of cars to steal. So, let's skip the apology crap and get moving."

"Yes, sir," Paul replied with a laugh. "How many of the supplies you want to move on this trip?"

"All of them," Mike answered as he made his way out the door.

"All of them?" Paul repeated incredulously.

"All of them. I have a feeling it's going to be a long trip to Miami."

Paul's smile broadened, and he shook his head while shouting, "You know, you really are a crazy son of a bitch!"

Mike responded, voice booming down the corridor, "Yeah, I've heard that somewhere before."

CHAPTER NINE

The room bustled with excitement as the students filled their backpacks, replacing books with vending machine snack food and bottled water. An uninformed observer would have assumed they had been trapped within the faculty room for weeks, rather than the forty-eight hours that had actually passed. Mike understood their need for action, for the feeling that they were not sitting around helpless, the feeling that—even in the chaos—they were in control of their fate.

During the night it had been decided that Derrick's minivan, a vehicle borrowed from his mother that had previously caused him much embarrassment, and Sean Reno's large Ford Explorer would be sufficient to transport the eighteen people to the military base. Mike had conceded that retrieving whatever weapons and supplies they could from Derrick's house was worth the stop. Not surprisingly, the other students had all begun demanding that stops were made at their own homes, but he laid out the risks of such actions, and eventually the others relented.

A night had passed since he'd announced their imminent departure and he spent the intervening hours rehearsing each stage of the plan. In addition to having two of the largest vehicles of the drivers in the room, Derrick and Sean had parked quite near each other in the rear lot. Armed with the remaining ammunition, the group would exit the building through windows in the English pod, which overlooked the rear parking lot. Exiting the school grounds would present the first hazard as it required passing through the infected that roamed the front courtyard. Though not relishing the idea, Mike felt it was more prudent to use the vehicles themselves as weapons than to use up ammo in bringing down any infected that attempted to impede their exit. Since they insisted on driving their own vehicles, Mike had taken the two boys aside to make sure that they would be prepared to drive through an attack. Satisfied with their resolve, he agreed to let them drive.

Once off of the school grounds, it would be a short trip to Derrick's to collect his father's arsenal and hopefully find Mr. and Mrs. Chancer unharmed. From there, it was another thirty minutes north on the parkway to the army base. Mike worried that the parkway might be congested with abandoned cars, but without knowing a secondary route well enough and not willing to pass through residential neighborhoods, he felt the choice was clear.

Before they left the faculty room, he tried to explain what the others should expect to see beyond the door. True, they had all heard the gunfire and heard the tales of each excursion, but facing the carnage they would have to pass through would require a strength they had not yet had to muster. There would certainly be faces of people they knew lying among the dead in the halls.

It surprised Mike that he had already begun to detach himself from the attackers' previous humanity. Fighting them directly, seeing firsthand the gruesome violence of which they were capable, had placed the infected outside the realm of human. Hoping the students were prepared, but knowing there was no way they truly could be, he instructed that the blockade securing the door be removed.

The hall leading to the stairs was, thankfully, still deserted. Quickly ushering them down to the first floor and past the main office, Mike could see the visuals begin to take its toll. With weak words of encouragement, he did his best to comfort them and keep them focused on the task at hand. As he entered the corridor leading to the English pod, Mike heard a scream behind him. Turning rapidly on his heel, he found two students helping a third back to her feet after she'd slipped on the blood-covered floor tiles. The girl understandably began to panic as she found her hands and backside covered with the remains of the victims beneath her. Desperately trying to quiet her, Mike looked out the doors to the courtyard and saw infected already making their way to the disruption.

"English pod. Run. *NOW!*" he shouted as the students realized their peril. Further screams and cries of fear erupted from the teenagers as they streamed past him. Mike and the five armed students formed a line blocking the entrance and began to open fire. Infected whirled as bullets tore into shoulders and legs. Within seconds, they rose again and continued their advance. With only Derrick and Jenni as marksmen with any experience, shots to the head of the attackers were few and far between. Once the others had reached the targeted pod, Mike ordered a quick retreat to rejoin them.

Derrick and Sean were the first out of the windows and they ran directly for their respective automobiles. As the rest of the students climbed through the first story window, Mike saw them running in haphazard groups. Cursing himself for not thinking to assign certain students into each vehicle, he watched as too many struggled to fit in Derrick's minivan, while too few entered Sean's SUV. Yelling for their attention, he waved wildly and pointed for some to break away from the minivan and head for the Explorer. Relieved when he finally saw recognition break across their faces, Mike looked behind him as several infected poured into the classroom.

Raising both firearms, and hoping that the short distance would allow for greater accuracy, he began to shoot. With screams and snarls, the fearsome beings fell dead, one on top of another. Still, as quickly as they had fallen, others soon pushed through to replace them. Mike continued to fire until both magazines were spent.

"Mr. A., get out of there!" yelled Erik, who now aimed his shotgun through one of the open windows, firing relentlessly. Mike quickly dove out, hitting the ground with a thud that knocked the breath out of him. Within seconds, he could feel arms dragging him along the soft grass towards the waiting Ford Explorer. No longer gasping for air, he got to his feet and jumped in the passenger seat, while Erik pushed in beside him and slammed the door shut. Sean pressed heavily on the horn and both vehicles squealed their tires as the drivers floored the accelerators. The force of the forward momentum pushed the passengers back into their seats.

As they rounded the slight curve that led to the front of the school, he was relieved to see that the infected that had previously occupied the courtyard had all headed into the building after they heard the screaming girl. As they pulled onto the main road, shouts and cheers erupted inside the car. For the first time in two days, Mike Allard could feel the warmth of happiness course through him.

* * *

The streets held no signs of life save for the ambling forms of infected people that attempted to chase after the vehicles, but proved no match for the speed at which the survivors travelled. Without incident, the small caravan reached the Chancer home and pulled into its long, curving driveway. Set far off the road, Mike hoped they would attract little notice from the infected that certainly lurked in the area.

Rolling to a stop, Erik stepped out of the SUV, with Mike quickly following. Exiting through the driver's door, Sean moved around the front of the still-running car and joined with them. With an increased familiarity, Mike removed the empty magazines from the guns and replaced them with the last two that remained to him. As he approached the minivan in front of him, Derrick rolled down the driver side window and wordlessly handed him the keys to the house.

Though agreeing that they would stop at the Chancer house, Mike did so with one condition. Derrick was to remain outside until he, accompanied by Erik and Sean, could make a sweep of the residence. He did not want to risk the young man finding his parents dead, or worse, still living but infected. Once he could rule out those two possibilities, Mike would signal the all-clear and Derrick would then be allowed to enter.

Easing through the now unlocked door, the three slid silently into the unfamiliar home. The entryway opened into a small living room on the left, dining room on the right, and a large staircase leading to the second level. Moving room to room, they made a cautious search of the first floor, and then headed up the stairs. The home showed no apparent signs of an attack, but also no sign of Derrick's parents. Making their way back down, Mike followed Derrick's verbal floor plan and located the door in the kitchen that led to the basement.

Since his adolescence, the history teacher suffered from a crippling fear of basements. His youthful imagination had always created fanciful monsters that for some reason chose to live in basements and waited anxiously to attack little boys that wandered into their lairs. With the rationality that came with age, Mike had always told himself that such things were impossible. Given the events of the past two days, he began to think his childhood fears deserved a bit more credence than his adult mind had previously given them.

Descending the wooden steps, Mike felt about for the string overhead to turn on the light. Thankfully, Erik thought to improvise a flashlight with the blue glow of his cell phone. The faint light provided enough illumination for him to locate the string and with a gentle tug, an exposed bulb sprang to life above them. Reaching the bottom step, Mike found and flipped on the switch that controlled the rest of the lights in the basement. The room was small; a well-worn work bench stood at the center, and one wall was filled with shelves of tools. The other walls, however, were lined with the unmistakable rectangles of giant steel gun safes. Mike counted fifteen as his eyes scanned the room.

"Damn," Erik exclaimed, the utterance matching Mike's own amazement.

"Sean, go get Derrick so he can open these things up."

As they waited for Derrick, Mike opened a tall metal cabinet that stretched to the eight foot ceiling. Stacked neatly on shelves were boxes upon boxes of various types of ammunition.

"It'll take an hour just to get these out of here," Erik said as he stepped behind Mike and saw the contents of the cabinet. Mike realized the teen was right; loading all of the weapons and ammunition into the vehicles would be a daunting and time-consuming task.

When Derrick entered the basement, he quickly began entering the combinations to open each safe. Mike was amazed that he could remember that many different combinations. Derrick explained that his father had used only three different codes for the fifteen safes.

Seeing how many weapons each case held, Mike sent word up for the other students to take shifts guarding the front of house, while others took brief showers in the two bathrooms in the home. Derrick, joined now by Jenni, began to show them how each weapon worked and the steps for loading and unloading. Mike's head spun with terms like clip, magazine, double barrel, spring action, bolt, hammer, and a slew of others that he struggled to remember.

Seeing the bewilderment etched across his teacher's face, Derrick presented Mike with a case holding twin black firearms.

"Mr. Allard, why don't you take these? They're Glock 17Cs with extended magazines. Each mag has thirty-three rounds, so you won't have to worry about loading and unloading as often."

"Yeah, that sounds like a much better idea for me," Mike laughed as he took the weapons into his hands. Expecting a greater weight, he was surprised as he lifted the guns, estimating the weight to be between two and three pounds. While he practiced removing and replacing the longer magazines, Derrick provided him with two hip holsters that snapped easily over his belt.

Days earlier, Mike would have declined the opportunity to possess firearms. Having grown up in the North, he had never been exposed to the pleasure and sport his new Southern friends had experienced while being raised in hunting families. He liked to consider himself a gun-control advocate, but now with the weapons holstered at his hips, he felt a greater sense of protection and confidence than he had expected.

As the automobiles were being loaded with the basement arsenal, he thought a third vehicle would serve their interests better. Heading in to the garage, he discovered that the Chancers had left a smaller red SUV behind. Derrick informed him that the mini-truck ran well and tossed him the keys from the kitchen counter. The extra car allowed the students to have more space, and provided additional room for the weaponry.

Two hours after their arrival, the students were freshly showered and a large majority of the weapons, as well as some various canned foods, had been loaded into their transports. Derrick asked for an extra minute in order to leave a note for his parents telling them he was safe and headed north to the army base.

The three automobiles slowly made their way along the gravel driveway and turned back onto the narrow back road. Driving the red SUV, Mike led the caravan at a steady pace, hoping to reach the parkway without any difficulties. Though his eyes were scanning the surroundings as he drove, his thoughts wrestled with how and when he would tell the young Chancer boy about the shredded bodies of his parents that Mike had discovered in the garage.

* * *

The cars wove their way through the many obstacles in the streets. The abandoned vehicles told the tale of the panic and frenzy that had most assuredly ensued when the infected had begun to attack. Mike tried to ignore the sounds of crunching bone and flesh when the many bodies that littered the path could not be avoided.

Soon, the convoy rolled steadily down his own street. The houses of neighbors stood vacant, the neighborhood resembling a ghost town more than the once thriving residential community it had been just days earlier. Through the rearview mirror, Mike could see the horde of infected in the distance that followed after the three cars. On his left, he saw the familiar mailbox he checked daily upon returning home after a day's work. The small, gray home sat twenty feet off the road, its short driveway allowing space for two cars. As the front door became visible beyond the large tree in his front lawn, Mike was startled to see four tattered forms throwing themselves against the entrance. Over their howling, Mike could hear a familiar sound. Acting on instinct, he slammed on the brakes and leapt out of car. Guns at the ready, Mike began firing and the four infected fell just as he reached the wooden steps leading to the front door. With a fierce kick of his left leg, the door crashed open and a gray flash of fur exuberantly jumped in circles around him.

"Hey, girl," he soothed as he crouched down to return the greeting of Gazelle, the small terrier he had adopted two years ago when he first moved to Tennessee. Scooping her up in one arm, Mike quickly grabbed a small bag of food from the kitchen cabinet and headed back out, pausing for a second to remove the short leash that hung on a hook by the door. Racing back to the car, he could see that the infected that followed them had grown in number and were now only a hundred yards down the road. Sliding back into the driver's seat, Mike passed the dog to Michelle, who sat to his right. As the vehicles resumed motion, Gazelle, with tail wagging and tongue licking, still brimmed over with excitement. Mike knew that it had been a foolish risk, one that endangered the students in his care, but in the moment he had been helpless to his instinct to save the beloved pet from the rapacious appetites of the infected.

Though clearly stunned by his hasty departure from the car, the students now played gleeful with the attention-loving canine. Mike found himself smiling as he listened to the cooing of the passengers with which he travelled. The paradox was not lost on him as he observed the students, each armed with guns, as they giggled like children, passing Gazelle back and forth between them.

Perhaps it was the adrenaline, or maybe the enjoyment of seeing the students' excitement, but the entrance to the parkway appeared before them faster than Mike had expected. Glancing into the mirror, he saw the other two vehicles following closely, and all three made the gentle left-hand turn towards the on-ramp.

While not as bad as he had feared, the parkway was a jumbled web of cars and trucks as far as the eye could see. Most sat idly with doors thrown wide as the occupants had attempted to escape on foot. Frighteningly common now, Mike barely noticed the numerous bodies that lay strewn about. Instead his eyes were drawn to the hundreds of figures that milled aimlessly, some standing upright, while others crouched, greedily feeding off a human carcass.

With his foot on the brake pedal, Mike revved the car's engine in an attempt to inform the other two drivers of what was expected of them. Receiving a thumbs-up from Derrick in the minivan behind him, he released the brake and the small SUV lurched into motion. Blurred forms bounced wildly as the car crashed into them. Knuckles turned white as he gripped the steering wheel tightly, aiming for the open spaces between the abandoned automobiles. Maneuvering onto the emergency lane which held far fewer mechanical obstacles, Mike glanced down at the speedometer as the red needle glided past first sixty, then seventy miles per hour. In the mirrors, he could see the two other vehicles still following closely behind.

In the distance ahead, he saw what appeared to be an over-turned tractor trailer, its hulking mass sitting sideways across the three lanes of the parkway. The emergency lane was entirely blocked with cars that had attempted to go around the disabled truck.

"Hold on!" he shouted.

The back end of the vehicle fish-tailed wildly when the smooth pavement changed to soft, wet grass as Mike veered the car off the road. More bodies slammed into the front grill as he struggled to maintain control of the car's direction.

"Mr. Allard, look!" Michelle screamed as she pointed towards the fast approaching tractor to the left.

Removing his eyes from the road briefly, Mike could see the outlines of four forms standing atop the over-turned trailer. What appeared to be a man and woman with two small children at their sides, waved manically at the three car caravan he was leading down the parkway.

"Dammit," Mike muttered, plans racing through his mind.

CHAPTER TEN

With a concerted effort, Mike, Pete, and Sara had managed to transport the supplies from Sub-Level 5 to the back of the building ahead of schedule. Sitting on unopened boxes of canned goods, the three conversed casually—the topic, of course, being the possible salvation offered in Cuba.

"Wanna bet that Castro is still alive and kicking?" Pete joked. For decades, the Communist dictator seemed impervious to all attempts at removing him from power. The idea of a surviving government system, communist or otherwise, was something Mike had not yet pondered. The American government had crumbled quickly after the outbreak. He recalled the final broadcast of the then-Vice President, urging patience and composure. It was the last vestige of executive law and order the country had known. The days that followed witnessed a steady decline into chaos, distrust, and isolationism. A once civil country by most standards had turned into a wildly barbaric, unforgiving wasteland.

As Mike kept an attentive ear tuned to the sounds of returning companions, his mind mulled through the possibility of an actual government, fully functioning, and supported by citizens that lived and worked as they had before the virus. The concept seemed so foreign to him now, having spent so much time surviving in that wasteland.

Though the refugee camp could only be described as rag-tag at best, the survivors had established basic ground rules aimed towards ordered cohabitation. Mike was understandably proud of the community he had helped create, but faced with the possibility of a truly prospering civilization, he began to realize how truly lacking the camp was. The brief time in the complex below, with its electricity and hot water, reminded him of the necessities the camp still lacked. The small, portable generators that provided minimal power were abandoned during the Tilian attack on the second camp. Since then, the refugees had survived as Neanderthals with only the advanced technology of fire.

The three continued to humorously debate the seemingly indestructible force that was Fidel, when the distant rumble of car engines sounded through the metal doors of the loading dock.

"Showtime," Mike said as he hopped from his seated position, drawing one of his weapons with his right hand. His left rested on the handle of the door, waiting to heft it open when the sounds seemed close enough, while Pete prepared to open the second door. Three short blasts of a car horn signaled the arrival of the others and with simultaneous effort, the two men lifted the heavy doors. As instructed, the four who had retrieved the vehicles stood poised behind open truck doors, taking aim at the throng of Tils that were pouring into the alley.

Shots echoed off the concrete walls, as Mike, Pete, and Sara quickly began loading the opened hatchbacks of two Suburbans. He had worried that some of the supplies would need to be strapped to the roof of the vehicles they returned with, a time delay he did not wish to be forced to concede. But Paul and the others had chosen well, and the massive SUVs easily accepted the numerous boxes.

"Grenade!" shouted Lisa, giving the others warning to expect the rocking boom that would follow. Her strong, battled trained arm hurled consecutive grenades into the Til mass. Explosion followed explosion as dozens of infected were torn apart by the blasts.

Minutes dragged on, and Mike could feel his strength depleting as he lifted the heavy boxes into the trucks. The deafening roar of gunfire and explosions filled the small alley, and reverberated through the cavernous interior of the loading dock. He could see Pete and Sara faltering under the strain of their exertion. By sheer force of will, his body continued lifting and stacking, each movement bringing him closer to collapse. His muscles screamed in protest as he shifted the last remaining supply boxes into the now-filled truck. Fighting his body, he rushed over to the second bay and aided Pete and Sara with the final boxes. Their task complete, the three vaulted from the loading dock and quickly piled into the idling Suburban.

With a shout, Mike signaled to the four engaged in laying down the suppressing fire. Hearing his call, Paul swiftly backpedalled and took his place behind the wheel, while Lisa jumped into the passenger seat. Andrew and Jon repeated the action with the second SUV. The mammoth automobiles sped forward and tore through the Tils before them.

The sounds of the skirmish had attracted more Tils than Mike had expected. The hundreds that had surrounded the hospital several blocks away had followed the racket and been joined by twice their original number. Even with the formidable horsepower of the Suburbans, the thick mass of Tils forced the vehicles to slow to a steady crawl. An endless tide of infected cascaded over them, pounding on roof, hood, and windshield. Violent images of the loss of Tim Cornell that had marred the start of the mission screamed in Mike's mind.

"Cover me," Lisa commanded from the seat in front of him. Raising a shotgun as she dropped her window, she shot two blasts that shattered through the Tils. Mike lifted his twin side-arms, shot out his own window and used the weapons to keep the infected that swarmed around the left side of the truck at bay. From his periphery, he saw Lisa pull herself through the open window until she sat along the door frame. Armed with the last two grenades, she strategically tossed them into the crowded street in front of the SUV. Seconds later, two explosions cleaved a twenty-foot long opening ahead. Hoping to build enough momentum, Paul floored the gas and the truck barreled through a thick wall of Tils.

With Lisa safely returned to the interior of the truck, Mike looked behind them and was relieved to see the second Suburban breaking free of the attacking horde. As he looked out the rear window, he saw a bloodied, bare foot dangling from the roof above. Raising his guns, he emptied the magazines of their remaining bullets, tearing through the roof as he did. The bodies of two infected crashed to the ground behind the truck and rolled wildly under the powerful tires of the second truck.

The immediate danger now past, Paul glanced over his shoulder and said, "You didn't tell us you wanted a sunroof, too, chief."

The city slowly receded from view as they travelled the twenty mile stretch back to the base of the mountain. As he watched the buildings grow smaller with each mile, Mike began to wonder if he would ever see it again. He had called Tennessee home for over eight years, two of those years spent in much happier times. True, most of his life he had lived in the North, but the state represented his first step towards independent adulthood. He had gone from his parents' home immediately to a college dorm. Once he graduated and settled here, he began to build connections with neighbors and bonds with friends that he had hoped would last a lifetime. He had believed that his evolution to maturity and the shrugging off of the last remnants of childhood naiveté would begin once he struck out on his own. Of course, he had not expected how quickly that evolution would have to occur prior to the outbreak. With a nostalgic sigh, Mike turned his mind to the future and said his silent farewell to the place that, for better or worse, had cultivated the man he was today.

* * *

The Suburbans reached the base of the mountain as the waning sun reflected its pink and oranges hues on the white hoods of the vehicles. It had been decided that they would bring the trucks as far up the path as possible and finish the rest of the journey up the narrowing trail on foot. With luck, the seven refugees could reach the mid-point and pitch camp before the full dark of night fell.

As Mike and the others worked to camouflage the trucks with branches and leaves, Paul removed various parts of each engine in an effort to make theft of the vehicles and their contents significantly more challenging to any interlopers that might happen upon them. Satisfied that the trucks and supplies were as secure as time allowed, the seven refugees began their hours-long hike.

Mike had been so consumed with the rescue and escape from the city he had been forced to detach himself from what awaited him at the camp. The lieutenant had looked barely alive from the massive amount of blood he had lost, his wound had reached down to the bone. Mike had grown to trust the old veteran implicitly. The man's gruff nature had been irksome at first, but Mike soon came to understand that he would always get honest feedback from the lieutenant. The security team was mostly comprised of soldiers that had served with Steven Olinder, the rest he handpicked from the camp and trained himself. While not impenetrable, the site was quite well secured thanks in large part to the man's military experience. Selfishly, Mike worried that Olinder had not survived his wound. If the camp was to head south, they would need that experience to survive the journey.

The sun set an hour before they reached the small camp, the exhaustion of recent events had slowed their progress.

Near collapse, the group ate quickly, more out of habit than any real hunger, and soon Lisa and Andrew took the first watch as the rest faded into sleep. After a few short hours, Mike was gently roused from his slumber so that he could take the last watch with Pete Marshall. Groggily, he positioned himself against a large rock, the brief rest doing little to alleviate the ache in his muscles. He always preferred to take the last watch on missions. In the sadness and rage of the world, he was still able to enjoy the few moments of beauty as the sun crested over the mountains. Its warming rays caressed him, body and soul, and provided a greater relief than rest. With the ever changing chaos in which he lived, the constancy of the sun breathed a sense of life and hope. He relished those too brief moments as the world came to life each day.

Remorsefully, Mike stood in the early morning dawn and proceeded to wake the others so that the final leg of their journey home could commence. The trail steadily rose upwards as they hiked, the passage growing increasingly dense with trees. Though eager to return, he also felt the familiar mental exhaustion return as they neared the camp. He had always wanted to be a teacher, spending his days in a classroom sharing with students his love of history. Many of his peers, however, had been working towards advanced degrees in hopes of becoming a school administrator.

That path had never interested him, though. The duties of a principal had always seemed to him both tedious and daunting. A classroom required him to focus on small groups, whereas leading an entire school was an educational responsibility he had never craved. Now—six years later—he found himself carrying the heavy weight of being responsible not for others' education but for their very lives.

Even with the extreme danger and stress an excursion away from the camp, Mike still felt more comfortable in action. The camp's requirements often enveloped him in an oppressive melancholy. There had been days over the last few years that he had thought about simply disappearing into the darkness of night. Yet his sense of duty always overruled and he remained as the leader he had never sought to be. He understood the others' optimism in going south. It was something he had felt many times over the years. In the beginning, he had longed to find a place of solace, a place where someone else could take charge and make the determining decisions. After the military base, and the other false glimmers of hope that followed, he had relinquished his optimism and surrendered to his fate.

The loss of so many lives as the survivors chased after each broken promise made Mike leery of salvation. It wasn't until Paul and he had spoken in the tornado shelter, that he realized that perhaps his flagging spirit was hindering the futures of the camp's refugees. The realization gnawed at him. *Maybe it's time to leave them?* his thoughts echoed without reply.

* * *

The sun stood at its zenith as the camp came into sight. One of the sentries shouted their arrival and quickly a crowd rushed to welcome them. An excited chatter immediately broke out amid the camp. Within minutes the news of the underground shelter and the Cuban broadcast swept through the refugees. Appreciating the exuberant welcoming, Mike struggled to make his way through the crowd in the hopes of seeking the stillness of his make-shift hut. Michelle Lafkin, arm now properly splinted, pushed to the forefront and threw her one good arm around Andrew. *Hmm,* Mike thought with amusement, *that's new.*

As he looked over the sea of smiling faces, he noticed that once again Derrick was absent. Making a mental note to speak with him, Mike's eyes locked with Dr. Marena. Unlike the others, the doctor's face was set with a grim, haggard look. Foregoing the comfort of his dwelling, Mike made his way over to the doctor.

"Glad you made it back," he said, extended his hand to

Mike.

"Thanks, you don't look it, though," he replied, as he shook the man's hand.

"It's been a helluva a few days since you left."

Now walking off to the side, Mike said, "Bring me up to speed, Doc."

In a hushed tone, Allen Marena updated Mike on the situation in the camp.

"The lieutenant isn't doing so good. By the time he got back here, he lost a lot of blood. We tried a few transfusions, which seemed to work, but the infection in the wound is my biggest concern. I'm pumping him with antibiotics, but honestly, Mike, he's still in critical condition. If I had an OR maybe, but there is just too much infected flesh and muscle to safely remove."

Mike processed the information, his fear of losing the lieutenant seemingly coming to fruition.

"What about taking the leg?" he asked the doctor.

"Again, with an OR maybe. I haven't done an amputation out here."

"Can you do it or not?" Mike's tone expressed his agitation.

"Yes, but that's not the biggest obstacle," Marena responded. "He said he doesn't want me to cut the leg."

"I don't give a damn what he wants! We need him, one leg or two. How soon can you be ready to operate?" Mike demanded, his volume reaching the crowd, which now grew hushed.

"I'll need an hour to get prepped. But, Mike, I don't think he..."

"Is he conscious now?" he asked, cutting the doctor off midsentence.

"Yes."

Mike began to walk with angry determination towards the medical tent.

"One hour!" he shouted to the doctor behind him.

As he threw back the tent flap, Mike was hit with the

stench of death. It was not like the smell of the Tils and their victims. Rather, this was the scent of human descent into death. Laying still on the cot, tubes running into arms and nose, the lieutenant was ghostly white, paler now than when he'd seen him last. His breathing was labored, each breath clearly posing a struggle for the once indomitable man. Whatever anger and frustration Mike entered with slipped from him quickly upon seeing the fragile figure.

Pulling a chair up to the bedside, Mike sat down silently.

"Hey, kid," Olinder spoke with a weakened voice, barely above a whisper. The effort required to speak was clear in his struggling tone.

"You know why I'm here, LT?" Mike asked gently.

"Yea, and you still ain't gonna get my leg," the withered man attempted to joke.

"We need you," he told the veteran with certitude.

"Nah, kid. They don't need me. And you just think you do. Truth is you're the one that's needed." His words, though soft, tore through Mike with a staggering force. It felt like the old soldier had been rummaging around in his mind, reading a hidden diary of thought. He had told no one of his conflicted emotions, yet Olinder's words carried such meaning that they had to be deliberately selected.

"I've seen the look, kid. I've seen it on the faces of the squad leaders I served under. Saw it in the mirror when I led my men in the second Iraq war." The veteran's breaths came in short, shallow rasps, like the tide as it retreated from the shore.

"I don't know if I can do this anymore. If I'm what the camp needs…I just don't know." Mike's voice broke with the exhaustion of both mind and body. He was surprised to feel a warm tear carve its gentle path down his cheek. He had let the years harden his emotions, fearing they would distract from survival. Yet in this moment, he let the dam break. He let the sadness, anger, fear, and uncertainty expose him to their power.

"I'd worry if you didn't doubt, Mike. I've seen more

people die because they were too certain. Good leaders doubt themselves."

The statement seemed quite contradictory to Mike.

"They all look to me for the answers. But I don't have any more experience with this than they do," Mike said. For only the second time in six years he vocalized the fear of leading that had weighed so heavily upon him. His eyes searched the lieutenant's face, pleading for an answer.

"Well, kid, that's when you trust your gut and hope for the best." Steve Olinder spoke the words with a compelling sagacity. Mike could not help but bark out a laugh; he was unprepared for the simple, Zen-styled wisdom from the ornery veteran. Laughing through his tears, he understood that what the lieutenant had said was exactly what he needed to hear, his plain words overflowed with more profundity than any eastern philosophy.

CHAPTER ELEVEN

Think, Mike, THINK, his thoughts screamed. The mini-SUV he drove was fast approaching the overturned tractor and the people stranded atop it. The metal shell of the trailer rested on its side, detached from the tractor. The number of infected that swarmed around it shocked him. *There's got to be dozens of them*, his mind took a quick tally. *Too many to ram*.

"We have to help them," Michelle pleaded.

"I know," Mike replied, though he did not yet know how.

Blaring the horn with the hope of drawing some of the infected away from the trailer, Mike continued to pull closer. The speed of the SUV and the soft terrain of the grass would not accommodate any hasty maneuvering. Within seconds the caravan sped past the trailer, and even at that speed, he saw the faces of the four people fall with disappointment, believing they were to be left behind. Once past the congestion, he eased the SUV back onto the hardened surface of the road. Easing off the gas, Mike allowed the vehicle to roll to a stop as the minivan and larger SUV pulled alongside.

"What do we do?" Derrick asked from the driver's seat of his mother's minivan.

Only a few of the infected gave up on the stranded strangers and followed the sound of the horn. Mike knew he had mere moments before they would be upon him and the students. Settling on a course of action, he quickly shouted instructions to the drivers of the other two vehicles.

"So, you're saying like cowboys and Indians?" Sean Reno, the driver of the larger SUV asked.

"If that helps you," Mike replied, surprised by his sarcasm in the situation.

Not waiting for a response, he put the mini-SUV into motion. Making a large U-turn on the parkway, he began the return to the trailer, with Sean's SUV following. The passengers of both vehicles lowered the windows and positioned themselves as Mike had instructed. The infected that strayed from the trailer were brought down quickly with shots fired from both trucks.

Let's hope this works, Mike thought.

As if ripped from a John Wayne movie, the two vehicles made a steady circle around the downed trailer. Students fired the new cache of weapons, inflicting deadly results on their targets. After two circuits, the number of infected still standing had thinned greatly. The racket of gunfire, however, had drawn other infected out of the woods that bordered the parkway. As the bloodied figures streamed out of the trees, Mike said a quick prayer that the next stage of his hastily devised plan would work. With a third circuit complete, the two trucks pulled alongside the trailer, the drivers positioning the vehicles a car width apart. Students now let loose a deafening roar of gunshots from the inside. Through the review mirror, Mike could see Derrick's minivan begin its approach. The infected swarmed towards them, their numbers far greater than those of the shooters.

Derrick pulled the minivan in between the two SUVs while another student slid open the large passenger door. Getting as close to the trailer as possible—no easy task with the number of fallen infected blocking the way—Derrick signaled for the four strangers to jump to the minivan's roof. With some trepidation, the four figures made the short leap down, then scrambled into the open side door.

As the door slid safely shut behind the newcomers, Mike shifted the gears into reverse. With great difficulty, he wove the mini-SUV backwards through the abandoned cars on the parkway. Several loud thuds on the rear bumper marked the final breaths of the infected behind them. Finally clear of the danger, Mike cut the wheel sharply and returned the vehicle to a forward facing direction. The other two drivers did the same with their automobiles, and soon the caravan was once again on its way to the military base.

A few miles further down the road, Mike signaled for the convoy to stop. The area was visibly clear of any infected and he wanted to assess the situation of the group's new additions. Assuming the strangers to have some injuries, he grabbed the first aid kit he had collected from the Chancer house. If nothing else, they could shift some people out of the already cramped minivan into one of the other vehicles.

Any medical ministrations were delayed, for as soon as all three vehicles stopped, Mike was enveloped in a grateful, and bone crushing, embrace by the woman they had rescued.

"Thank you, thank you, thank you," was all the woman said tears of relief flowed unrestrainedly down her face.

Once she collected herself, the woman introduced herself as Sarah Weyland. She explained that both she and her son, Andrew, had been attempting to escape from their town when the parkway filled with infected. Drivers had swerved to avoid them, causing a massive pileup that brought all traffic to a halt. The two managed to go unnoticed as they huddled in the backseat of her car, and several hours later, she and her young son had started walking. They came upon Bryce Glassion and his daughter, Annie, a day later and the four continued their journey together. Another attack of infected forced them atop the trailer, where they had remained for the last eighteen hours.

Without direction, Michelle and Jenni brought the strangers food and water. Mike knew they should not linger long, but allowed the four haggard looking survivors a few moments to settle down and gather themselves. He informed them of their intent to head for the military base and extended an invitation to join them, which the four readily accepted.

The caravan soon resumed its journey with the passengers more evenly divided among the three vehicles. What was once considered a scenic road now more closely resembled a warzone. The carnage of mangled corpses, infected and uninfected alike, lay scattered in all directions. The burned out shells of automobiles still smoked in the afternoon sun. The peaceful suburban area had turned into an unbelievable scene, similar to those of a war-torn third world country from the evening news. It was impossible to feel any sort of satisfaction from the rescue of the four strangers when the hell outside the vehicles starkly showed how many had been lost in just two days. Even Gazelle, usually overflowing with energy, seemed subdued, perhaps sensing the anxiety of her human companions.

As Mike drove, Michelle scanned the radio stations finding only static. For years, complaints about the sensationalistic tendencies of the twenty-four hour news networks made for entertaining debates. It seemed unreal that a nation as powerful as the United States of America could so quickly be crippled to the extent that there was no media information. Even the emergency broadcast system had ceased its shrill, warning tone.

The silence was unnerving, and Mike was grateful to direct the vehicle towards the exit ramp where large white letters on a green sign announced the safety of "Fort Campbell Military Base."

Following the markers on the road, the caravan soon pulled into the main gate of the compound. An uneasy sensation gently gripped Mike's nerves as his eyes took in the empty sidewalks, roads, and guard stations.

They probably had to pull back to secure the buildings, he told himself. The self-encouragement did little to relieve his anxiety as their progression onto the base showed no signs of life. Unlike the parkway and the streets of his town, the meandering roadways of the base were devoid of any bodies. Mike could only hope it was a good sign.

The vehicles came to a stop in front of what looked to be one of the main buildings. Twenty-two eager passengers stepped out of their three transports and formed a tight group in front of Mike. Their attention focused on him as they awaited instructions.

"All right, guys. We need to stick close together. The base is big, so it means we have to look around so the soldiers can find us. Everyone armed just in case?" It was a question the education professors in college had not prepared him to ask while he was training to become a teacher. "Nobody pulls a trigger, unless I say so! That clear? We don't need to accidently shoot one of the good guys."

Hoping that trigger fingers remained un-itched, Mike led the mostly-student militia inside the large doors of the building. The room was immense, its walls stretching two stories to a vaulted ceiling. Various flags hung loose and stirred slightly from the breeze through the open doors. As with the guard stations, the room stood empty. The group explored several of the adjacent rooms, finding halls that led to even more halls. The complex was a veritable maze that challenged him to commit each turn to memory in case a swift escape was needed.

It took several hours to search the entirety of the massive building, and fatigue mixed with disappointment as they netted no results. The offices they found were neat and orderly, no indication of an attack or hurried exit. The apparent abandonment of the building confused Mike. The base, and the soldiers that trained at it, were world-renowned. He could not accept that the military—either through orders or defeat—would have completely deserted it.

For now though, he could see the weariness that had overtaken the rest of his companions, especially the four new additions who had had little sleep during their time atop the trailer. They graciously accepted his decision to return to the front entry room and set up for the night, and though the twists and turns they had taken disoriented him, they soon managed to find their way back. In the large windows of the room, Mike was surprised to see the sun already beginning its descent. *Searching this place took longer than I thought,* he mused.

The mood of the students in his care had greatly improved since leaving the small confines of the school's faculty room. The goal had been to reach the military base, which had been accomplished without any great injury. As he had suspected, simply being active in their survival had filled them with a greater sense of confidence. Mike still turned over questions in his mind as to the whereabouts of the base occupants, but even he felt a bit of tension ease as the group ate and talked into the evening.

Using rolled-up hoodies and spare clothing as pillows, the small band of survivors began to drift into sleep. Mike noticed that even though the room was significantly larger than their previous nights' quarters, the students still sought the security of close proximity as they huddled together.

His mind restless, he stood at the doors and stared out into the night. *What if everyone's gone?* he thought. *It can't be. There has to be soldiers out there somewhere. Tomorrow we'll split into groups and search the other buildings. It's the damn military! They have to be out there!*

Retrieving a cigarette Erik had given him earlier from his shirt pocket, Mike stepped quietly into the moonlight and lit it with the strike of a match. As his lungs filled with smoke, his eyes stared off into the darkened sky. The stars still shone, appearing to twinkle as clouds and gasses passed in front of them. To his left, the moon gleamed in a sliver of silver light.

He instantly felt miniscule as he gazed towards the heavens. *Everything's changed down here. Our world seems to be coming to an end, but out there things just keep going.*

He had not been one to ponder mortality and eternity in

the past. Yet in that moment, after three days of trying to survive an unspeakable terror, he could feel the strands of time that pulled him into the future. Time marched relentlessly onward, dragging along even the most resistant. He felt helpless as he understood that no matter how much he willed it to be so, the world he had known was indeed over.

His thoughts turned to the students who slept in the room behind the doors. Their futures were irrevocably changed. What plans they might have had, he now realized, were on a different road, one forever barred to them as they travelled down this new path. He thought of his own family, knowing how many of them had fallen ill. No foolish hopes existed for him that they had somehow survived the infection; the only hope he held was that their ends had come swiftly and peacefully. He had come south for independence, but now felt utterly alone. An orphan wandering aimlessly in a foreign land.

The cigarette had long since burned itself out when Mike flicked the filter from his hand. His somber mood kept him from returning inside, preferring to surround himself with the sounds of crickets and the life of evening nature. Some time had passed when he heard the panicked voice through the doors.

"Annie? Annie!"

Mike quickly came through the doors to find Bryce Glassion standing and shouting for his daughter. Seeing Mike, his voice called out. "I can't find my daughter!"

The others soon woke to his frantic calls of her name. With two small flashlights, Mike and Derrick began searching the room, hoping to find the girl sleeping soundly. Seconds passed when they noticed one of the doors leading into the rest of the building stood ajar. Without hesitation, Mike, Derrick, and the girl's father rushed through it into the hall.

"ANNIE!" he father screamed into the darkness. Mike and Derrick echoed his calls as they splashed the flashlights' beams into the rooms leading off the hall. The three men broke into a run as room upon room showed no sign of the little girl.

Racing down the hall, shouting her name yet hearing no response, Mike's heart began to sink. As Derrick turned his light from an empty office back into the hall, the small circle of illumination flashed across the face of a startled four-year old girl. The angelic-looking child said innocently, "I had to go potty, Daddy."

With an agonized cry and tears of relief, Mr. Glassion rushed to his daughter. Gazelle, who had not strayed more than a few feet from her owner's side, began to sound her high-pitched bark punctuated with low growls.

"Wait!" Derrick shouted into the night.

Mike was stunned by the swift horror of an infected grabbing the child from behind and lifting her to its snarling lips. Teeth broke flesh as the creature tore into the girl's shoulder. Her father, just a few feet from his child, screamed, "NOOOOO!!!"

With guns drawn, Mike and Derrick rushed forward yet were unable to take a shot as Glassion leapt at the infected, and all three forms went crashing down. Though it was just seconds to reach them, the pair discovered the still form of the little girl, her neck savagely torn apart. Her father began to rise from the tangled mess of limbs. He stood with his back to them, his head drawn down towards the form of his deceased daughter.

Words abandoned him, and Mike stood, silently unable to take his eyes from the sickening sight on the floor.

"Mr. Glassion?" asked Derrick, his voice gentle.

The man struggled to speak, his words a choking gurgle over his tears of anguish. His head shook from side to side in an apparent refusal to accept the reality before him.

"Mr. Glassion?" Derrick intoned again.

Mike motioned for the boy to withdraw, to allow the man to grieve in peace, when he noticed what Derrick had clearly concluded before him. The murmuring sounds of

Bryce Glassion were not caused by grief. His eyes widened with realization as the man's head snapped violently to his shoulder, his body spinning to attack.

Before Mike could react, his right ear exploded in pain when Derrick fired a single shot that tore through the newly-infected man's skull. As the body slumped to the floor, Mike struggled to ease the piercing ringing that echoed endlessly in his brain. Derrick tugged on his arm, pointing the flashlight further down the hall. The two turned quickly and retreated back to the main room as wave upon wave of infected filled the hall and chased after them. Pausing at the end of one hall, both men stopped to unleash a flurry of bullets at their pursuers. Though the ringing in his right ear still throbbed, Mike could distinctly hear through his left the sounds of gunfire and screaming from the room where the others waited.

Continuing their retreat, Mike pushed open the doors to the front room and found it was now filled with infected pouring in through every entrance. Students armed with a variety of weapons struggled to keep the crushing wave from sweeping over them. The infected pushed forward, two replacing each one that fell to a bullet. Others of the overwhelming number crouched greedily over human bodies, feasting on flesh and muscle. He could hear the sounds of infected drawing ever closer behind him.

Derrick rushed straight into the room and joined his friends in their fight for survival. Mike Allard—high school history teacher—stood frozen, shell-shocked as the events moved in slow motion before him. His eyes found the ravaged body of Amanda Piper, the girl who had remarkably survived while her classmates died. Sean Reno, the boy who had helped the others escape in his SUV, lay on the floor, his body riddled with bullets after he had become infected. *So many,* Mike thought, his emotions detached from his body.

Wordlessly, he reloaded the twin firearms and turned to face the infected that were racing towards him. Through a cloud of disbelief, he began firing round after round. His shoulders ached from the recoil of the powerful weapons, but he continued undeterred as the bodies of infected began piling before him. Screams and gunfire roared distantly, as if a world away.

With a glance, he saw the remaining students inching further and further back. Soon, he could sense them only feet behind him. Derrick and Jenni joined him in his defense of the hall, while others continued firing into the entry room.

You're surrounded, a voice screamed from within. As the infected closed the distance in front and behind, the voice—Mike's voice—spoke again, this time with no emotion.

Tonight...we die.

CHAPTER TWELVE

The service was brief, several members of the camp taking turns sharing stories of Lieutenant Steven Olinder and the mechanic Tim Cornell.

At one end of the camp, a small patch of land held markers memorializing the refugees that had died since the camp had been established, yet, the lieutenant's was the first body to be interred in the space. The loss of the military man sent a concerned shock through the camp. If Mike had learned anything in his study of history, naming a successor that the people trusted and respected would go far to alleviate their fears. Paul Jenson had rejected the offer of security command. In anticipation of the expected refusal, Mike had thankfully asked him privately. He did not want Lisa Velazquez to know that she was his second choice.

The council met directly after the burial ceremony to discuss plans for the exodus south, as well as other camp business. As the members took their seats, Mike entered the tent dressed in what passed for the more formal clothing he had donned for the funeral.

"Before we get to the Cuban broadcast, let's run through the status updates first," he said, bringing an official start to the meeting. The doctor shared his concern regarding the low stock of antibiotics in the camp's medical supply. The intensive treatment of the lieutenant's infection had put a severe drain on their resources. Upon the veteran's request, Mike had agreed to administer the lethal dose of morphine that ended the proud man's suffering. Dr. Marena had refused to perform the action out of ethical and moral convictions. Mike respected both men's decisions and therefore took the duty upon himself. Marena continued his situation report with an update on Abby Jarvis' condition. The young pregnant woman seemed to be in fine health. Pregnancy was a new quandary for the camp, and one Mike believed they would soon face again. Eighteen months in the camp had allowed many of the refugees to transition from a mode of survival to one of relative security, marked by romantic bonds that were beginning to form among several refugees. Michelle and Andrew's clinging embrace two days earlier was just one example of those bonds.

Michelle Lafkin announced that she would lead a team to the hidden vehicles to inventory the contents. Having loaded many of the boxes, Mike knew that food would not be a concern for some time. The situation not having allowed for a thorough search, he hoped that some of what they had removed from the tornado shelter included medical supplies for the doctor. The meeting progressed as each member updated the group. Derrick Chancer had little to say regarding the community, which caused Mike to worry again that his time spent in the isolated tent was beginning to distract him from his responsibilities.

Soon the conversation turned to Cuba and its alleged promise of safety. Even the loss of the lieutenant had not dampened the excited buzz that marked most conversations in the camp over the last two days. Mike knew no vote was needed; the eagerness to believe the message and head south was evident.

"Lisa," he addressed the new head of security. "I need you to determine the fastest and safest route south."

"Well, I've been looking at the maps since we returned. The trip will be close to nine hundred miles. Given our numbers, I'd like to try and get our hands on at least two buses for the main portion of the camp. The rest can divide among smaller vehicles to scout ahead and provide security."

Mike was impressed that she had already begun the preparations. He knew the loss of her commanding officer struck a deep blow. Her dedication, however, drove her to honor his memory through determined efficiency.

"Okay, the less vehicles the better. Biggest obstacle, though, is going to be gas. Any thoughts?" Mike offered the question to the assembly.

Lisa again had already begun to develop a plan of action. "With rotating excursion groups, we would need at least a month to secure enough fuel for the journey. The other option is to leave sooner and hope to find fuel along the way."

"I think it will be better to wait the month," the doctor added. "I know everyone is eager to head out, but a month won't change much and it will allow us to prepare more comprehensively."

"Agreed," Mike responded. "Derrick, what do you think?"

The young man's mind was clearly elsewhere and seemed startled when he heard his name.

"Huh? Oh, yeah, right. No, a month is good," he said. Mike could feel the disapproval emanating from Paul behind him. *He's right, I have waited too long with Derrick,* he thought.

Seeking to swing the attention from Derrick, he turned to Michelle. "When you get an inventory of the supplies, bring it directly to me. We can't assume the trip south will take only two or three days. I don't want the camp thinking they can feast for the next month. We continue with the ration sizes we have now."

The discussion continued for some time. Lisa agreed to

send the first recovery team out the following day. Without Tim, they would be forced to find transportation in relatively good working order. Some in the camp had basic mechanical skills, but none could rival the knowledge level of the deceased mechanic. As the council departed, Mike asked Derrick to remain behind. As Paul exited the room, he glanced back to Mike and gave a slight nod of encouragement. The camp leader knew the time had come, but dreaded the conversation he was now forced to have.

With the room now empty save for the two of them, his former student spoke first.

"I know what you want to talk about. I've let you down, and I'm sorry for that, sir." Even with the amount of time that had passed and experiences shared, Derrick still addressed Mike formally with either "sir" or "Mr. Allard."

"Derrick, we all know that what you're dealing with is unimaginable, and I respect what you're trying to do. But I just don't think it's healthy for you, and it certainly isn't safe."

The young man stared at the table and nodded his head gently. Though time and horror had taken its toll, Mike could still see the young boy who had once sat in his classroom, the boy who had dreams of college football and marrying his high school sweetheart.

"How is she?" Mike asked.

Derrick raised his head, his eyes giving the answer as he shook his head in despair.

"Derrick, this next month is going to take all of us giving all we have. For the time being, I'm going to ask Paul to take over your responsibilities managing the camp." The words tied Mike's stomach into a painful knot.

"But, more importantly," he continued, "I'm worried that you're holding on to something that isn't there anymore. I can see it consuming you. She wouldn't want that."

With more force and energy than he had shown in months, Derrick snapped back. "I'm not giving up on her! She wouldn't have given up on me! It's so easy for you. You don't care about anyone like I do. We're all expendable to you. You were going to kill her! Just like you killed the lieutenant and all the others! You haven't even seen her in months."

"I haven't seen her because she is not there, Derrick," Mike said calmly.

"No," the young man spat, his anger seething. "You haven't seen her because you know what happened to her is your fault!"

There, Mike thought, *it's finally been said.*

Derrick kicked back his chair and stormed out of the room, leaving Mike alone as the accusation lingered in the air.

* * *

The air on that fall day six months earlier, had been crisp. From the height of the mountain camp, the changing leaves of the trees stretched for miles in a tapestry of golds, reds, and oranges. Derrick, Jenni, Paul, and Mike had departed the camp at dawn for their hunting trip. The food supply had been fairly stable, but with winter fast approaching, Mike hoped to pad their inventory with a few extra deer and rabbit. The rest of the council didn't see the need, and in truth, he was using the excursion to spend some time away from the daily responsibilities of his post. Jenni had been all too eager to join him, as she also felt the turn of the seasons and knew that future chances away from the camp would steadily become fewer until spring.

Mike could sense the tension between Jenni and Derrick, the latter loudly protesting the trip prior to setting out that morning. Paul seemed ambivalent, but his sense of duty required him to shadow the camp leader on any expedition beyond the camp's security perimeter, and so the four had set out several hours earlier, but had yet to turn up any quarry.

"You 'bout ready to head back, Chief?" Paul asked.

Mike looked up at the sun before he replied, "We can do another hour or so and still make it back before dark."

He led them through the woods, each member of the group well practiced in moving silently amid the undergrowth that carpeted the ground. A few moments later, Jenni motioned to her left, and Mike could see the flickering white tail of a large buck a hundred yards away. Armed only with crossbows, the deer was too far away to ensure a kill shot. With a flurry of quick hand gestures, he signaled for Jenni to circle forward on the right, while he moved to the left. The other two members of the hunting party would hold their current position.

As Mike advanced, he completely lost sight of the lone female among the group as she blended seamlessly with the foliage. *Dang, she's good,* he thought. An experienced hunter before the outbreak, Jenni's skills hand increased tenfold over the last few years. Much of the venison the camp enjoyed came as a result of her ability to track and hunt in the wild mountain woods.

As the distance closed between hunter and prey, Mike stopped short as the antlered animal raised its head in sudden alarm. Assuming the creature had picked up on their scent, Mike stood unmoving, hoping the deer would return to its grazing. Instead, the deer cocked its head towards Mike's right and immediately bolted through the trees. Having not closed enough distance with the animal, he did not pursue the deer with its much greater speed. As he turned to make his way back to the others, he heard sounds of a commotion from Jenni's direction. The sound of branches snapping was quickly followed by the sound of a single shot. Mike then understood that had not been the scent of humans the deer had detected, but rather that of the Tils.

Slinging the crossbow over his shoulder, Mike drew his weapons and raced towards the gunshot. Paul and Derrick burst through the trees from their position, with Derrick calling out for his girlfriend. Mike was the first to reach her and found the young girl convulsing on the ground, the body of a Til a foot away from her with the entry wound of a bullet marking its skull.

Mike's heart fell as Jenni lifted her head towards him, her eyes filled with fear, as her body shook beyond her control. Tears stung his eyes and his vision blurred with moisture as he raised his gun to her. His emotions made his weak, and he hesitated to end the life of the vibrant young woman who had survived so much with him. He could hear Derrick running up behind him and he did not want the boy to see her change, so he marshaled his strength and gently squeezed the trigger.

The shot rang out, but went wild as Mike felt himself thrown to the ground from a thundering weight crashing in behind him. The force of the tackle sent his guns from his hands as his body collided with the soft earth. Dazed and breathless, his eyes could see the blurry form of Derrick rushing to Jenni's side.

"Derrick, no!" Paul shouted.

As the adrenaline poured through him, Mike was able to catch his breath, and as he stood, he turned to see Derrick restraining the now fully-transitioned woman.

With lips pulled back into a vicious snarl, Jenni fought against her captivity with wild abandon. Mike reached for the other gun strapped to his leg as Derrick continued his struggle to contain her.

"No! You can't shoot her. There'll be a cure! The doc will find a cure!" he pleaded, tears streaming down his face.

"Derrick, you can't do this," Mike implored. "She's not herself anymore. There isn't a cure now, and there may never be."

"Stand aside, Derrick," Paul ordered, his own gun aimed directly at the struggling pair. Mike could see him weighing the options. Positioned as they were, a bullet that killed Jenni might also pass through into Derrick, the result would either kill him or infect him.

"No! You kill her, you kill me."

"Listen to me," Mike tried again to reason with him. "She's gone. What's left now would kill you and anyone else that got near her. Jenni's gone, Derrick. She's gone."

"There'll be a cure, Mr. Allard. I know it! Please, let her get cured."

Seeing reason was not going to succeed given the young man's current hysterical state, Mike did the only thing he could.

"Cuff her."

"Mike," Paul began, quickly silenced as his leader barked the command again.

"Just do it, dammit!"

* * *

Mike sat alone in the council room, a gray ball of fur curled around his feet where Gazelle slept. Many nights he woke violently from tortured sleep, covered in a thin sheen of sweat, as the memory played in his dreams. He cursed himself for the second of hesitation on that fall day. Derrick was right. Mike did not visit the tent in which Jenni was chained because he could not bring himself to face his failure. He did not blame himself for Jenni being attacked. He had lost many over the years to unfortunate twists of fate. No, he was wise enough to not accept blame for that which he could not control. Rather, the fault he felt was for letting his emotions prevent him from doing what had needed to be done.

Paul ducked into the room, pausing for permission to intrude. With chin on hand, Mike signaled consent with the raise of his eyebrow and a deep inhalation.

"You okay?" Paul asked as he crossed the room and occupied the chair to Mike's left.

"You should have known him when he was my student. That kid was so determined to make something of his life. Even when the virus hit, he still kept everyone going," Mike said, his hand gently scratching the side of his face. "I wanted to save him from this. I should have pulled the trigger a second sooner, but I was weak. I was weak and now they're both gone."

"It wasn't weakness, Mike. And you can't keep blaming yourself for that. Someone you knew for years was changing in front of you. You were in shock," Paul said, trying to ease his friend's guilt.

"That shot, yeah. But, I knew that letting her live would destroy him," Mike continued, his voice soft and confessional. "I knew it when he pleaded with me for her life...I knew he was just as lost to us as she was then. That was the shot I needed to have taken."

"No one would have taken that shot, Mike. I was there, remember? I could have pulled the trigger, too. It's one thing to kill someone that's transitioning, but no one can blame you, or me, for not killing someone that's still healthy."

Mike shook his head as he spoke, "Don't you see, though? It will happen again. What we set in motion by letting her live, letting her be chained in a tent while we wait for a cure that may never come, it's all going to happen again. Someone will get bit, and someone's going to plead for mercy for their loved one. What happens when this camp is filled with infected chained in tents?"

"That's not going to happen. That's why we're going to Cuba, Mike."

Mike laughed. "Cuba. Yeah, and what do you think is going to happen when we reach the coast and they see us bringing an infected along for the trip? Any place that has cleared itself of the virus has certainly had to have been more decisive than we've been. Once they see we have an infected with us, they're either going to refuse us passage or simply shoot us down where we stand."

As Paul began to understand Mike's reluctance to place all his faith in the supposed salvation of the southern island, the conversation drifted into a silence that stretched on into the night.

CHAPTER THIRTEEN

The infected coalesced from both directions as Mike Allard and the small group huddled with him continued empting round after round into the seething mass. His supply of ammunition was dwindling quickly, yet the numbers of infected seemed to multiply with alarming alacrity. The hall before him offered no opportunity for escape. Unable to turn around, Mike forced his memory to recall the large entry room, scanning the mental images for some means of egress. His mind's eye passed quickly over the main doors, the thick glass windows, and the other doors of the room that led off to various hallways. Mike knew those exits were now impassable, having seen hordes of infected stumble through them moments earlier. His eyes drifted above him as an unlikely chance began to take shape in his mind.

"Erik," Mike shouted over the loud din. The second-year senior, with shotgun blasting, stood with his back to Mike.

"Take down the ceiling above me!" Mike instructed, hoping the young man could hear him. In response, drywall and insulation rained down on Mike's body. Two subsequent shots of Erik's firearm had created a gaping hole in the ceiling above Mike, exposing the second floor.

Understanding Mike's intentions, Derrick quickly boosted Jenni—with Gazelle tucked under her arm—into the darkness above them. Her hands grasped onto the metal support beams that framed the building. One by one, those around him were pulled up by outstretched arms, leaving just Mike and Erik losing ground as they tried to hold back the infected pressing down upon them. The congestion of dead bodies had slowed the advance of the infected as they scrambled over the fallen. Those behind, however, faced no such barrier.

"Go!" Mike ordered as he turned to hold back the infected in the entry room so Erik could escape. Once the young man reached the safety of the second floor, Mike stood ready to face the mortality that loomed darkly before him. Any attempt to climb up would allow the infected to charge unhindered, their predatory hands surely strong enough to pull him back down. The decreasing weight of his weapons indicated that the last remaining bullets were soon to be fired.

"Mr. A," Erik shouted down above him. "The fire extinguisher!"

With a split-second glance to his right, Mike saw the debris-covered red canister that was hooked to the wall. Instincts beyond comprehension directed him to grab the extinguisher and hurl it forward at the infected who stood just a few feet from him. Hoping his aim would prove true, he directed both weapons downward and fired into the canister. The resulting explosion sent a thick cloud of white powder in all directions.

Holstering his firearms, Mike used the brief moment of blind confusion to jump towards the jagged opening ripped in the ceiling. He could feel hands clasp around his wrists and forearms as his body was dragged through the hole.

Without pause, he struggled to his feet and led the others through the moonlit hallway towards the emergency exit door and the staircase beyond. As they raced upwards, Mike could hear the grotesque raging growls of infected following several floors below. Reaching the top floor, he threw his weight against the metal door.

The unsullied evening air was a welcome relief from the scent of gunpowder and decay that hovered thickly within the building. Thinking quickly, Derrick slammed the door shut behind them and tried to find some way of locking it closed. Erik pulled a large metal cover off a ventilation unit and jammed it under the door handle. While it would not hold indefinitely, the hastily rigged blockade would allow the survivors a head start once the infected broke through.

Mike's eyes strained in the dim light as he searched the rooftop. At the far end of the roof he could see the steel bars of a fire escape. Leading the others to it, he looked down the side of the building and was relieved to find no infected at the ladder's base. Derrick, followed by Jenni, began the steep descent as Mike waited warily, eyes locked on the door as it was pounded relentlessly from within. As the last to start down, he kept one gun in his left hand, using his right to support his passage down. When he reached the halfway point, he could hear the door give way to the escalating pressure of the infected. Feet finally meeting the ground, Mike brought a finger to his lips to caution silence. Their shadowed forms moved through the night towards another building in the distance. Mike hoped that this building was far enough from the main hall and the infected that now filled it.

Moments later, the still-stunned escapees found themselves in what was clearly a small barracks. The one-story building was compromised of a sleeping area with a dozen or so cots, a bathroom with multiple showers and stalls, and an undersized living area furnished with two couches and a television. Mike quickly set about making sure all exits were secure. The barracks lacked many windows, which he counted as a blessing given the number of infected on the base. Once several large trunks had barricaded the front and rear entrance, he turned to assess what remained of the party that had originally sought refuge that afternoon.

Of the twenty-two that had reached the base, only nine

now remained, himself included. Mike found the familiar faces of Jenni, Derrick, Michelle, and Erik. Sarah Weyland sat on one of the cots as she clung to her son Andrew tightly. Blaine Grimson and Josh Sorenson occupied two other cots, the latter shivering with fear. *So few,* Mike thought to himself. Anger grew within him as all the efforts he had expended to keep his students safe had been erased so violently and so quickly. *We left one hell only to be stranded in another.* Reaching the military base had been the full extent of his planning. Desperation and disappointment placed their icy grip upon him as his mind searched fruitlessly for the answer to the screaming question, *What now*?

The faces of those around him were paralyzed with fear as tears tracked their faces, the horror of what had occurred filling them with defeat. Mike could not find the words to console or encourage. His own heart hung heavy with the same emotions. No longer able to lead with strength and conviction, he simply took his place among the weary, sitting with them in silence as the dark of the night passed into the waking of the dawn.

* * *

The nine refugees, as Mike had begun to think of them, had found no sleep since the attack. They kept their movements infrequent, fearing the slightest chance to alert the infected to their presence. When the faint slashes of light cut into the room from behind the barricaded window and doors, he knew it was time for action, but, try as he had during the last few hours, he could see no viable plan. The prolonged silence served as evidence that none of those present knew what to do next and were unwilling to put voice to such a dire predicament.

"Yeah, so we're pretty much screwed, right?" Erik intoned. In the two years Mike had known him, the teen had never been one to follow the social norms of any situation. In the classroom, he had often delivered scolding looks towards Erik when he made such remarks. This new world however, had already broken previously held standards, and Mike found himself amused by the youth's impudence. The comment, perhaps inappropriate, had served well in opening the discussion as to what their next steps should be.

Wherever they headed, it was clear that they would need to retrieve at least one of the vehicles since travel on foot would be highly dangerous. How exactly they would manage that endeavor was tabled for later discussion. As for the destination, the small group seemed to agree that the less populated their goal the better. Surprisingly, it was the twelve year old boy who provided them with the solution.

"When we went camping last summer, remember that cabin we saw on the cliff?" Andrew asked his mother. "Why don't we go there?"

Mike looked to the boy's mother for further explanation. She informed the group that the family had indeed gone camping the previous summer. On a wilderness hike, they happened across a small stone house tucked into the side of a cliff wall. The steps carved into the hard rock leading to the structure were weather-worn. Sarah's husband dared the journey in order to photograph the unusual home.

"It was clearly abandoned," she said, concluding the now-painful memory.

"Which campground?" Derrick asked. Though Mike was unfamiliar with the location, Derrick recognized it immediately.

"From here, it's probably like thirty-five to forty minutes southeast," he told Mike. "I've gone there a lot with my parents."

Mike realized that he still had not told Derrick of the discovery in his family's garage. *It will have to wait,* he told himself.

"Well, if we're agreed then it sounds like that's where we are going," Mike looked to the others as he spoke. With affirmative responses all around he, joined by Derrick and Erik, set out to retrieve the vehicles from the front of the main building. Having proceeded with the necessary stealth, they were surprised to find the journey mercifully free of any infected, and the vehicles remained untouched where they had left them the previous day.

Mike was grateful for the tinted windows of the building as they concealed the carnage of the night's attack. After removing the weapons and the few supplies from Sean Reno's SUV and leaving it behind, Derrick and Mike drove the other vehicles the short distance back to the barracks where the others waited anxiously.

He was surprised that no attempt had been made to follow them, wondering where the endless number of infected that had ravenously assaulted the survivors were hiding themselves. So much was unknown about the behaviors of the infected, and he worried that his lack of knowledge would have further deadly outcomes. In the four days since the outbreak, so much had changed, yet so little had been learned.

Michelle, Erik, and Sarah and her son joined Mike in the small SUV, while the others piled into the minivan. Derrick, the only one with sure knowledge of the directions, took the lead position as the two vehicles exited the military base. Mike had been tempted to search the complex for food and water, but without knowing the location of the infected, he did not want to risk such a search. *Whatever we have with us will have to do for now,* he concluded.

Though Derrick had estimated a forty minute drive, the blocked roads forced them to make several detours along the way. During the journey they were chased several times by the infected, but they posed no serious threat to the fast moving vehicles. Gazelle dozed lazily in Michelle's lap, oblivious to the world beyond the car doors. Mike wished his eyes could also have escaped the sick scene of infected feeding on the corpses that lined the roads. He envied the small dog her peaceful slumber.

Three hours passed before they arrived at the small painted sign announcing the entrance to *Willow Falls*

Campground. Maneuvering the vehicles onto the dirt road, they proceeded deeper into the camp. Still closed for the off-season, there were relatively no signs of life, healthy or otherwise. Mike moved the SUV ahead of the minivan as Andrew began directing the route to the best of his memory. In short order, the curving road soon proved too narrow for automobiles. As the passengers disembarked, Mike asked the boy if he knew how to lead them to the stone house.

"Yeah, if we take this path there's a cutoff that goes into the woods and then you just have to hike up to the cliff," the young boy asserted with confidence.

"You're sure?" Mike asked.

"Of course I am sure," the boy replied with the typical disgust of a preteen being doubted by an adult.

In the end, though, the boy was not that sure as the party of nine had to double back the way they had come several times before finally discovering the stone steps that led up to the home. Mike was still impressed with the boy's recollection, and could not bring himself to recriminate the youth over wrong directions. *Without him*, he thought, *we'd probably still be sitting in the barracks deciding where to go.*

As Sarah had remembered, the stone steps had seen much better days. It was little wonder that only her husband had risked the climb to reach the house. With each precarious step, the refugees slowly made the accent up the cliff's face until finally reaching the stone structure. Like the steps leading to it, the house had been the victim of passing years and many storms. The small window frames stood vacant, the glass long ago shattered and littering the interior. A thin, wooden door swung on rusted hinges that creaked loudly as the company passed through, the sound causing them to cringe.

Once inside, Mike was amazed to find a cavernous living area that opened into four other rooms. Whoever had designed the home had cut directly into the stone to form the interior. The process resulted in the exterior hiding the true size of what laid within. Three of the adjacent rooms had clearly served as sleeping quarters and were sparsely furnished with worn, wooden dressers and metal bed-frames. The fourth room off of the main area consisted of an old-fashioned desk and several sturdy looking-chairs. Returning to the large front room, he placed his pack down on the long table, encircled by six chairs.

Noting the faucet-less sink and woodstove in the left-hand corner, Sarah confirmed that in addition to lacking power, the home also had no running water. Erik, returning from his exploration of the area behind the house, announced that an outhouse existed down a steep, stone path.

"Well, guys, it's not the best, but it is safe," Mike tried to reassure the doubting faces before him. Their responding expression clearly showed his words had fallen on deaf ears.

Trying to support his efforts, Sarah announced with forced cheer, "Come on Andrew, there's a broom in one of the bedrooms. Let's clear out the leaves and broken glass." The boy dutifully followed his mother while Mike gave the six teenagers a withering look intended to spur them into action.

Jenni, quickly comprehending the unspoken directions, began to collect some of the larger branches that had made their way through the open door. As she did, Erik inspected the front door, looking for ways to secure it shut. Soon, the others set about doing various tasks to improve their new—and Mike hoped—temporary home.

Satisfied with their contributions to the marginal renovation, he began to explore the area behind the home with Gazelle gleefully padding alongside him. There was indeed a dilapidated outhouse at the bottom of a dozen barely serviceable steps. *That's going to be tricky,* Mike mused. Easing his way down, with his back pressed tightly against the hard rock of the cliff, he followed the narrow stairwell to the outhouse. While he struggled with his footing and refused to look down, Gazelle bounded gracefully down the steps.

"Show off," Mike mumbled. Realizing he had been holding his breath during the descent, he exhaled with relief as he reached the final step. The outhouse fit with the rest of the rundown nature of their new refuge. A large pipe ran from the seat of the toilet out over the cliff to dispatch any human waste. Though he found the concept interesting, he knew he certainly would not want to be walking a hundred feet below when someone needed to relieve themselves. After the inspection of the outdated bathroom, Mike began to search the rest of the ledge. Passing a stone fire pit, he followed a small path that led around a sharp curve in the rock wall. The short twenty-foot span ended abruptly into a small clearing that, like the back rooms of the house, had been cut into the stone. *No escape,* Mike thought, *but we could hold off the infected for days on those two stone staircases.*

Man and dog made their way back into the house and he was surprised with how much had been accomplished in making the space even remotely livable. The floor had been swept clean of all debris, the chairs flanked the table neatly, and the front door was shut firmly thanks to a large plank of wood resting in two brackets bolted onto the door frame. After expressing his shock and admiration for their fast work, Mike joined his students as they hiked back to the vehicles to collect all the weapons and supplies.

Jenni proved extremely helpful in finding the automobiles without having to correct any wrong turns. Shortly after reaching the SUV and minivan, the seven made their way back to the stone house, pausing intermittently to gather small branches and logs along the journey. The sun was beginning to sink low in the sky when they reached the shelter.

Having been raised in the North, Mike was quite familiar with wood-burning stoves and immediately checked the flue for clogs and, finding no obstructions, lit a warming fire. With some hard-used cast iron cookware recovered from a cabinet in the room, Mike and Sarah worked together to heat up several of the canned goods the students had taken from the Chancer home. When the cooking was complete, he continued to keep the fire burning, not for any lack of warmth in the spring air but rather he knew the comforting effects a welcoming fire had on people. Even Gazelle had inched as close as she dared before curling up to sleep, stomach full with the food Mike had put down for her. Enjoying their first warm meal in days, the nine refugees sat around the table and ate with what could almost pass for happiness.

What a difference four days makes, Mike ruminated over his can of beef stew. He had never expected to find such satisfaction in scooping warm stew into his mouth. He wondered what further surprises lay in the days ahead.

CHAPTER FOURTEEN

As the days matured to weeks, Derrick Chancer retreated into even greater seclusion from the camp community. He now ate and slept in the tent that held the chained remnants of what was once Jenni Calente. His presence in the camp had become ghostly and peripheral. Mike had not spoken with the young man since their heated exchange of words two weeks earlier. In truth, he felt that there was perhaps nothing left to say. Both men had made a decision six months prior and now they had to accept the respective consequences of those choices.

It was not a situation Mike desired, but he resigned himself to its seemingly inescapable authority.

The last two weeks had also required the camp's reluctant leader to focus his attention to the preparations underway for the departure south. Lisa Velazquez and her security team had managed to acquire one school bus and a number of smaller vehicles for the journey. The automobiles were in fair condition and could be expected to make the trip without failure. Gasoline was still a major concern for the camp, however. The years since the outbreak had seen many people using whatever ever gas they could find for transportation, heat, and cooking. It came as no shock when Lisa's daily updates showed only small increases in the fuel reserves. Their best estimation placed the needed gasoline amount in the four hundred gallon range. Two weeks into the search and the camp could only claim possession of less than half of what it needed. Though neither Mike nor Lisa wanted to continue the search while on the road, unless their luck changed drastically in the coming days, that option seemed to be forcing itself on the camp.

Where gas proved sparse, Michelle had far greater success regarding the food supply. The crates and boxes taken from the underground shelter would be able to feed the camp's population for several months without concern. Mike had willingly upped the refugees' daily rations slightly due to the extra physical effort everyone in the camp was exerting in anticipation of leaving the mountain settlement. The increase had also added to the heightened morale of the energized the camp.

Paul Jenson, Mike understood, was also a major contributor to the community's mood. Since taking over Derrick's duties, the residents of the camp showed clear signs of relief as they now felt there was someone to truly help with the day to day management. Mike realized, much to his chagrin, that he had indeed waited too long to remove Derrick from the post. His attempt to spare the young man further pain had actually negatively impacted the population as a whole. Rather than eating their meals in their separate tents, many now gathered together in a large common area Paul had cleared and filled with as many spare seats he had been able to find. Mike had even taken to joining them for the evening meal. In nights past, he had preferred the quiet refuge of his own cabin, seeking to ease the dull ache in his head that came regularly after a day spent managing the camp. But—much like the other refugees—Mike's constant tension seemed to ease over the preceding days. Though still not optimistic about the Cuban prospect, the rejuvenated atmosphere the other residents created had taken a positive toll on him.

With the day's work complete, he stepped out under the

dusky sky. The mountain air was warm even at this height. *Summer's coming,* he thought. As he made his way over to the common area, several refugees called out greetings to him. Pausing briefly to speak with each, Mike shared a hearty laugh when he stopped to talk with a small gathering of men who were responsible for the structural maintenance of the camp's makeshift buildings. They regaled him with a story of the day's events which had led to one of them, Jim Blournier if Mike recalled the name correctly, coming into unfortunate contact with poison ivy when he went to relieve himself during a wood-gathering trek into the woods.

"That'll teach ya to check what kinda leaves you're grabbing next time," howled Bill Demart, who served as the group's foreman.

Through his laughter, Mike spared a pitying look for the man who sat uncomfortably on a log, his desire to itch fighting with his reluctant amusement at his own predicament.

"I think the doc has some creams. Check with him before you turn in for the night," Mike instructed as he left the group and continued to the common area.

Grabbing a plate from the stack of mismatched dinnerware, Mike ventured over to the large pots steaming with aromas that made his mouth water.

"What are we having tonight, Alice?"

Alice Johnson and her husband Marc were two of the older residents of the camp and had owned a very successful pair of restaurants in the Southern Kentucky area. From the moment they joined the camp, the meals had greatly improved. The two chefs had a remarkable talent for utilizing the camp's minimal food and spice collection to make very savory meals.

"Venison stew, chief. We found some dehydrated vegetables in the goods you brought back," Marc answered. It seemed that Paul's honorific for Mike had spread throughout the camp; Mike noticed more and more of the refugees addressing him as "chief."

"Well, it sure smells good, Marc," he acknowledged. He thanked the man for the generous portion and turned to find an open seat. Across the crackling fire in the center of the cleared area, he saw his security chief wave him over. He took a seat with the small group comprised of Lisa, Paul, Andrew and Michelle. As he sat, Paul offered him a bottle of the mountain water collected from a stream near the camp.

Mike enjoyed the company of those with which he now sat. The time in the camp had formed bonds among the community, but he and the rest of the council had focused so intently on their tasks that most conversations consisted of camp business. Now, however, the idle banter of daily living, discussions of memories and shared experiences, were a welcome relief from the work of running the camp. Since the installation of the common area, Mike eagerly looked forward to sharing his evening meals with those who had become his friends. There were moments, before settling in this most recent camp, that he doubted there could ever again be a time when he could simply relax with companions. Now he and his companions sat comfortably in the calming evening, lightly debating the merits of certain films.

"Hands down, *The Godfather* is the best mob movie ever made," Paul said. The former ranger began a comically poor impersonation of Marlon Brando's character of Vito Corleone.

"No way, man, *Scarface* is ten times better," Lisa corrected, still laughing from the soft rasp Paul imitated.

Mike interjected with his own favorite, "Yeah, but what about *Goodfellas*? The bar scene with Joe Pesci is classic!"

The three elders of the group began re-enacting the humorous lines from the movie scene while Michelle and Andrew sat with blank amusement. Just twelve when the virus hit, Andrew had never seen the movies being discussed. Mike wondered to himself if the world would ever see a new movie in a theater again.

The moon loomed high on the blackened sky when the

gathering dispersed and Mike found himself back in his small cabin. With a basin and half-empty jug of water, he washed the day from his face and stripped down to his underclothes before sinking into the soft sheets that covered his cot. His constant canine companion jumped onto the bedding and circled twice before finding a satisfying spot alongside Mike's left leg Sleep found him easily that night, and when he woke he was pleased to note that no dreams had tormented him.

With a sigh and a stretch, Mike rose from the cot and gave himself a quick shave over the basin, the cold water stinging his face and forcing him to full wakefulness. Donning his usual attire of jeans and t-shirt, he soon found himself at the small desk that had grown heavy with the journals discovered in the tornado shelter. Carefully pushing them to one side, Mike began to study the various maps that added to the clutter. Lisa had identified two routes south, the first employing use of the interstate systems, while the second relied more on back roads as much as possible. The latter option would certainly add more time to the journey, but the former risked a very visible trek across potentially clogged parkways.

For the better part of the last two weeks, Mike and the council debated each route's merits. As of yet, no consensus had been reached. He had listened keenly as the two factions of the council presented their respective arguments during meetings. He knew a decision deadline was drawing near, and given the deficient results of the fuel search, Mike was leaning to the more direct, and shorter, route. As soon as he was close to finalizing his decision, nagging doubt always gave him pause and forced him to refrain from an announcement as he re-weighed the options.

In many ways, he believed the decision could prove to be the most critical one he would make as the camp's leader. Feeling the now too familiar headache stirring in his skull, he was relieved when Lisa and Paul entered his quarters. The relief was short lived as he took in the serious expressions each wore.

"Good news, I'm guessing?" he asked the pair.

"Only if the definition of 'good' has changed a whole heck of a lot," Lisa countered as she and Paul took seats opposite Mike.

"We may need to speed up the departure," Paul added.

Lisa explained that one of the fuel search teams had returned moments earlier to report sightings of a massive number of Tils less than twenty miles from the mountain's base.

"How many?"

"Several hundred, maybe a thousand. It was tough for my guys to get a solid count without risking notice."

Mike was stunned by the number. "Tils have never gathered in such a large group. And they certainly have never scavenged across miles."

Dr. Marena's research had shown that once a person became infected with the virus, the victim's sympathetic nervous system suffered serious disturbances. The fight-or-flight response in humans reached extremes in the Tils. Without stimulus, they tended to remain docile. Yet once agitated, rage and aggression soared to uncontrollable levels. The predatory urges only ceased when the stimulus was removed, thus allowing the infected to return to a state of docility. Other findings of the last few years indicated a proclivity to scavenge within a small range of one or two miles. Though not completely solitary beings, most dens Mike and the refugees had discovered consisted of small numbers. Only a stimulus would attract numbers like they had seen at the hospital weeks earlier.

"Could they have followed us out of the city?" Paul asked.

"It's possible," Lisa replied. "But that would be highly unusual for them. We're talking about a several mile chase over weeks. Tils have always given up once their prey was out of range."

"Are they following something else?" Mike wondered

aloud.

Shaking her head, Lisa replied. "Not that my guys could see. And the Tils didn't seem frenzied, just walking steadily down the turnpike."

"How long until they reach the mountains?"

"A few days, maybe a bit more."

"And the camp?" Mike asked. "How vulnerable are we?"

He could see that Lisa had already assessed the situation and was prepared for the obvious questions he posed.

"Assuming they're headed for us, and assuming they make it up the mountain, and those are big ifs, Chief, then I'd say we're pretty vulnerable. Our numbers and weapons can hold off many, but any prolonged fight will attract more Tils. And our people will need rest, something I've never seen the infected require when they are in their frenzy. We might be able to survive two days, three at best."

* * *

"So that's the situation, folks," Mike said, concluding his speech to the camp. He had continued to speak with Lisa and Paul for another hour before calling the council together. It had quickly been decided that the entire camp needed to be updated before the inevitable rumors made the already bleak situation even worse.

With the news of the approaching horde, the council determined that the refugees would begin to make their way south within the next five days. The decision on which route to take was no longer in question as the council agreed that the faster they could put miles between the refugees and the infected the better. Mike hoped that a two-day head start and the more direct route of the interstate would be enough to avoid the veritable army of Tils.

He could see the worry stamped clearly on the faces of the refugees that gathered before him, however he was not surprised to see numerous backs stiffen with a resiliency he had become used to seeing among them. None of them could have lasted six years without having proven their fortitude time and again. Mike hoped that their courage would continue to see them through the coming days.

The crowd soon dispersed and set about the tasks he had gone over in his announcements. The next days would necessitate a hasty loading of supplies into the vehicles that had been acquired for the journey. More time would have allowed Lisa's teams to perhaps locate more automobiles, but with what they currently possessed, the refugees and supplies would fit, if being somewhat cramped, for the trip.

The camp quickly sprang to life as people began forming groups to transport the supplies down the mountainside. Others packed clothing, toiletries, and the like into duffle bags and suitcases that had been scavenged over the years. Surprised, Mike even saw the good doctor pitch-in with the efforts. Normally one to stay buried in his research, the man had made the least attempt to assimilate into the camp after he joined them.

As the others engaged in their tasks, Mike found himself standing outside the tent everyone else in the camp avoided. He envied the uncomplicated tasks on which the camp's residents were now focused. His own task was far from simple. Yet, he had been unable to find ground to disagree with the council's decision in the matter. Mike sighed deeply, the action mixed with regret and inevitability, as he took the remaining steps inside the small tent.

CHAPTER FIFTEEN

"You're up early," Sarah Weyland said, announcing her presence in the lifting mists of early dawn. She joined him on the fallen tree Mike now used as a bench.

"Is that what I think it is?" he asked, accepting the steaming mug she offered him.

"It's no Starbucks," she responded, "but it is coffee at least." Over the past two days Sarah had worked wonders in the small kitchen area of the stone cabin. Even with the few supplies taken from the Chancer family, she had been able to create warm meals for Mike and the children. As he thanked her, the two gazed out over the vista before them. The sun, still on its ascent, had lit the morning enough to see the deep canyon below and the wild trees that seemed to stretch to the heavens.

"You know, I can probably count the times I've actually seen the sunrise, but, it seems different now," he said. He sipped from the mug and the strong, black brew spread its comforting warmth throughout his body.

"When Andrew was first born he was a difficult sleeper. My husband worked nights back then, so I would sit in a rocking chair and just hold him as I tried to get him to fall back asleep," Sarah reminisced. "I was a young mother, and didn't have a clue what I had gotten myself into. But sitting there, rocking him in that chair, no matter how scared I was, every time I watched the sun rise with this amazing little creature drifting to sleep on my shoulder…all the fear and doubt just seemed to wash away."

Mike considered her words as the two sat in a prolonged silence watching the last beautiful moments of the sun's rise into the sky. The magnificent colors of dawn soon faded and merged into a cloudless blue. He could hear the stirring from the cabin as the adolescents within roused from their slumber.

"I'm going to take a couple of the kids into town today to see what supplies we can find," Mike said as he stood from the make-shift bench.

Laughing as she followed him to the stone structure, Sarah responded. "I'd give you a list, but we pretty much need everything."

* * *

The drive into the nearby town was free of any interaction with the infected. Mike began to wonder if the virus would eventually be fatal to its victims. *It could all be over already*, he thought without conviction. Though the last two days had been spent in and around the stone house at the campground, and there had been no sightings of infected during that time, Mike was still hesitant to trust that perhaps the worst was over.

The warm spring weather had begun to aid the decomposition of the bodies that lay along the roads and sidewalks. Though most corpses had seen flesh and muscle stripped to the bone, a few of the carcasses had remained intact and were now showing the first signs of maggots. As the small SUV rolled quietly into the parking lot of a grocery store, Mike began to realize that the corpses rotting were mostly those of fallen infected. *They don't eat their own*, he made the mental note.

Mike was joined by Erik, Blaine, and Michelle. Though hesitant to allow her to accompany them, Michelle argued that it would fall to her to procure the necessary feminine items she and the other two females would need.

"Unless you're going to pick out what we need?" she asked, the rhetorical tone clear to all. With awkward mumbling, Mike and the two male teens assented, and Michelle won her place among the group, though the men found her tactics somewhat devious. Parking the vehicle directly in front of the store's glass doors, the four exited the truck with firearms at the ready.

Mike approached the door as Erik asked over his shoulder, "Need me to shoot the glass out, Mr. A.?"

"I would if the doors were locked, which they're not. But you know, thanks Mr. Trigger Happy," Mike replied as he pushed the doors inward.

The lights suspended from the store's ceiling were dark, leaving Mike to assume that, like the military base, power was indeed out everywhere. The clear day provided enough illumination to move about surefooted. Blaine and Michelle each commandeered an available shopping cart and the four refugees set out to collect the much needed supplies. The carts filled quickly with canned beans, soups, fruits, vegetables, as well as some fresh produce that seemed in good condition. Soaps, shampoo, and deodorant were some of Mike's chief priorities since none of them had had an adequate chance to clean themselves in days and it was quickly becoming evident in the minimally ventilated stone cabin. Clothing detergent was also a sorely needed necessity, and Mike placed several jugs of it in the carts' undercarriages. A variety of pastas and sauces added to their cache, as well as large amounts of bottled water. Several flashlights and many packs of batteries were likewise scavenged along their tour of the aisles. Blaine, notorious for his sweet tooth, ensured that a pile of candy and chocolates found room in the crowded carts.

Once the supplies had been secured in the SUV, Mike and the teenagers returned to the interior of the grocery store. Relieved to find the water still working in the bathrooms, the four eagerly used dishtowels from the "home" aisle and washed up. Mike was surprised at how long the water ran dark as he washed the grime from his hair, arms, face, and chest. The evidence of their ordeal stubbornly clung to their bodies. Even with several repeated attempts, he could still see dark patches of skin that dirt refused to abandon. Though not as ideal as a hot shower, he did feel better from having cleaned himself as much as a grocery store's sink would allow.

Mike could see the same effect he was experiencing from the bodily refreshment in the three students as they piled back into the SUV. The conversation during the drive back to the others was more playful than it had been in past days. A casual banter had broken out among the four when Mike was forced to bring the vehicle to a halt in front of an extended passenger van that blocked both lanes of traffic.

"You take a different way back, Mr. A.?" Erik asked.

"No," Mike answered slowly. His mind itched with unease as his eyes flashed to the left and right of the truck. "Guys, make sure you have your guns ready."

He quickly put the vehicle in reverse. As he twisted in the seat to see out the rear window, he saw another large van approaching quickly. Stifling a curse, Mike returned his foot to the brake. Now boxed in from the front and rear, the small SUV was rapidly surrounded with armed men that swarmed out of the wooded sides of the road. A mountain of a man stepped out of the newly arrived van and began to walk towards the blocked vehicle.

"How about y'all step out of there real slow now?" the man's voice boomed. Though it was a question, it was clear he expected only one answer.

"Mr. Allard, what's going on?" Michelle asked nervously from the back seat.

"I don't know. Just stay calm," he tried to sound

confident in his reply, but in truth Mike did not feel it. With his left index fingered he pressed a button on the door and the driver side window rolled down.

"We don't want any trouble," Mike shouted. "We just want to pass through."

He had his eyes glued to the rear-view mirror and the man that loomed ominously in it. As a result, he did not see one of the armed men reach his door. With a start, Mike felt himself forcefully pulled from the vehicle and roughly pushed towards the side of the SUV. The man that accosted him took possession of Mike's two firearms. He stood helplessly, a gun jabbing into his spine, as the others were removed from the truck and relieved of their weapons.

As the large man that had spoken earlier approached them, Mike was able to get a better view of him. The man stood several inches beyond Mike's own above-average height. He was clothed in camouflaged pants and a ribbed, white tank top that exposed a well-muscled frame. His arms, neck, and the visible parts of his torso were covered in a variety of tattoos, skulls and naked women the most common designs on him. Even the man's fingers were tattooed to spell out four-letter expletives.

"Look we don't want any trouble, man," Mike repeated his earlier plea while attempting to disguise the building fear in his voice. He and his three companions were now unarmed and outnumbered two to one. He knew that this situation, as bad as it was, could take a drastic turn to the worse if not handled delicately.

"We don't want no trouble either," the man said. He stood but a few feet from Mike, with thumbs tucked nonchalantly through his belt loops. "We just want your guns, your truck, and your supplies." As he concluded his heavily accented sentence, he spit a large amount of brown liquid onto Mike's right shoe. The men that followed him laughed uproariously, either from the words or the spitting, or both.

"There're a lot of supplies in town," Blaine interjected,

clearly in an attempt to rationalize with their captors.

The man turned his head to the teen and slowly drawled, "Why should I go shopping when I got delivery right here?" Again, his followers laughed at the leader's paltry witticism.

Trying his best to assess the situation, Mike estimated that they were still five miles from the campground. On foot the trip would take at least an hour. Without weapons, he and the three in his care were at the mercy from any attack of the infected along the way. Yet, overpowering this band of thieves was unlikely, and he was old enough to understand that rationalizing with the mindset of these men was equally improbable.

"Take the guns and the supplies. Just leave us the truck, man. We're sitting ducks out here without it," Mike tried to counter-offer even though he believed the attempt was made in vain.

The tattooed man laughed loudly, "I'm sorry. Were you thinkin' this was a negotiation?"

"Dude, come on, what the…" Erik began, but was cut off abruptly as the man's fist collided with his face. The two men restraining Erik took advantage of his current shock and weakness and drove him to his knees.

"No one was talkin' to you, boy!" the band's leader followed his words with another spit of his snuff-induced saliva, the second glob aimed at Erik's hair and bleeding face. Michelle cried out in protest, and Blaine struggled against his captors who quickly subdued him with a blow to his right kidney. He crumpled under the pain and soon joined Erik in his kneel.

"They're kids!" Mike shouted. "Leave them alone! You want our stuff, take it. Just leave them alone!"

Crackling his knuckles in a needless display of intimidation, the towering man drew close to Mike's face and smiled.

"See, I told ya I didn't want no trouble," he said. His noxious breath stung Mike's eyes and nose. "But, now y'all done went and made me get violent. 'Cause of that, the price just went up."

"We don't have anything else. You're leaving us out here to die, what else could you take?" Mike spat the words as his angered boiled inside him.

"Oh, I think you got something else we could use," he said as he cupped Michelle's face in a filthy, tattooed hand. The gleam in the man's eye was not unlike that of the infected. Not just a thief, Mike realized, but a predator as well.

Michelle flinched at the touch and Mike shouted as he struggled against the men that held his arms, "You sick, bastard, get your hands off of her!"

The young girl could no longer fight her fear and a withering sob escaped her. Her body shook uncontrollably as the man leaned in close to her face and began to sniff her neck and hair. His inability to defend Michelle turned his stomach as much as the sight of the man's action.

"Yeah, this one is gonna be good, boys," he called out to his men, who replied with disgusting taunts and slurs. Turning his attention back to Mike, the man's smile grew even more sinister as he spoke. "We got a new world to populate, brother, and she's gonna have to do her part."

From the corner of his left eye, Mike saw a flash of Erik's arm, which was then followed by a grunt from the tattooed man.

"That'll be tough to do when I blow these off you," Erik seethed as he spoke. Mike moved his head lower and saw that Erik now held a gun jabbed into the crotch of the band's leader. Erik's right pant leg was pulled up slightly, enough to reveal the holster strapped to his ankle in which he had concealed the weapon.

"You're making a big mistake, kid," the man said, though his tone clearly showed his surprise and faintly decreased bravado.

"Move an inch, and it'll be you that made the mistake," Erik warned. "Now, tell your guys to drop their weapons, or your voice is gonna get a lot higher."

Mike could see the indecision on the man's face. Several tense seconds passed until he finally ordered his men to place their weapons on the ground. Mike and Derrick moved quickly to repossess their own weapons from the ground. Once control of the situation shifted in their favor, Erik slowly regained his feet and backed away from the tattooed man.

"Mr. A., take their guns," Erik said, though his eyes never left the figure at which he pointed his weapon.

"Erik, let's just go!" Mike tried to break through the boy's trance. "We're not them. We're not leaving them out here helpless."

Mike wasn't sure if Erik's slight turn was to argue with him or instead agree, but in the brief half-second his attention was diverted, the tattooed man lunged forward. The shot rang out loudly in the tension and plunged deeply into the tattooed man's forehead before it exited the back of his skull. The man's body jerked backwards from the force of the blow and smashed lifelessly to the pavement. It was not until Mike felt the familiar reverberation through his left arm and shoulder that he realized that he had pulled the trigger. The slow motion of the moment ended abruptly as he heard three shots fired behind him. Whirling around, he found that Blaine and Michelle had both shot and killed two men that had used the confusion to attempt to retrieve their own weapons from the ground.

The remaining five men stood in stunned silence. With their leader ended, Mike could see their resolve shatter. Though the tide had changed, he still felt as if the situation was not fully in his control. He had hoped to salvage some fragment of civilization by denying Erik's request to leave the men unarmed. He had not necessarily cared about the fate of the thieves, he had acted out of the hope that ethics and morals still played a part in the world.

"Kick your guns forward," he finally said to the bandits. They complied without hesitation, and Mike slowly bent to collect their weapons while the other three members of his group kept steady aim.

"Where are the keys to the van?"

"In…inside," one of the men stammered in reply. Blaine moved to the van that blocked their forward progression and confirmed that the keys were inside. Once Blaine repositioned the van, Mike told the others to get into the SUV. Through the open windows, his students made sure the unarmed men made no attempt to escape. Mike walked over to the vans that were now parked parallel to each other, drew his weapon down, and fired shots that quickly deflated two tires on each vehicle.

Within seconds of resuming the driver's seat of the SUV, Mike had them speeding down several back roads hoping to reach the campground before the thieves could offer pursuit. He doubted they would, but he used the idea as a way to avoid thinking about what had occurred. His students remained silent during the drive either of their own accord or from sensing Mike's mood.

The short distance and the fast speed brought them to the campground's entrance minutes later. Mike slowed the vehicle substantially as he turned into the dirt and gravel driveway. Several yards in, he brought the truck to a complete stop before he exited. Gathering several branches from the ground, Mike began running them over the tracks the SUV had left behind. Once he was satisfied that their path was sufficiently disguised, he drove the rest of the way to the trails.

Assisted by the rest of their companions, the supplies were unloaded and carried to the stone dwelling. Upon seeing Erik's swollen jaw and split lip, Sarah's motherly instincts immediately went into action. At first refusing any care, Erik eventually relented and allowed her ministrations. When she asked what had happened though, Erik as well as Blaine and Michelle, downplayed the situation. Later that night Mike told Sarah the entirety of the day's events as the two sat in the night-darkened front room.

She tried her best to improve his melancholy, but her

words proved paper tigers. He accepted the necessity of firing at the tattooed man to protect Erik. It was the acts of the band of men that troubled him more. Mike and those with him had struggled to survive so fitfully over the last several days, but that struggle had been against a diseased, maddened creature; today's battle was against other men. He had read the fiction, seen the movies, never thought it would happen so quickly in reality.

Six days, he thought, *That's all it took. Six days for humanity to end.*

CHAPTER SIXTEEN

"So you're abandoning us? Kicking us out?" Derrick shouted with understandable anger.

"It's not safe, Derrick, and you know that. If we had more time then maybe, but as it stands now we have no way to contain her during the trip," Mike repeated the statement he had said several times in the past twenty minutes. Once the council had made its decision, he had volunteered to be the one to inform Derrick of the news. His guilt in helping create the young man's situation drove Mike to accept that the words had to come from him. With barely enough vehicles to transport the refugees, a separate vehicle could not be spared to isolate the infected Jenni Calente.

"So, that's it then? After all these years, after all we have been through together, you're just going to leave us behind?"

Mike could not bring himself to repeat the rationale again.

"We're so close. She can get better once we get to Cuba. You know it, she can get better. They'll be able to help her. You can't do this to us! Please, don't do this to us!" Derrick implored. His pleas were steadily becoming more frantic, tears streaming down his face. Their voices and movements had incited the caged, infected Jenni to snarl wildly as it thrashed against its restraints. The moment grew to be too much, and Mike knew he had to leave the confining tent.

"I'm sorry," he said, the words catching in his throat. He turned quickly and exited through the tent flaps into the pre-dusk mountain air. Avoiding the camp proper, he instead took himself into the wooded area that marked the edge of the refugee stronghold. His vision began to blur as his own tears welled up. Mike could still hear the pleading screams of Derrick in the tent.

"Please, don't do this to us!"

Mike quickened his steps, hoping to get far enough away to no longer hear the repeated imploring of his former student. Branches stung his face as he shifted into a run, the thin wisps of wood whipped and lashed at him. He welcomed the pain as a form of required punishment, a self-mortification that could bring absolution of his sins. Several minutes passed before his blind sprint resulted in a stumble and he crashed to his knees. The free-flowing tears mixed with the thread-like trails of blood on his face. Breathing heavily, he cast his eyes upward as a primal scream ripped from his lungs and filled the silent woods. Six years of pain, loss, fear, and defeat took control of his voice as he continued to scream into the fading light. In time his throat became raw and the shouts weakened to thin rasps until silence once again claimed dominion.

Rising from the softened earth, Mike could make out lumbering shapes in the distance. As his vision cleared from the tears, the violently bent necks of the figures became obvious. Still in a cathartic meditation, he instinctively reached his hands towards the double holster on his chest. He felt complete, felt whole, as his fingers wrapped around the warm steel. Easing them from the leather restraints, his arms straightened and dropped to his sides as the figures advanced. His eyes did not move yet his vision perceived his surroundings with uncanny certitude. *Seventeen*, his mind stated lifelessly.

The infected quickened their pace, yet Mike kept his guns lowered. Soon they were thirty feet away, then twenty, fifteen, ten…

With a dark glare and half smile that bordered on demonic, he slowly raised his arms and began firing his weapons into the group of infected. Ignoring his own rules for Til encounters, he did not take head or heart shots. Instead, he filled the diseased bodies with lead in arms, legs, and stomachs. The force of the shots caused the infected to stumble and fall. He did not want to give them a quick death, he wanted to give them pain, though they could not feel.

"Come on! Get up!" he screamed at them. In that moment, he no longer cared if he got bitten. In that moment, he almost envied the creatures before him and their inability to feel pain, physical or emotional. He envied the carefree reality in which they existed. *If I get bit*, he thought, *then it all ends*.

Mike shouted again for them to rise. And so they did. And again he squeezed the triggers; the rhythmic percussion of the blasts lulled him into a stupor. The infected continued to fall from the bullets tearing threw them. Soon, though, they no longer were able to rise. The loss of blood or the ruined leg muscles prevented them from offering any further threat. Only one still lived and was using its arms to drag itself closer to Mike.

The creature howled in rage as Mike stood his ground above it. From practiced memory, he knew that he had one round left in each gun. Pity, not anger, drove him now as he lowered one weapon and delivered a killing shot to the tormented figure. Returning the spent weapon to its holster, Mike turned and retreated through the woods back to the camp. His left hand still held the gun that contained one unspent round when, several minutes later, he reached his destination.

Having heard the screams and gunfire, a concerned

crowd had gathered in the darkness. Mike met their stares with a measured look. Locking eyes briefly with Paul, whose own eyes expressed understanding and pity, he moved to his left and entered the stigmatized tent he had been in earlier. His eyes took in the sight of Derrick as he sat before the cage that held his high school sweetheart. As the infected-Jenni raised her head, she greeted him with a snarl and a growl. Derrick turned his attention to follow her gaze.

"What? What do you want?" the young man asked him. His tone showed his exhaustion and contempt.

"I'm sorry." They were the only two words that he could manage without breaking his resolve. When he spoke them, he slowly raised the gun and squeezed the trigger to expel the final shot. Derrick's eyes widened and the shout had barely formed on his lips when the bullet whizzed past his head and sunk deep into the creature in the cage. Her body convulsed with one spasm before falling lifelessly to the dirt floor, a shallow pool of blood forming around her head.

Mike felt the air leave his body as Derrick tackled into him. He put up no resistance as the younger man landed blow after blow into his face and chest. He took the beating as punishment for not allowing this scene to play out all those months ago. In truth, he could not feel the pain. His body was numb and his mind had disconnected from it during the screams in the woods. His daze continued as he heard Paul Jenson rush into the tent and struggle to pull the enraged man off. Derrick screamed wordlessly, and Mike understood the sound, having been its owner an hour before. There were no words to express the emotions that now raged through his former student. Even so, Mike recognized each one as if translated in some fashion.

Others soon filled the tent and Mike could feel arms and hands pulling him up from the ground. His eyes stayed locked on Derrick as the boy fought for freedom from the men that held him in check. The voice of Dr. Marena shouting orders to bring Mike to his medical tent seeped into his hearing, though their meaning was distant and incomprehensible. The smell of alcohol and sterilization were the only indications to Mike that he had reached his destination.

"I'm fine," he mumbled with a voice that felt borrowed.

Did someone say my name? his mind inquired. *I'm fine,* he repeated, yet his mouth did not move. *Why won't you listen to me? I'm fine. I'm fine!*

Dr. Marena's face hovered before him and Mike felt himself being lifted off the ground. His eyes now stared at the dark gray fabric that lined the interior of the tent.

I don't want to lie down. I'm not ready to sleep.

He could see Dr. Marena's mouth move but could not hear the words. He felt a pinch in his right shoulder and soon a warm sensation spread across his body.

I don't want to lie down. It's getting dark. Why is it dark? Hello? Hello? Is anybody in here?

* * *

Pain. That was the first sensation Mike could register as he slowly opened his eyes. *Correction,* he thought, *make that a lot of pain.* His blurred vision began to clear and he recognized the familiar accoutrements that marked the medical tent. His eyes shifted side to side. Mike tried to turn his head, but he could feel something attached to him to prevent such movement.

"Hello?" His voice sounded rough and scratched. He realized how dry his throat was when he spoke, but the dryness paled in comparison to the pain that shot through his mouth when he spoke the word.

"Don't try talk, Mike," came a voice from behind him. The shadows in the tent shifted and Dr. Marena entered his field of vision at his left side.

"You have a broken jaw, among other things, so keep your mouth still," the doctor instructed.

"How long?" Mike asked doing his best to keep his jaw immobilized.

"You've only been out for a few hours. I had to use Demerol to knock you out. I was able to reset your jaw. I don't have the equipment to wire your jaw shut, so I had to immobilize it with a strap. It's not my best work, but it'll hold. Your nose was broken in three places, and I reset that as well so it should heal fine. You had a pretty nice gash around your right eye, which I stitched up. Your lip was split, so you have a few stitches there, too. Both of your eyes are pretty well swollen, and I have given you some anti-inflammatories to help bring that down. Oh, and you lost a tooth, but not much I can do about that."

Mike listened to the doctor as he rattled off the list of injuries. *Well,* he thought, *guess my modeling days are over.*

"Chest?" he asked the doctor.

"Bruised and cracked ribs. Without x-rays I can't tell you how many, but there is nothing punctured, so if you keep them wrapped and don't lift anything heavy for a while, you'll be fine."

"Thank you," Mike managed to say after the doctor helped him sip water through a straw. The cool liquid eased his parched throat with welcome relief.

The doctor nodded in return and informed him that he would be back shortly. Once the man left, Mike broke orders and began to rise up from his prone position. Pain seared through his body with a staggering force. At first trying to grit his teeth against it, only to find that increased the unwelcomed sensation, Mike forced himself to sit up on the gurney.

"Didn't he just tell you to stay put?"

On instinct, Mike tried to turn himself to the direction of the voice. His sore ribcage screamed in protest, drowning out his neck's own complaints. As the pinpoints of light faded from his vision, Mike moved more cautiously and turned to find Paul sitting in a chair in the corner of the tent.

"Where's Derrick?" Mike said through his teeth.

"Locked up in his tent," Paul replied.

"Release him tonight," he ordered.

"You sure about that? What if he decides to finish what he started?" Paul asked him as he indicated Mike's current condition.

"Then he does," Mike answered, getting used to speaking without moving his jaw. "But, he won't, and I won't have him chained up like a criminal. He and I both did what we had to do. If he decides to stay then it's on his terms. If he leaves, then we give him what we can spare."

Paul nodded in consent.

"So, how are you feeling?"

"Well, my legs don't hurt," Mike tried to joke, but the laugh caught in his throat as pain throbbed in his chest.

"That's not what I meant."

Mike had hoped that his broken face and chest would have allowed him at least a brief reprieve from having to assess his emotions so quickly after the event.

"She died months ago. It's up to him now if he joins her, or decides to live." Though he would always carry the guilt of not having acted sooner, he did feel an increased lightness in his soul. He had acted out of contrition by ending Derrick's torment and with his penance complete, Mike hoped both he and the young man could find whatever peace still existed in the world.

Derrick, having been released from his physical and emotional bonds, left the camp sometime in the night. He left no note, no farewell.

* * *

With the threat of the approaching Tilian horde and the precipitous departure it forced, Mike had little time to rest his sore body. He was pleased to find that the camp had accomplished much in those few days. The majority of the supplies had been loaded into the transport vehicles. In their eagerness to depart, some of the refugees had even taken down their tents and chose to share with others.

Moving slowly through his own quarters, Mike began to

box up his belongings. When the virus broke out, he had escaped with the clothes he had been wearing, and the small gray canine that now rested comfortable on his cot. Gazelle seemed to sense the approaching relocation for she kept her eyes half-cocked and had taken to staying even closer to Mike than normal. She was his only real reminder from his life before the virus. The items he placed into the small box consisted of essential documentation and maps; nothing of personal consequence.

On the third day after receiving his injuries, Lisa updated Mike regarding the Tils advancement. With their closer proximity, scouts had been able to more accurately place their number at eleven hundred. The number still staggered Mike whenever he thought about it. Unfortunately, their pace had increased. Though hoping to gain a two day head start, the refugees would only be one day ahead of the massive force of infected. If the parkways were not passable, or something happened to the vehicles, Mike feared that the infected would be able to over-take them quickly.

The remaining days passed quickly and soon the refugees found themselves waking on the morning of the departure. Not immune to the nervous excitement, Mike found that even he had woken well before the scheduled time. Stepping from his cabin, Gazelle by his side, he took in the broken-down camp site. The mountain camp had been his longest home over the last six years. Its establishment had offered him and the other refugees the first feeling of permanence and routine.

There was a part of him that yearned for this island salvation to exist, but he had learned not to give in to those emotions, so it was with guarded optimism that he joined the other refugees as they began the final descent down the mountain. Mike at first felt foolish for the nostalgia he was experiencing as he travelled further away from the camp. However he soon came to accept that *home* can come in many different forms, and somehow along the way their mountaintop camp had become its latest definition.

CHAPTER SEVENTEEN

If pressed, Mike would have been unable to pinpoint when it had happened, but somewhere in the two months since relocating to the stone home in the Willow Falls Campground, the survivors had settled into a routine. Though he still keenly felt the desperation of their situation, he had begun to accept the enormity of what had befallen him and his companions.

As the temperatures steadily increased, and the rains began to fall more frequently, the current inhabitants of the house had developed into a family. Meals were always shared together, and much of the daily work became group activities. After the first foray into town to gather supplies, Mike had grown significantly more cautious on the two subsequent trips. Michelle, still recovering from the trauma of what had almost happened, declined to join them on those trips, opting instead to stay behind with Sarah, her young son, and Gazelle. Mike could see the change in the teenage girl. Perhaps more than the horror of the infected, what her fellow man had attempted traumatized her even more.

Both journeys into town since the altercation had been fraught with anxiety. Mike, along with Blaine, Josh, Erik,

Derrick and Jenni, made sure they were very heavily armed and alert as they had gathered additional supplies. Once, they spotted a small group of survivors travelling along the road. With distrust still strong, Mike had ordered the others to hide in an alley as he warily watched the strangers. He saw no sign of weapons, but unsure as to their intentions, he chose not to reveal himself to them. While he loathed the suspicion of others that had replaced his compassion, he could not bring himself to jeopardize the safety of those already in his care. When the party had passed safely into the distance, he and the others resumed the scavenging and made their return to the campsite.

Of the many routines adopted by the survivors, operation of the battery-powered shortwave radio receiver was the one upon which they placed much faith. Derrick had discovered the radio in the small groundskeeper's house on the eastern edge of the campground. Mike shared the responsibility with the others of scanning the radio waves for any incoming communication. Hopes rose at each interruption in the usual static, but quickly plummeted when the static returned without a message. On only one occasion did they discover signs of life in the world.

Andrew Weyland had been manning the radio several weeks into their stay when a voice was faintly heard amidst the static. The young boy jumped excitedly at the sound and immediately called out to the others. Like a black and white, World War-era photograph, they huddled close to the radio as Mike adjusted the dial slightly until the voice rose above the ambient noise. In what sounded like an Asian dialect, the male's voice spoke calmly. Though unfamiliar with the language, Mike soon realized that the voice was repeating the same message several times. The message ended as abruptly as it had begun, and in the days that followed, continued to be absent from the radio waves. Not knowing its meaning or content, the group continued to spend much of their time scanning the frequencies with diminishing hope.

The supplies scavenged on the trips to town had not only kept the refugees adequately fed, cleansed and clothed, but also worked towards making their new home more livable. Blankets, sheets, pillows, and inflatable mattresses had been taken from a big-box chain store. Several small area rugs from the same store now covered the cold stone floor of the house. Sarah had even managed to hang curtains over the lone window in the large front room. Not soon to be featured in any interior design magazines, the dwelling had improved greatly since their arrival.

Each day after breakfast, everyone got to work on the various chores that had proven essential to the happy cohabitation of nine individuals. Laundry, food preparation and clean-up, and firewood collecting were perhaps the most time consuming tasks. The teenagers took to their various jobs with eager abandon. The steady enhancement of the house, as well as an increasing sense of security, had lightened their previous moods of despair and defeat.

In the evenings, once the chores had been completed and the evening meal served and consumed, it became common for several of the group to engage in card games, book reading, and even board games, all of which had been scavenged during their two month stay. Mike understood the need to resume some normalcy, but he also refused to allow complacency any entrance into his thoughts. While the stone home certainly proved serviceable, he doubted that nine people could continue to live in such close quarters. Additionally, the food supply would become cause for major concern. It was fine to rely on what could be scavenged from stores and homes in neighboring towns, but Mike feared that those sources of supply would soon reach an end. Each day that the radio aired no broadcast indicated that there was still no formal survival base. *We have to begin thinking in the long term,* Mike told himself often.

Lacking any real experience with agriculture, save for handing his grandmother tools in her garden when he was a young boy, Mike understood that this was the time for planting. If events did not change, and no help could be found, then the refugees would need to rely on their own food production if they hoped to survive through the winter. He knew the campground, with its thick canopy of trees and stone outcroppings, was not going to allow the growth of much.

Though he disliked the idea, and had not yet mentioned it to the others, Mike was quickly becoming convinced that, sooner rather than later, a search for a more habitable locale would need to begin and the stone house would have to be abandoned.

* * *

Another month had passed and the southern summer was evident with temperatures well above ninety degrees, and a humidity that was debilitating in its oppression. Mike had yet to broach the topic of relocation with the others. His remembered exhaustion and anxiety from the first days of the outbreak held his tongue. The dangers of staying versus leaving soon became his main thoughts, yet his mind could not determine a victor. The idea of being out in the open, on the road, gave him chills, yet starving in a frozen stone home did little to soothe him.

As he had suspected, the availability of food supplies in the neighboring towns had diminished substantially. Most stores were picked clean of non-perishable items, leaving only the rotting meats, fruits and vegetables to create a burning stench. Mike estimated that their current stock should, if well rationed, last this new family of his through the summer. The daily portions were adequate for basic nutrition but he could easily see the weight loss of his companions. His clothing hung far more loosely than similar sizes had before the outbreak. Though his gym attendance was certainly non-existent, the daily labors of this new life had continued to work his body to extremes.

Stripped to the waist, Mike carried a heavy bundle of

wood across the stone walkway leading to the house. As he stacked the timber into a pile against an exterior wall, Sarah stepped out of the home to speak with him. In the months since their settlement, Sarah's optimism never flagged. Whether out of motherly protection for her son, or a genuinely positive disposition, her spirit remained unclouded. Today, however, he could see an anxiety and wild fear in her eyes as she approached him.

"He's sick," she said to Mike as her hands twisted the hem of her yellow shirt. Her hair, normally pulled back into a neat pony-tail, now fell haphazardly to her shoulders, with some larger locks still held in an elastic band.

"Andrew?" Mike asked, assuming that her state could only be brought upon by concern for her own flesh and blood.

Nodding, Sarah's eyes quickly filled with tears. Mike reached his hand to her shoulder to steady her and offer comfort.

"What's wrong?"

"He has a fever. He woke up this morning looking a little pale, and then he complained that he was cold. I took his temperature…it's high, Mike. And he can't keep anything down," she said in a nervous ramble.

Mike immediately understood her concern. Having lost the rest of her family to the virus, Sarah was quite familiar with its initial symptoms.

"What if he's…sick, Mike?" she asked. Her eyes betrayed her and it was clear that she had intended to say *infected* but could not bring herself to voice the possibility.

"You can't think like that. Sarah, kids get sick all the time. It's been three months, he would have gotten sick long ago if it was the virus."

He spoke the words, yet his emotion lacked much conviction. There was so much about the virus they did not know. When the outbreak first spread, news reports had limited the potential victims to certain blood types. *If that was true*, Mike wondered, *then why did people who got bitten change? And, how could they change so rapidly?* He detested the lack of information available to him. On one of the missions into town, he'd even ordered a stop at the local library to collect as many books as possible on viruses, specifically the Inclusion Body Disease virus, the reptilian illness that had started it all.

Though some of the erratic behavior in infected humans mimicked diseased reptiles, Mike was unable to learn much else. Over the intervening months, he began to worry that the virus had struck with such devastating rapidity that maybe no one had had a chance to truly study it.

Following Sarah into the house, Mike soon found himself looking at the unconscious and frighteningly pale young boy. His mother had covered him with as many blankets as the small group had in their possession; with the warm summer air, the other children had no longer been using them when they slept. The boy's small frame was cocooned in warmth, yet still his body shook while he slept. To Mike he looked like a typical person with the flu, but having not personally been near to anyone with an earlier stage infection, he could not rule out the possibility that what Andrew had was a danger to them all.

"Is he…?" Sarah asked him, but could not bring herself to finish the question.

"I don't know," he answered honestly. "Have the others been around him today?"

Sarah shook her head in response.

"Okay, for now, until we can be sure, they need to stay out of this room. If it's not the virus, he still looks in pretty bad shape."

Mike sat down on the bed and placed his hand on the boy's forehead. The skin felt like fire to the touch. Searching his mind for answers, he recalled watching an episode of a hospital-based drama where the doctors helped break a patient's fever through a warm bath. Hoping the method was grounded in some reality, Mike immediately went outside to retrieve the metal tub used for laundry. Bringing the tub into the room, Sarah helped him fill it with water from jugs. Though not large enough to fully accommodate a pre-teen boy, the tub was sufficient in submerging the boy's trunk beneath the room-temperature water. Now out from under his shelter of blankets, Andrew's body shook violently with shivers.

After twenty minutes in the tub, Mike removed the boy as his mother wrapped him in a large towel. He was unsure if the method had worked, but he thought Andrew felt somewhat cooler to the touch. *Wishful thinking most likely.*

Over the next two days, he and Sarah kept a steady vigil in the small bedroom. Mike had been forced to alert the others to the situation. He could see their emotions twist with concern for Andrew, and fear for themselves. After two days of being in close proximity with the boy, neither Sarah nor Mike showed any symptoms, which led him to believe that Andrew suffered from a strong flu, but not the Tilian Virus.

That hopeful assumption, however, did little to relieve his worry for the boy. His fever had diminished slightly, but still remained precariously high. Andrew had not eaten in over two days, and his already thin body seemed to be caving in upon itself. Though unconscious most of the time, when he did wake Andrew spoke with unintelligible words and sounds, the fever clearly clouding his motor skills and cognitive ability.

Not only worried about the young boy's survival, Mike was concerned what effect his death would have on the others. Sarah, who had already suffered so much, seemed to live only for her son. Without him, Mike feared what would happen to her will to survive. His students, as he still liked to think of them, had grown very attached to Andrew. Just as Mike felt the responsibility for their well-being, so too had they undertaken the role of protector with regards to the youngest member of their campground clan.

By the third day, the routine of the house had come to a grinding halt. Mike and Sarah alternated between sleeping and watching Andrew, while the others desired to stay in the large front room waiting for some sign of the boy's return to health. Mike closed the door to the sick boy's room behind him and found the gathering of his students. Arrayed around the large table, their gloom was palpable. He took a seat in one of the empty chairs. He had intended to go to sleep in the room he shared with Erik and Blaine, but the expectant faces before him pleaded for information.

"No change, yet," he said with a voice clearly marked with exhaustion. "How long have you guys been out here?"

"Since this morning," Derrick offered.

"You can't stay inside all day, guys. There's work that needs to be done, and it's not good for you to just sit around and wait," he told them.

"No offense, Mr. A., but the little man is probably the only family I got left. So, picking twigs in the woods can wait until he gets better," Erik said. The look he leveled at Mike showed that he would accept no argument.

Mike nodded his head with an understanding smile. *For better or worse,* he thought as he rose from the table and shuffled to bed, *we're a family.*

On the fifth day of Andrew's illness, Sarah's strength had begun to crack. Mike held the heart-broken mother as she cried on his shoulder. The boy had shown no sign of improvement. What little food and water he consumed had to be forced down his throat. His skin seemed to stretch over his bones as muscle dwindled underneath it. Mike knew the boy could not last much longer in his condition. Sarah's sobs came from a place of deep sorrow, a place only a mother losing a child could understand. As he held her, his eyes caught the slightest flash of movement from the bed. At first dismissing the movement as further shivering, Mike then heard a soft, rasping and weak whisper.

"Mom?"

Through her tears, Sarah had not heard the sound. In fact, Mike was unsure if he had even heard it, or his imagination had willed it, but again the boy's voice rose.

"Mom?"

"Sarah," Mike said as he pulled back from his hold of her. He turned her towards the bed, and she gasped as she saw her son struggling to sit up, his eyes open and clear.

With a startling scream, the mother rushed to her son and scooped his near weightless body into a tight embrace. Her tears of sorrow had quickly been replaced with ones of pure relief. Mike found himself unable to hold back his own emotions as twin wet lines rolled down his face.

Having heard Sarah's exclamation, the teenagers rushed into the room. Mike smiled through tears as he watched them join the pair on the bed. Overcome with emotion, he exited the room and sought fresh air outside the stone walls. With a deep inhalation, he filled his lungs with the clean mountain air. Running his hands over his face to wipe away the wetness, he shook his head with a laugh.

In the following days, the routine returned to normal. Chores were completed and meals were again shared as a group. Andrew had regained his strength quickly, as well as his appetite. Mike could not help but remark to himself on the resiliency of youth. Free to admit it now that the danger passed, he had been sure the boy was on his deathbed. Now, however, he watched Andrew playing with Gazelle in the stone grove beyond the home.

Mike found himself on laundry duty that day and was returning to the house just as Blaine approached from the other direction, his arms loaded heavy with wood for the stove.

"I don't care how young you are," Mike warned jokingly. "You carry that much at once, you're going to hurt yourself."

"Well, I am definitely going to hurt myself if you don't open the door soon," Blaine replied with a smile.

Mike quickened his step up the worn stone path and shifted the dry clothing to one arm as his left hand reached to open the door.

A loud sound ripped through the canyon, its echo

reverberating along the stone walls. Mike felt the left side of his face splashed with liquid as his body reacted to the startling sound. He turned in the direction of the sound as Blaine released the wood he carried, letting it crash to the stone path. Mike glanced quickly at the falling logs, and then brought his eyes to meet Blaine's own; they were wide and lifeless. As his body fell backwards, Mike saw the red exit hole of the bullet that had gone through Blaine's skull.

Turning, Mike saw the forms of the five men at the head of the path leading from the woods to the stone house, each armed with either a rifle or handgun. On instinct, he hurled himself through the front door just as the men opened fire. Crashing to the hard floor of the house, Mike suddenly recognized the faces of the men—they were the same faces that had attacked him and the other refugees months earlier, the faces of the men he had mercifully let live.

CHAPTER EIGHTEEN

The progression down the mountain was occurring at a much slower pace than Mike had anticipated. With over seventy people making the trek, it was well into the night before the group was able to make camp at mid-point. Few among the survivors had ventured away from the main camp as much as he and, the security and scavenger teams had. He had mentally prepared himself for delays, but Mike had not expected them to occur so soon into the journey.

The trail down that Lisa had selected was the widest of the ones used for an excursion off the mountain. Even so, the mid-point camp could barely contain the large number of people that now milled about. Not wanting to risk a visible fire, the refugees had dined on dried and salted meat prepared days in advance. Though the texture was unappealing, the taste of the jerky was good, and the meal helped fill the many rumbling stomachs that complained loudly during the march.

Dr. Marena was busy tending to various requests of assistance, severely blistered feet being the most common. Mike was surprised at how quickly the refugees had lost their travelling skills. In just the year and half spent in the mountain camp, they had grown soft compared with the earlier years of frequent relocation. No complaints were voiced, but he could tell that just the one day hike had taken its toll.

"They got comfortable," Paul said, lowering himself down near Mike on the ground. He was always amazed at how well Paul could read his thoughts.

"And we still have another day's hike before we reach the transports," Mike said dully.

"After years on the road," Paul began in reply, "you can't blame them for welcoming the relief the camp offered."

Before Mike could respond, Lisa and Michelle joined them on the soft undergrowth.

"How we looking for tomorrow?" Mike addressed the question to Lisa.

"If we keep moving like we did today, you're going to have to make the call about leaving."

The debate had already begun in Mike's mind earlier in the day when he saw how little progress the group had made. At the current rate, the refugees would not reach the transports until dark. Mike would have to decide whether to make camp and wait for dawn, or risk starting the drive in darkness. Experience had shown that the Tils did sleep, but the vehicle headlights would be more than enough to draw them into the open and kick off their frenzy. Sleeping out in the open, however, was also an undesirable risk.

"What do you think?" Mike asked her.

"It's a crap shoot either way," she said. "And I follow the lieutenant's example, I advise but don't decide, Chief."

Mike could not help but join in the laughter of the other three. Memories of the lieutenant were a welcome break from the decisions ahead. The small group sat for some time reminiscing about the gruff man and his idiosyncrasies.

With an early morning start to the final leg of the descent, Mike indicated his intentions to retire for the evening. His unspoken influence over the refugees motivated them to follow his example, and soon the campsite grew quiet, save for the soft footsteps of the security team that patrolled the perimeter.

Mike's sleep was fitful as his mind continued to deliberate over the next night's options. Even in college, he had been prone to weigh the potential outcomes of major decisions, trying to will his mind to follow the successive ramifications of each course of action. Serving as the leader of the refugees, that tendency had served him well and kept him from making rash moves that could endanger the lives of others. The cost had deprived him of many restful nights, and he could feel the effect the past years had on him. Though only twenty-nine, his time as leader had tired him, and aged him, more than six years should have.

Dawn came too quickly, as he had grown accustomed, and the camp's activities stirred to wakefulness those that remained asleep. If Mike had been pleased that the travelers voiced no complaints last night, he was highly agitated by the conversations he overheard as he convened with the council. People immediately began grousing about sore feet and legs, stiff backs from the bare ground, and exhaustion from too little sleep.

With a quick glare from Mike, Paul broke away from the council and began to navigate through the griping crowd, employing whatever magic skill he had to turn the mood around. Mike hoped it worked because the day's journey would be just as arduous as the day before, and his patience for unnecessary complaints was thin. He had intended to speak with the refugees once the drive south began. He wanted to caution them about the potential dangers, and to encourage them for what he believed would be a monumental journey that would change their fates forever. He certainly was not planning on giving a pep talk to get them down the mountain, which would most likely be the easiest part of the trip.

Once again, Paul succeeded in his task, and by the time he rejoined the council's discussion, Mike could already sense a drastic reduction in negativity as the refugees made ready to depart. He gave Mike a playfully arrogant smirk, as

Mike shook his head at his friend's charismatic abilities. Not wanting to waste the current good mood of the travelers, he ordered their departure, and the final trek down the mountainside was underway.

* * *

The pace did not increase that day, and it was close to midnight before they reached the road and the guarded transports. Having accepted a moonlit arrival during the hike, Mike decided that they would wait until first light before continuing their exodus.

"Lisa, I want everyone not part of the security team, scavenging team or the council loaded up. They're not going to like it, but they are sleeping in the vehicles. We may have to make a quick exit tonight, and we can save a lot of time if most everyone is already in the transports," Mike informed her.

"Yes, sir," she replied with military formality.

Turning to Paul, he said, "Make the rounds and do your thing. Make sure they all know that even a whisper could do us in. And anyone that complains about sleeping in a cramped car or bus, you can tell them that I have ordered that at the first sighting of a Til, the transports are pulling out of here with whoever is on them."

"I'm on it, Chief," Paul affirmed, smoothly switching from friend to subordinate.

"What shape are they in?" Mike directed his next words to the doctor.

With a shrug, Dr. Marena replied, "They're a bit worse for the wear. We have a good supply of pain relievers for the more serious bruises and soreness, but the rest can do without, I think."

"All right, do me a favor Doc, and check in with the security and scavengers first. You're authorized to bench any of them that you believe unfit due to exhaustion, etc. They will be our only protection tonight and I need clear, alert people out there." Mike had thrown in the favor remark since he learned long ago that the doctor's feathers ruffled whenever he thought he was being given an order. With Dr. Marena, he always had to use a good amount of honey to catch the flies he needed.

Mike smirked inwardly as the doctor set off to his task filled with self-importance and temporary authority. He was pleased to see that many of the refugees loaded into the school bus and other passenger vehicles with heightened attention to silence and, thankfully, a decreased attention to protestation.

"Just let us get through tonight," he whispered to the darkness. Mike said a silent, ironic thank-you for the truly late hour of arrival. Dawn would be just five hours away, so the refugees would not have to linger too long in the open.

After completing his check of the security detail, Dr. Marena made his way over to Mike who rested atop the hood of the large, yellow school bus.

"How's the mending going?" the stout physician asked him.

In truth, the journey down the mountainside had proved more difficult than Mike had expected. He had begrudgingly allowed his pack to be carried by a fellow refugee as the weight and straps painfully compressed his broken ribs. Even the double-holster vest he wore had to be loosened often during the trip to avoid sharp pangs of pain through his chest. Worse yet, though, was his inability to eat much food due to his still-swollen jaw fractures. Thankfully the swelling around his eyes and nose had drastically diminished, leaving behind a yellow and purple colored mixture of bruised flesh.

With a muted laugh, Mike responded. "It's going. I'll definitely pass on any more mountain hikes for the next while."

"Well, it would be easier going if you would just take some of the painkillers," Marena admonished.

Mike shook his head in response. He had refused the

medication once the journey began. The trek south would be hazardous and he had no intention of letting his mind be clouded when immediate decisions were sure to be required.

"Listen, Mike, I need to tell you something," the doctor said. His voice took on an even more hushed tone, speaking now in barely a whisper. Through his time with the camp, Marena had always seemed unconcerned and aloof with regards to the camp's well-being. Now Mike could clearly see the anxiety written across the man's face.

"After the situation with Jenni, I ran some tests on the body," Marena began, holding his hand up to forestall Mike's recriminations for such an action.

"What's done is done, so spare me your disdain. That's not the important part. After analyzing the samples I noticed some irregularities."

"You mean other than being infected with the virus for the past six months?" Mike cut in.

"You can be sarcastic or you can listen to what I am telling you," the man replied.

"Go ahead."

Taking a second to enjoy his scolding of Mike, the doctor continued with his explanation. "The irregularities were with the virus itself. We know the virus attacks the frontal lobe—the rational, decision making part of the brain—and concurrently boosts activity in the hindbrain, or reptilian brain. But with Jenni, that part of the frontal lobe was in far better condition than any of the previous subjects."

Mike could not find the cause for any alarm in the doctor's words.

"So…what? You're saying she had a weaker strain of the virus?" he asked.

"I thought that at first, too. But then I went into the woods to collect samples from the Tils that attacked you that day. Though you didn't leave me much to work with, I was able to find three other subjects with the same decreased frontal lobe damage." Dr. Marena paused to allow Mike to mentally sift through the information.

"And you're thinking it's unlikely that all four had weaker strains of the virus?" Mike asked.

"Highly unlikely. Add to that the fact that each of the four had varying degrees of frontal lobe damage. Jenni's samples showed moderate to severe impairment. Two of the other subjects had even less impairment."

"What are you suggesting, Doc?"

The doctor shifted, gently placing his weight from one leg to the other. In his eyes, Mike could see the look of a man who relied on facts and evidence, evidence that now caused him to present true anxiety.

"It certainly isn't conclusive," he stammered. "But, even though the hindbrain in all four still exhibited severe functional increases, I think the frontal lobe may be healing itself."

For six years, Mike had heard people talk of a possible cure. They had shared an improbable hope that sometime in the future someone somewhere would be able to create a medicine to reverse the effects of the Tilian Virus. Those expressions of hope and faith had steadily dwindled over time, but still Mike knew that unlike him, there existed in people a resilient loyalty to the idea that one day the world would be made right again. For the first time, he heard the word "heal" removed from its previously abstract existence, and replaced as the drum beat of reality.

"If the brain is healing, then won't the Tils eventually stop being…well, Tils?"

"But it's not the entire brain healing, just the frontal lobe."

"Which means what?" Mike asked, becoming frustrated with the doctor's reticence.

"I don't know what it means, Mike," Marena replied with his head shaking in concern. "I don't know what it means, and that's what has me worried."

The doctor's words weighed heavily on Mike as the dark of the night slowly ticked along towards dawn. His seat upon the bus's hood grew uncomfortable and he spent the next few hours slowly pacing the improvised camp. With his mind restless from thoughts of the coming days and the doctor's discontent, Mike barely noticed the dull throb emanating from his various healing bones.

Just as the faintest bit of light broke over the eastern mountains, Mike's attention was drawn to the hustling form of one of the camp's scouts. In a quick flurry, Lisa, Paul, and the scout made their way over to Mike's position. During their approach, he saw Lisa's eyes furtively glancing westward down the main road into the city.

"What's wrong?" Mike asked, bracing himself for further bad news. He wondered to himself if a day would come when there would be any other type of news delivered.

"The Tils, sir. They've gained a lot of ground. They're about one klik from our position," the scout reported as he tried to regain his breath from his rush back to the refugees.

"Are they frenzied?" Mike asked.

"No, sir. They're just walking."

Looking to Lisa, he gave the command to get the refugees mobilized. With luck the camp would be out of range of the Tils' sight before the horde descended on their location.

Members of the security team moved about the survivors, rousing them from their sleep. Even in the dim light of the early morning, Mike could see the look of panic on the faces of those around him.

Turning back to Paul he asked, "How did they get that close? What's the point of the damned scouts if we only get a warning minutes before an attack?"

"Our guys only ranged out two miles. It's not like the Tils carry torches or lights, Mike. There's no way he would have seen them until they were close enough to actually see them," Paul replied with a tone of defense.

The two men stared at each other for a moment, before Mike turned away in abating anger. He knew the nervous tension of the mission was getting to him. He likewise knew that any continued conversation with his second in command would have only served as an outlet for his aggression. Bottling his frustrations and sparing Paul his misplaced anger, Mike gathered his pack from the front of the bus. The weight of it caused his injuries to voice their pain, but he welcomed it as a distraction from his mental irritation.

The daylight he had longed for hours before now came far too quickly. Within minutes the refugees had loaded into the convoy vehicles and were beginning to move southward down the highway. From the passenger seat of a large SUV, Mike craned his neck to the west. Though too far to be individually distinct, he could see the large mass of figures making their way down the city's access road. A shudder passed through him. He had never seen such a large number of Tils gathered as they were now.

Once the engines had sprung to life, the sound filling the quiet dawn, the horde increased its pace. Still a half mile off, the mass of Tils had identified a prey and entered into their frenzied state of attack. Though the vehicles could only move at half the posted speed limit due to the congestion of abandoned cars and debris, the refugees were well on their way as the infected spilled into the area in which the refugees had been sleeping only fifteen minutes before.

CHAPTER NINETEEN

Pain seared through his right shoulder as it collided with the floor's hard, stone surface. Ignoring the jarring effect of the impact, Mike brought himself up into a crouch and retrieved his handguns from the leather holster slung across the back of one of the wooden chairs. Bullets echoed off the stone walls of the exterior, while others found entrance through the small glassless window.

With a commanding shout, Mike told Sarah to stay down as she rushed into the living space from one of the bedrooms. He could see maternal anxiety in her eyes, and determination as she realized that Andrew was not within the relative safety of the house. Derrick and Jake, were inside and quickly joined Mike by the window as he sporadically shot towards the figures of the armed intruders. From his vantage point, he could see three of the men hunkering down behind trees and boulders, while the remaining two hid somewhere beyond his vision.

Returning a volley of bullets, Mike hurriedly tried to assess the survivors' position. With four inside the home and a large supply of ammunition, he knew they would be able to hold the attackers at bay for quite some time. His main concern was the location and safety of the other members of their group. Over the din of the gun battle, he could hear the high-pitched barking of Gazelle from behind the house. With her he knew, were Andrew and the two teenage girls, all three were most likely unarmed.

As he reloaded, Mike asked Jake, "Where's Erik?"

"He was collecting firewood with Blaine," the young man replied as he fired two shots of his rifle.

As he glanced to the hand of the dead boy that was visible through the doorway, Mike feared that Erik may have met the same fate if the attackers had come upon him during their approach. Mike knew that the armed men would offer no quarter, they were here to settle a score and kill the remaining survivors. Even with the adrenaline that now coursed through his veins, he felt uneasy about a full-scale shoot out with human opponents. Since the outbreak, he had allowed himself to view the infected as some sort of "other." He was able to justify those killings because he placed the infected outside of the human race. Now he was defending his life, and the lives of those with him, against an all too human enemy. As the months wore on, he suspected that the previous encounter with these men was but a precursor to a struggle for survival that would define the new world. But, faced with that reality, he began to question his own resilience.

A brief lull in the sound of gunfire stirred him back to focus. Indicating that Jake and Derrick should cease fire, Mike cautiously peered through the window. One of the attackers was standing several yards down the path leading to the house. With a high-powered rifle cradled in his right arm, the man began to speak.

"You're pinned down," he shouted. "Give up and no one else needs to get hurt."

Mike could hear the lie, but responded in order to give him more time to think.

"What do you want from us?"

"We need food and supplies. The Tils are all over the towns," the man said, as he continued his attempts to convince the survivors to surrender.

It took a moment to understand that Tils referred to those infected with the Tilian Virus. It seemed he was not the only one trying to distance himself from the previous humanity of the sick. The "other" he had divided them into now had a name.

As Mike opened his mouth to reply, a soft shuffle of rocks and dust cascaded down in front of the window. At first assuming the cause to be bullet-loosened debris from the home's roof, Mike saw a glint of deceit in the man's eyes as they drifted upward.

"They're on the roof!" he shouted. The brief pause in the fighting had not been an attempt to coerce them out of the home, but rather to allow the two unaccounted-for attackers time to scramble above the dwelling.

Without sparing a second for Jake and Derrick to understand his words, Mike quickly raised his weapon and fired three shots at the man standing on the path. The bullets found the target and brought him crumbling to the ground. Derrick raced to the door and veered left towards the rear grotto. Rising from the wall's protection, Jake aimed his rifle out the window and joined Mike in providing cover fire for Derrick.

The battle regained its former intensity as both sides aimed, fired, and reloaded in rapid succession. In the distance Mike could see a shadowed outline slipping from tree to tree behind the attackers. *Erik,* he thought with relief.

The tall, young man used the cover from the sound of the shots to quickly close the distance. As he neared one of the attackers, Mike could see Erik raise a handgun and expel several shots into the man's back. With surprise, the remaining man on the path spun quickly to address the assault from the second front. Before he was able to complete his turn, Jake delivered a killing shot to the man's head. The body had not yet hit the ground before Mike raced to join Derrick behind the house.

"I got one, but the other is still on the roof," Derrick

informed him. The teen stood with his shotgun trained on the roof, while the body of an attacker lay prone at his feet. Mike could see the two girls, Andrew, and the dog huddled safely behind a stone outcropping.

"You're friends are dead," Mike yelled into the air. "Throw down your weapons and surrender!"

A second later, first a gun, then a man slipped off the rooftop. Erik and Jake reached the rear grotto and kept their weapons raised, the wariness of the last attacker evident in their pose. With a streak of fabric, Sarah rushed past them and quickly embraced her son.

Mike approached the man, who stood with his arms raised.

"Why did you come here?"

"We didn't mean no harm. We was just hungry," the man stammered.

"You killed a teenage boy. Is that no harm?" Mike asked the man as an icy coolness replaced the adrenaline-fused heat in his body.

"I didn't shoot nobody. Jimmy had us come here. Said we was gonna pay you back for leavin' us with nothin' that day," the man's tone grew increasingly panicked as he spoke.

Mike studied the man. Of an average height, the man was clearly once muscular but months of malnutrition had stripped a great deal of bulk from his body. The sandy blonde hair of his head was greasy and dirt filled from lack of washing. His calloused hands were equally caked with filth. A t-shirt and jeans hung loosely over his form, the articles either his own from days of plenty or looted sometime after the outbreak. The man's age was difficult to discern, but Mike guessed that he was approaching his thirties.

"What's your name?" he asked him.

"Mike. Mike Stevenson."

The shared given name struck Mike strangely. Though a common name, Mike Allard could feel the anger towards this man rising in him for having the same name. It was an irrational response, he knew, but he began to see himself in the man before him. The infected—the Tils—had no choice in what they became. But this man had been the master of his own fate. He had, at some point in time, chosen the path of brutality and ruthlessness. To Mike, it made this haggard person a far darker enemy than the infected would ever be.

"You shouldn't have come here, Mike Stevenson," he said with a lifeless tone.

As the man looked into Mike's eyes, searching for mercy, Mike slowly raised his gun and ended the man's life with a bullet through the skull. In the years to come, he would acknowledge that day as the death of two Mikes. One that had chosen violence and murder and met his end with a bullet. The other, a kind and hopeful man that had been thrust into a world beyond his control, thrust into a struggle for survival, who met his end by delivering that bullet.

* * *

There was little conversation as the survivors set about clearing the area of evidence of the horrific battle, their movements determined and coordinated. The security the stone home had enveloped them in over the preceding months was irrevocably shattered. The bodies of the attackers were dragged to the cliff's edge and unceremoniously cast over into the deep canyon below. A wordless agreement had been made among the survivors that the men would not receive the same type of burial Mike now presided over for Blaine.

The teen boys had dug a shallow grave into which the body of their friend was placed. The excavated dirt had been returned to the hole and several large rocks now covered the site. Arrayed in a horseshoe around the grave, the others stood with bowed heads as Mike struggled to find the proper words for the primitive ceremony. As he spoke the half-prayer, half-eulogy, his tear-filled eyes looked over those gathered. Michelle unsuccessfully fought back tears as he spoke, she and Blaine had grown close during their time in the wild. Sarah, her hands still tinted red from her scrubbing of the blood in the home's threshold, clung tightly to her son. The boy pressed his face into his mother's side. Jenni and Derrick held hands, while Jake and Erik clenched their jaws against the emotion of sorrow.

As he stood before them now, Mike could not shake the image of their disbelieving eyes as he had lowered the weapon that took an unarmed man's life. Hours later, he still could not bring himself to feel remorse for his actions, but he knew the faces of his companions would haunt him in the days to come.

"Amen," he said in conclusion, which prompted the others to repeat the word. He had not been overly religious before the disease laid waste to the world, and he had struggled since to find any claim to faith. If pressed, he would have admitted an unorganized belief in God prior to the outbreak. Perhaps from the way he was raised, or just from the ease of accepting a higher power, Mike had never considered himself to hold any atheistic beliefs. In the long, quiet nights at the campsite, he struggled with his current view of God. He questioned, as he was sure others that survived did, how any god could allow such devastation to exist in the world. His theological musings, however, always came to the same conclusion. He could not relinquish an acceptance of God because the current world would be too dim without it.

After the youngest of the survivors had taken to their beds early that night, Mike found himself sitting alone at the table in the front room. Sarah had relentlessly swept the floor clear of any shell casings and bullets. Mike wished such a method could cleanse his mind of the day's events. His hands, rougher now than when he had been a teacher, warmed themselves around a mug of coffee. Though the nights were still warm, he could not shake the chill that had clung to him since pulling the trigger.

Sarah quietly emerged from the room she shared with her son. As she gently pulled the door closed behind her, Mike asked, "How is he doing?"

"Still shaken up, but no worse than the rest of us," she replied as she poured herself some coffee and eased gratefully into a chair at the table.

"How are you doing?" she asked, after sipping from the steaming mug.

"My shoulder's going to be pretty bruised for a while," he answered.

Both took a long drink from their respective mugs and sat in silence for several moments.

"You did what you had to do," Sarah whispered, breaking the tension.

"I could have let him go," Mike said. The words seemed appropriate, though he said them without conviction.

"You did that once already. They had a second chance that *you* gave them, which was more than what they were going to give us. What happened today wasn't your fault. If things had gone differently, they would have gladly killed us all, or worse."

Mike knew Michelle had confided in Sarah how terrified she had been months earlier when the men had tried to take her.

"I keep telling myself I should feel bad, that I should regret it, but I can't, I don't," he admitted. "I shouldn't have done it in front of Andrew, though. He didn't need to see that."

"Yes, he did."

For the first time in the conversation, Mike raised his head and looked into Sarah's eyes. There was a force behind her words that made the utterance even more shocking.

"Before all this happened, months ago, I would have said you were right. But, this is the world now. This is our reality. We can hide as much as we want in this cave, but it doesn't change what's going on out there.

"It's funny. I would never buy any video games for him

that had violence or guns. I thought I could protect him, shield him somehow from the bad influences. But I can't do that anymore. Maybe it's cruel, I don't know. What I do know though, any day something could happen that takes me away from him. He needs to understand what is happening. He needs to know what the world is like now, that there are people in it who mean him harm and would kill him for no other reason than to see him die."

"That's a harsh lesson for a kid," Mike said.

Nodding, Sarah replied. "Maybe. But today he also saw that sometimes good people have to do difficult things to protect what is right, to protect the ones they love. As his mother, I think it's a fair trade."

Mike rose from the table and poured himself another cup of coffee from the still-warm pot. He had no intention of sleeping that night for fear of another attack. Knowing the others needed to rest both body and mind, he did not ask for any help in splitting the night's watch. Instead he resigned himself to the aide of highly caffeinated coffee.

"We can't stay here much longer."

"I know."

"Not just because of today, though that probably means we need to leave sooner. With winter coming, we need to be able to have shelter and food that this place can't provide," he said as he leaned against the wooden countertop.

"I can start packing things up tomorrow. But, where are we headed?" Sarah asked. It was the same question that Mike had been unable to answer for the past several weeks.

"I don't know, yet. I was thinking maybe a farm, something we could fortify with fencing around the house."

"Well, wherever you decide, we'll follow. You've steered us right this far."

"More like we have been lucky this far," Mike said as a joke, but his self-doubt was conspicuous in his tone.

Sarah left her seat and placed her empty mug on the counter. With a motherly gaze, she stood before him and lifted his chin so his eyes were forced to meet hers.

"We all owe our lives to you, Mike. You may not think it, but you're the leader we all look to."

As she stepped away and turned towards the bedroom door, Mike looked at her retreating form and asked, "What if I don't know what I am doing?"

Sarah reached the door before she turned around and, with a face full of feigned gravity, she answered the question that Mike had struggled with since the first night huddled inside the school's faculty room with several frightened students.

"Fake it," she said. "We won't know the difference."

Mike could not help but let out a bellowing laugh, which promptly turned into a fit of giggling shared with Sarah. With the exchange of goodnights, he settled back into his chair, placed his guns on the table top, and settled in for the long night.

CHAPTER TWENTY

Hours after departing, the convoy had only covered a little over one hundred miles. Though Mike had wanted to press on, the refugees—having left so precipitously that morning—required a bathroom pit stop. Conceding to their needs, the convoy now sat idly on the side of the highway. The security force was in a hyper-vigilant mode. The Tils that had been sighted earlier were now many miles behind, but still the men and women responsible for the refugees' safety kept their eyes scanning the area for fear of another force of infected. After answering his own call from nature, Mike received updates from Paul and Lisa regarding the convoy.

"The vehicles seem to be holding up okay," Lisa relayed from her discussions with the few refugees with mechanical inclinations. "The bus is overheating a bit, so we may have to schedule a stop here and there to let it cool down."

"That's the one vehicle we can't risk losing. After this break, I want to cover another two hundred or so miles before we stop for the night. We can schedule a break half way for the bus," Mike instructed. At their current pace, they would reach the Florida coast the day after next.

"Any thought to what we do when we get down there?" Paul asked.

Though the message from Cuba purported to offer safe haven from the infected, there was little in the way of information regarding how to reach the island nation. There would, supposedly, be ships that ferried survivors across the sea, but the frequency of the ships had not been mentioned in the notes.

"We wait, I guess," Mike responded. "We might find that our destination is packed with other survivors, and we might find nothing. If there are ships, we could be waiting a day, a week, or a month. We don't know, but as soon as we reach the coast Lisa, I want your people to set up as secure a fortification as possible. If the wait is an extended one, we'll need the area to be safe for us."

"Yes, sir," the woman replied. "The camp won't like it, but we will need to keep our area as condensed as possible. It will be unfamiliar territory, and I don't want us spread out too thin."

"Agreed," Mike said with a nod.

"What about the other possibility?" Paul asked with some hesitation. The council had discussed the risk that the message might turn out to be a trap to lure survivors to a renegade camp that wanted their supplies and weapons. Over the years, the refugees had had several encounters with those that had used the chaos of the pandemic to establish lawless societies. Those groups had survived through greed and aggression and were, in many ways, as irrational as the infected.

"I haven't decided, yet," Mike answered honestly. "When we make camp tonight, let's get the council together to weigh the options."

Soon after the discussion came to a close, the convoy was once again making its way south along the highway. As the miles slowly passed behind them, Mike turned his mind from thoughts of the future and focused them on the vistas beyond the truck's windows. The road stretched through rural communities with fields of untended grass, overgrown and wildly high. He could only assume that cattle once grazed in the fields, but now the only sign of domestication and civilization were the sporadic wooden fence posts that had enclosed the grazing land. Even those posts were infrequent as much of the wood had long ago been looted for fires.

The road itself in these areas was marked by the encroaching power of nature reclaiming its dominion. The black macadam was riddled with pot holes from several winters. Strong weeds and other flora had pushed through the hard surface and stood brazenly amidst the work of man. Downed trees, either from storms or age, blocked lanes and forced the convoy to travel through some back roads before once again finding the highway.

Though like any interstate, the rural areas it passed through were as abundant as the remains of metropolitan cities. The stark contrast of "once" and "now" was thrust into a greater vividness. Wind-tattered billboards beseeching travelers to visit various locales flapped unhindered in the wind, the colors of the advertisements having long ago faded and blended together to resemble the ink blots of a Rorschach test. Felled trees no longer impeded the convoy's progress, but were replaced exponentially by abandoned automobiles and the sun-bleached skeletons of old victims. Whether having fallen to the Tils, renegades, or the ravages of time and starvation, the remains gave no indication to the final moments of their respective lives. *Guess it doesn't matter anymore,* Mike thought to himself, *there's not enough of us left to mourn them.*

He had traveled through cities several times over the last six years, but there had always been a task or mission to focus on. Now Mike was able to observe the sights as he passed them. Tall skyscrapers reached to the heavens. A few stood relatively intact, but most had windows blown out from their facades. Others had toppled to the ground, while some remained standing yet completely burned, leaving only the steel skeletons that had supported their immensity. *Bodies, fences, and buildings,* he mused. *All skeletons now.*

Empty businesses and store fronts lined the city blocks. It was difficult to recall the times when people bustled along those streets, wrapped in a contended self-oblivion. Mike acknowledged he had been one of them, once. He could picture those days when he woke in his bed and begrudgingly set about his morning routine. His outlook for the day had often depended on the quality of that first cup of coffee. He wondered how many moments he had missed in a cloud of what he had considered important.

Thinking back to his long journey south to begin his life of independence, he was unable to bring to mind the sights he was sure to have passed. Instead he had been focused on the destination. Well-kept farms had meant nothing to him then, save for the thought that the people who tended them surely were living in the "wild." Now, even the wild west of early America seemed tame when compared with his reality.

The steady rhythm of the tires soon lulled Mike into a deep sleep. Exhaustion and his injuries kept him unconscious even during the second stop to cool the bus's engine. It wasn't until the early hours of dusk, as the convoy rolled to a stop, that he woke to feel the press of the passenger window against his head. A half-remembered dream, a scene from his youth where he had built a fort with his brother in the woods behind their family home, slowly evaporated as he regained his bearings and exited the truck. A dense field of tall grass stood off to the right, while on his left a truck rest stop and disused gas station were beginning to fill with the other refugees. Ahead and behind, the highway stretched interminably.

"You should've woke me," Mike said to Paul as the other man approached.

"Were you asleep? Huh, I didn't notice," the ranger replied with a smile.

"Yeah. I'm sure. What's the status?"

"Lisa took two of the smaller cars and scouted the area. There doesn't seem to be much around in the way of Tils or human, so we decided this would be a good stopping point for the night."

Mike was slightly surprised that Lisa had taken part in the scouting herself. He assumed word of his earlier dissatisfaction with the short warning had gotten back to her and she had taken it upon herself to verify the camp's safety.

"How far?"

Paul handed him a map, indicating with his finger their current location in Florida, just south of the state's border with Georgia. Mike estimated that the party had exceeded his goal of three hundred miles by another fifty.

"Well, we're certainly committed to it now, aren't we?" Mike joked.

"If the road ahead is like what we've already seen, we'll arrive the morning after next," the man replied, unable to hide the hope from his voice.

"Yea, and in your mind you think we'll be smoking some Cubans by that night," he teased.

"Of course," Paul shot back with a smirk. "And having drinks with little umbrellas in 'em. Heck, I bet my buddy Fidel even greets us personally."

"You have a demented little mind. You know that right?"

With a slap to his commander's back, Paul continued. "This could really be the end of this nightmare, Mike. Even you have to admit you're hopeful."

"I am," he allowed. Mike realized that once the journey began the same infectious optimism that had spread through the camp had reached him, though perhaps to a much lesser degree. His wariness, however, was undiminished. "Maybe once I light that cigar, I'll relax. Until then, we still have some five hundred miles to cover, and who knows how long of a wait after that."

"I think the camp is torn between crippling fear and blinding excitement," Lisa interjected as she joined the two men's conversation.

"As long as everyone keeps themselves in check," Mike responded, adding, "Thanks for taking scouting detail before."

He hoped the mild praise would assuage any further guilt or embarrassment his security chief might feel as a result of the morning's rant. Lisa's reply was a simple nod of the head. Her years in the military had prepared her well both in terms of combat training and also in hearing apologies in the masked words of superiors too proud to voice them outright.

With Gazelle eagerly pacing alongside him as he walked along the site, Mike could hear snippets of conversations as the refugees spread out across the truck stop. There was muted talk of what might lay ahead, the hope of an ending to so many years of struggle and sacrifice and loss. *Just once,* he thought, *let there be a light at the end of this tunnel.*

Finding a relatively level patch of ground, Mike gingerly lowered himself down, hoping not to aggravate his many aches. Fishing her bowls and food from his pack, he poured a generous portion of the hard, brown bits into one bowl and filled the other with water from his bottle. The dog buried her head into the food and crunched hungrily before taking several laps of water. When she was finished, Mike picked her up and placed the small canine on his lap, her tongue licking his face to express her gratitude and devotion. He thought back to the first days of the struggle when he risked his life, and those of his students, to rescue Gazelle from the infected that had surrounded his home.

His fingers scratched her soft fur, and he knew his instincts had been correct. She had been a constant companion through his journey, a source of solace and peace in times darker than he had ever imagined possible. It occurred to Mike that perhaps Gazelle was the only one among the camp that was unfazed by the interceding years.

The conversations steadily died down and were replaced by the stillness of the camp members wrapped in sleep. As planned, the council gathered to discuss the plan for the arrival in Miami. Speaking in hushed tones, the topic soon focused on the possibility of treachery.

"As much as the others are going to be impatient to reach

the city, I don't think it is wise to send everyone in without first inspecting the area." This from the doctor, who shared a rare opinion in camp policy and security.

"Lisa?" Mike asked the security chief.

"I agree with the doctor. It will be early enough when we get there for a small team to go ahead, inspect the site, and return to the convoy. I'd say the rest hang back about a mile while my people secure the area."

"That's fine. But, we need enough to remain with the convoy for protection," Paul added.

"Okay," Mike said as he brought the debate to an end. "Take eight to scout and the rest stay with the convoy."

There was no further need to discuss the possible eventuality of a prolonged wait for rescue. The council had spent several hours planning in detail the establishment of a temporary perimeter to secure the refugees. Mike wanted to take no chances thus the plan had been hashed out to allow for as many potentialities as the council could imagine. Confident that the camp's leaders were working in strict cohesion, he disbanded the meeting. Though the others left and sought sleep before the morning journey, Michelle stayed behind.

"What's on your mind?" Mike asked as he studied the girl. Any shadow of the shy, naïve girl he had taught years ago were gone when he looked at her. Twenty-three years old now, Michelle's face revealed the maturity and experience few should ever have had to carry. Her blonde hair, once long and flowing, was now cut short, the disheveled strands framing her face. Many women in the camp had adopted the shorter cuts due to ease of maintenance and diminishing supplies of shampoo.

Michelle had, as a result of Sarah's death, quickly taken on the role of the nurturer among the survivors of the early days. Mike knew the other refugees looked to her as a strong leader and caretaker. To him, as hard as it was with the figure before him, Mike still was able to see her as the girl who had once so timidly asked for extra homework.

"Nothing, really. But…I can't help but think what happens next," she replied.

"Is there something about our plans that worries you?"

"No, it's not that. I mean *after* all that. If Cuba works out, what do we do? Do we just go back to living normally? Do we get jobs, live in houses, start families like we would have done before all this?"

"Wouldn't that be a good thing?" he asked her.

She sat quietly for a minute before responding, "Can it really be that easy? After everything we have seen, all we have been through, all the people we lost…can we really just go back to…life?"

Michelle had been the first to learn that members of her family had been infected and what infection meant. Even in the chaos of those last televised moments, she had been taken aside and told of her father's death. Like so many others in the camp, she rarely spoke of loved ones that were forever lost. Mike understood the reasoning. He had spent many isolated moments in those first weeks tormenting himself with wonderings of what had become of his own family. Eventually time and events forced him to bury those thoughts deep, survival demanded the sacrifice of mourning.

"I suppose it will take time to adjust," he told her. "But we're used to that I think."

Michelle looked up from tracing lines in the dirt in front of her. "Everyone else seems to think it will be just picking up where we left off."

"We know better, don't we?" he smiled.

She returned the smile in kind, and in her eyes Mike could see it was sincere.

"So…you and Andrew, huh?" Mike teased.

"Shut up," she laughed, tossing a small pebble at him.

* * *

The rest of the night passed without incident and by the

early light of dawn, the refugees once again assumed their seats in the convoy's vehicles and began the long drive through Florida. Mike recalled a handful of family vacations he spent in the state. Following the lead of many retirees, his grandmother had lived out the remaining years of her life in the warm sea air. His parents had made the obligatory trip to Disneyworld and the Epcot Center for which he and his brother had begged relentlessly. As a late teen, Mike had joined his friends on a spring break excursion to Miami. During this drive, he reflected on how vastly different this trip would be from the one with college kids eager to try out their fake IDs.

Several hours into the trip, one of the cars in the convoy suffered from a flat tire which forced an unscheduled stop. Two of the refugees worked feverishly to change the tire. Several passengers used the stop to relieve themselves, while others patrolled the perimeter against any intruders. One of the men signaled to Mike and Paul, both of whom were looking over the map. Upon reaching the guard, Mike could already see the cause for his beckoning gesture. Scattered some distance off the highway's shoulder was a rotting heap of carcasses. Mostly animal, but he identified several pieces of human bodies. With flesh and muscle still clinging to some bones, it was clear that the deaths had been recent. The discovery of the tell-tale signs of nearby Tils spread quickly through the refugees, and propelled even greater haste in replacing the tire and reloading the convoy. Only once the vehicles were moving again did Mike relax slightly.

The further south they went, more indications of the Tils presence became evident. Mangled corpses littered the highway at every turn of the head. Even the bodies of Tils, weak from starvation, could be seen crawling across the hot black surface of the road. An anxious vigilance could be felt at the two subsequent stops to prevent the bus's engine from overheating. As the sun was setting, the hunt for a secure place to make camp for the night began.

Eventually, the council settled on a long stretch of an overpass. The decision was supported by the limited number of possible entries for any attack. Before letting the refugees exit the vehicles, several members of the security team undertook the regrettable task of removing any corpses from the area. Once the sound of bodies hitting the water below ceased, Mike allowed the passengers to begin setting up for the night. The football field-sized section of road was heavily guarded at both the northern and southern ends. With every capable member taking up arms, Mike hoped the guards had slept well the night before, since there would be no shifts to relieve them that night.

Refugees sat in huddled masses, the scent of fear over their exposure to the trials of darkness filled the evening air. *I doubt anyone gets sleep tonight,* Mike suspected. Too restless to sit idly, he alternated between the two guarded ends of the overpass. Paul joined him as he spoke with the men and women protecting the southern exit. The conversation was trivial, a result of the participants only half-focusing on the whispered chatter. All eyes peered into the darkness, focusing and refocusing on each shadow and piece of debris the soft wind moved.

As Mike began to take his leave and return to the northern front, a faint scuffling sounded from the darkness. Immediately, guns were raised, cocked, and aimed in the direction of the noise.

"Easy," he said. Worried that the sound was benign, he did not want any itchy trigger fingers giving away their position. With the moon only a sliver in the sky, Mike agreed to let one of the men use his flashlight to scan the area beyond.

As the soft glow fanned out over the highway, it came to rest on one lone, still figure standing a few dozen yards away. With its head bent severely to one side, it was clear that it was a Til before them. Instead of rushing towards them, the infected continued in its unmoving stance. The stand-off resembled an old film save for tumbleweeds blowing across the ground.

Mike turned to one of the women in the group. "Can you make the shot with the crossbow?"

"Our bolts are for short range. I don't know if I can make it," she replied.

Hesitant to have the night's silence torn by gunfire, Mike instructed her to take the shot. The woman quickly holstered her sidearm and retrieved the crossbow at her feet. Loading the bolt, she knelt to the ground and braced the bow securely to increase accuracy. With a click and a whoosh of air, the arrow sped through the distance and nicked the arm of the infected before it passed by the target. The Til, unfeeling of any pain, simply turned and beat a fast retreat into the darkness.

"Did it just run away?" Paul asked in amazement.

"Sir, do we give chase?" another guard asked.

Mike paused for a second, considered the risks and declined the man's offer of pursuit. With tension still in the air, Mike ordered Paul to quietly let the guards at the other end know that contact had been made. He stressed that Paul should do so without needlessly alerting the other refugees.

"They're scared enough already," Mike explained. He remained at the post for the rest of the night. In his mind, Paul's earlier question was persistent in its nagging. *It ran away,* he thought. *Why would it run away? Can it feel pain? No, it didn't even flinch when the arrow cut its arm. Could it really have been scared off?*

* * *

The refugees were so eager to leave the area the next morning that it was not necessary for Mike to give any instructions for haste. Within minutes of waking, the gear had been packed and the convoy loaded, and he gave the order to move out. There were some sixty miles left in the journey, and he hoped that the next hours of travel faced no obstacles. A light rain began to fall and Mike listened to the steady pattern of the windshield wipers slide across the glass of the front window. Again as before, the miles were marred by tens, if not hundreds, of corpses left to rot in the baking heat of Southern Florida.

A little more than two hours later, with less than five miles left before the convoy would reach Miami, Mike's attention was drawn ahead as Paul began to decelerate the SUV. The lead car had come to a stop and now the remaining vehicles of the convoy were following suit. The numerous lanes of the highway were completely blocked with abandoned vehicles as far as the eye could see. Following their training, the security team immediately set up in formation around the convoy.

As Mike stepped out of the truck, his eyes scanned the surrounding area. The highway was bordered by the typical foliage used to block the sounds and sights of traffic from the residential neighborhoods in the distance. As he and Paul walked forward to assess the situation, Lisa jumped down from the roof of the lead car.

"There's no way we're getting the bus through. I don't think we could even get a car through it," she informed the pair.

Not doubting her assessment, Mike still stepped first onto the car's hood then its roof to see the blockade for himself. Hundreds of cars, trucks, and buses filled the lanes of the highway in both directions. Easing down off the car, Mike winced slightly as his ribs reacted to the contortions of his descent.

"What do you think?" Paul asked him.

"I don't like it, that's for sure. It could be cars left by others that heard the Cuban message. Maybe so many have come that the road's become a parking lot. Or…" he answered, his tone showing worry.

"Or, it could be a trap," Paul said, finishing his sentence.

"Yeah," Mike replied, drawing out the word as his mind debated the camp's next steps. "How much further before we reach the city?"

"Best guess, I'd say two, maybe three miles," Lisa said.

"All right, it's walkable," Mike admitted, though he distrusted the idea of travelling even such a short distance in unfamiliar territory on foot. "Lisa, have your men stay on point. Paul, get the camp gathered."

"Yes, sir," the two responded in unison and set out to execute his orders.

Within minutes the entirety of the refugee camp was assembled on the shoulder of the highway. From the hood of one of the convoy's cars, his hair and clothing clinging wetly to him, Mike informed them of what needed to be done.

"Okay folks, here's the situation…we're going to have to walk from here." As expected, several groans could be heard among the survivors, but mostly the mutterings were fearful. Mike continued, "I know you're tired. I'm tired, too. I'm tired of waking up each morning not knowing how many of us would live to see the night. We have three miles ahead of us and six years behind us. We knew this journey was going to be tough. I don't know what dangers are ahead of us," he pointed down the blocked highway. "But I know all the dangers we have already overcome."

He paused to scan the faces of the crowd before him. He could see their fear, but that fear was matched by their determination.

"We will take only the necessities we can carry. Everyone with a firearm needs to have that weapon ready and accessible. We *will* get through this, folks. We will because we owe it to our family, to our friends, and to our loved ones that did not live to see this day." As he stepped down from the car, the crowd dispersed and began to ready themselves for the final miles of the trek.

"Very Bill Pullman of you," Paul deadpanned. "I half expected you to shout that this was our Independence Day."

With a laugh, Mike replied. "What do you want? It's all I had on the fly."

Within a half-hour's time, the party of refugees, over seventy in number, embarked on the weaving path down the highway. Thankfully, the rain had stopped soon after his impromptu speech. The going was slower than he would have preferred, but the vehicles were so tightly crammed together that often assistance had to be given to help people over hoods and trunks. The return of the sun worked to dry Mike's clothing and remove the discomfort of moving about in wet jeans.

It was difficult to judge how much distance had been covered, but he estimated the group to have already walked a mile when word came from the rear of the group that a guard needed to see him and Lisa urgently. In an attempt not to arouse worry, the two walked calmly and steadily to the rear guard.

"What's the situation?" Lisa asked him. The short man, coming up only to Mike's shoulder, seemed hesitant to respond.

"I can't be sure, but I think we're being followed," came his nervous reply.

Mike quickly snapped his head up and stared into the distance. "Why do you think that?" he asked, searching the road they had come down.

"That's the thing, sir. It's just a feeling, like someone's watching us. And once in a while, I'll see a flash of movement, but it's gone before I can focus on it."

Though not overly familiar with the man, Mike did know him to be very competent in the field. The lieutenant had spoken quite highly of him, thus he was reluctant to discount the man's information as simply nerves.

As he turned to Lisa to discuss what the man had said, a series of shots from what sounded like several machine guns erupted at the head of the group of refugees. Dropping quickly behind a wood-paneled van, Mike could hear the shouts of the refugees as they sought cover of their own.

CHAPTER TWENTY-ONE

The buzz of activity woke him from a dreamless sleep. Tossing the thick covers aside, Mike stepped from the warmth of the bed and cringed slightly as his feet met the cold, smooth wood of the farmhouse bedroom. Winter's reach could still be felt, though the calendar had already turned to March. Embers from the previous night's fire were all that remained in the fireplace. As he shrugged into an oversized flannel robe, he made his way over to the window.

Tying back the thick drapes allowed for the bright light of morning to flood the room. Looking down from his second story window, he could see the scurrying figures of his companions setting about the morning tasks. In the time they had lived in the farmhouse, several other survivors had joined them, swelling their population to forty-eight. Normally, Mike would have felt a pang of guilt for sleeping so late into the morning, but the security meeting of the night before had stretched well into the predawn hours.

When they had first come upon the abandoned farmhouse, the remains of its former occupants stained the green grass of the front yard. The gruesome task of removing and burying the bodies was well worth the price of security and lodging the discovery offered. The property itself stretched out over a few hundred, relatively flat, acres. A three-foot high wooden fence encircled the farmhouse as well as a small cottage. While the initial height was certainly not an effective barrier against the infected, Mike immediately developed a plan to dismantle some of the other, outer structures around the farm and use the salvaged wood to raise a taller fence.

Though the previous residents had not survived the outbreak, several of the farm's animals did manage to evade the hunger of the infected. His urban upbringing provided no knowledge of animal husbandry, which forced Mike to rely on the skills of his far more rural students. The animals had been rounded up, their respective pens had been rebuilt, and soon the small group of refugees had a plentiful amount of fresh eggs and milk each day.

The main building was more than adequate for the eight of them, though as their numbers grew, the farmhouse's new tenants had been forced to double and triple up in the bedrooms, as well as convert the large dining room and ever more massive basement into shelter-style sleeping quarters. The winters had been survived with relative ease, in large part due to the numerous fireplaces and wood stoves that filled the home. The trees that covered the outer edges of the property provided ample firewood.

After the first winter and its subsequent thaw, Mike and the other refugees began planting myriad types of vegetables in the hopes that the community would eventually become self-sufficient. A childish glee had enveloped them when the first sprouts of green poked through the ground. With the additional hands now living among them, the harvesting of their crops was made less arduous. The nearby Tennessee River provided an abundance of trout, bass, carp, and other aquatic protein sources.

It was with wariness and trepidation that Mike consented to accept the first band of survivors. Though Blaine's murder and the battle with the renegades had been months earlier, any interaction with strangers was cause for alarm. Gradually, after lengthy discussions, the initial band of refugees welcomed the new members to the group. As months passed and cycled into years, more and more survivors had followed the same thoughts Mike had had to seek an isolated area.

The newcomers hailed from several counties in Tennessee, as well as the northern neighbor, Kentucky. One small family of three had managed to survive their journey from western Kansas. With each arrival, the strangers would provide information about the world beyond the security of the farm. There was still no government presence, military or political. No one had heard or seen any broadcast communication since the airwaves shut down at the beginning of the outbreak. As for the infected, they still roamed freely, attacking and feeding at will.

Once dressed for the day, Mike headed downstairs and found Michelle and Sarah feeding split logs into the kitchen's large wood stove.

"Morning," he greeted them and he followed his nose to the still-warm pot of coffee.

"Hey, Mike," Sarah returned. "Surprised you're up already. I heard the meeting went late last night."

Relishing the warmth of the coffee, he took a seat at the table while he waited for the morning's collection of eggs to be brought in. "Yeah, some of the guys on patrol reported that two areas of the fence have been broken down. They couldn't tell if it was just accidental, animal-related, or something else."

Though everyone was aware of the security patrols and the purpose they served, many—Mike included—still preferred to leave the "something else" undefined in casual conversation. The refugees would never be able to escape the reality of the infected, but over the last two years they had developed coping strategies. In order to create some sort of normalcy, it had become an unspoken rule, one of many, to save talk of the Til for only the most necessary occasions.

"How worried should we be?" Sarah asked.

"I'm going to take a ride out to the sites in a bit and see what we're dealing with," Mike informed her. Though he was concerned with the report, he preferred to keep his feelings to himself and spare others what could be unnecessary worries.

Derrick and Andrew soon entered the kitchen through the rear door that led out to the yard and chicken coops. Each of them was carrying a basket heavily laden with the morning collection of eggs. Since their time at the farmhouse, Derrick had eased into the role of overseeing the management of the daily tasks. Mike marveled at the young man's natural acumen with recognizing and evaluating the various details of maintaining a thriving farm community. For his part, Derrick seemed to enjoy the work. In high school his focus had been sports, but now it was clear the youth was impressed with his newfound skills. In addition to gaining Mike's respect, the other refugees praised him regularly for his success in the challenging undertaking.

Perhaps his most adoring supporter was Andrew. Sarah's son had grown considerably in the last two years, leaving the lankiness of the pre-teen years behind in favor of a body made strong by the hard rigors of farming. Having lost his father to the virus, he had slowly grown to view Derrick as the male role model boys his age so desperately needed. To Derrick's credit, he understood the younger boy's needs and took him under his wing as a little brother.

Many of the refugees throughout the farm had steadily developed the same sort of familial relationships. Michelle and Jenni, previously good friends, had soon developed the rapport usually visible in only the closest of sisters. Fathers, mothers, and siblings had begun to emerge regardless of the lack of actual blood relation.

Mike, however, found himself thrust into a drastically different role. For him, no bonds of family had formed. He served none as a surrogate father or brother. Instead, he had become their leader, an untrained general in a war not of his choosing. As he felt the shackles of leadership tightening around him, he soon realized that no matter how much he cherished those around him, he could not serve them if his thoughts diverted from the task at hand. While the others had slipped back into a form of normalcy, he had found he could not relax his anxiety with regards to their plight.

Life bustled around him on the farm, but Mike maintained a constant wariness and an expectation for the proverbial other shoe to drop. The isolation and independence he had sought when he first moved south had now amplified to a level from which he could see no escape. Only now his independence was marred by having so many dependent on him.

After his breakfast of eggs, scrambled as usual, Mike headed out, making his way towards one of the two still functioning cars. Along the way, he was greeted by several of the refugees as they went about their work. A few small children ran through the yard chasing after chickens that squawked loudly at the pursuit. He smiled as he saw them at play, their carefree spirits oblivious to the danger that surrounded them. Few children had survived the initial outbreak and the subsequent hardships of life on the road—only three of the farm's occupants were under the age of ten.

Hopping into the old Jeep Wrangler, Mike turned the engine over and began the short drive to the location of the first broken fence. Several cows and the bull that were grazing in the outlying fields barely lifted their heads as he drove by, accustomed to the movements of humans since birth. Reaching his destination, he was met by two men, Tyler and Phil. In his mid-forties, Tyler Aaron had spent much of his life tending to a farm of his own in Eastern Kansas. He had arrived at the refugee farmhouse that winter with his wife and teenage son. The Aarons were the only ones in the camp that had survived the virus with all members of their immediate family unscathed.

Phil Armstrong, a rail-thin thirty-two year old, was one of the most recent arrivals, having joined the group in late

January. A drifter by nature, his years spent on the road had honed many scavenging skills that had proven invaluable among the refugees.

"Morning," Mike said as he stepped from the Jeep. The men returned his greeting and gratefully accepted the warm thermos of coffee Sarah had given him before he departed.

As the trio walked closer to the fence, he could see a four foot section where the additional boards they'd used to increase its height, had been splintered and ripped free from its tethering.

"Like I said last night," Tyler began. "I ain't never seen an animal do that. Horse might could if panicked, but there've been no sightings of one as such."

"Wind?" Mike asked.

"Not likely. Any wind that did this would have been felt at the house, and the weather has been pretty calm," answered Phil.

Gazelle padded cautiously along the winter-hardened ground, her nose taking in the scents of the area. As she neared the broken section of fencing, a low growl rumbled in her chest. Her reaction was the final confirmation Mike needed to be sure that it had been Tils that had damaged the structure. Certainly not of a size to be considered a guard dog, the terrier mutt had a keen sense of smell that had proven reliable in the detection of the infected.

"The other site looks the same?"

With affirmative nods from the two men, Mike continued. "I'll send some guys out with supplies to patch them up. For now, keep the patrols focused on the breaches. Moving forward I want daily inspections of the entire barricade."

As he took his leave, Mike was tempted to turn back to instruct the two not to discuss the damage with others, but he continued on, knowing that a request of silence was fruitless in the small community. With Gazelle leaning her head out the windowless vehicle, he made a quick pass to the other breach, informing the men there that supplies would be sent.

That Tils had in fact been that close to the farmhouse had Mike's brow creased with concern. Since establishing themselves at the farm, sightings of the infected had dramatically decreased. Untended fields that stretched for miles had served as an herbaceous deterrent for the carnivorous Tils. The few sorties beyond the farm's acreage had reported some signs of them, but those had all been located near previously well-populated areas. *Food must be getting sparse for them to venture out this far.*

After surveying the entire perimeter, Mike returned to the main house and signaled to Andrew, who was engaged in a comical battle trying to herd the roaming chickens back to the rear of the house. Try as he might, the birds found every possible means of escape.

"Have you seen Erik?" Mike asked him.

With a chicken cradled under each arm, the youngster informed him that Erik was at the barn. In recent weeks, several members of the community had begun construction on a lookout platform atop the barn's high roof.

"Do me a favor and tell him I need to see him ASAP, okay?"

"Okay!" the boy said, eager to pass his Sisyphean task onto another.

As Andrew ran off on his new errand, Mike climbed the steps to the house's porch, entering the house. The lightweight screen door closed with a bang behind him, as he walked down the long hallway to the small study that the refugees used for conducting camp meetings. After they had moved in, Jenni had discovered a file drawer that contained several surveyor maps detailing the surrounding land. The documents were now marked with symbols added by the refugees to indicate various important features of the farm's defenses.

In addition to the maps, the previous tenants had collected a wealth of genealogical and historical papers regarding their farm and holdings. The Tuft family had owned and worked the middling-sized farm for the better part of one hundred years. The photographs that adorned the walls of the farmhouse chronicled the generations that had dwelt there and the evolution of the farm and its many structures. As the family grew, so too did the size of the home, first expanding horizontally and then eventually receiving a second and third level.

Mike had spent the first few months at the farm pouring over the Tuft history as he sat by the fireplace after his companions had gone to sleep. Twinges of guilt eventually subsided over time, a decreasing sense that he was in some way invading the privacy of the former occupants. Diaries and logbooks recounted the daily activities of the past century, with special attention given to the many births and deaths the years had seen. Mike cherished the documents, losing himself in a history of an era long gone from time and familiarity.

Now his attention focused on one of the large maps that sat atop the massive wooden desk occupying the majority of the small room's space. Marking the two breaches with a pencil, Mike involuntarily began to chew his lip, puzzling over what else could be done to keep the Tils out.

"You needed to see me, Mr. A.?" Erik said as he entered the study.

"How's the platform coming along?" he asked in response, moving to the large leather chair behind the desk.

Taking a seat of his own, Erik wiped the sweat from his brow with the back of his forearm, a testament to the strenuous labor in the still-cool days of early spring.

"Not the prettiest thing I've ever built, but it's sturdy enough. Probably have another few days of work left."

"Good," Mike replied before changing topics. "Listen, we have a problem. Some of the guys came to me last night about two breaks in the fence. I checked them out this morning. It's the Tils."

With a nod of acceptance, Erik leaned back in his chair. Since coming to the farm, he had been devoted to the security of the refugees. Though for the most part a loner in school, he had considered Blaine a friend and had taken his death hard. A drive of relentless vigilance had quickly settled over the young man, which Mike had leveraged to the benefit of the entire community. In truth, the majority of the security plans that had worked to keep the farm safe had originated with Erik.

"I'm going to send some guys out to repair the damage, but if the Tils have gotten this close then it is likely they have either seen us or picked up our scent."

"Which means they'll be back," Erik said matter-of-factly.

"Exactly. I need you to get with the other security folks and start thinking of ways to strengthen the fence. Also, we may need to up the number on patrol."

"That's going to be tough, Mr. A.," he began. "Half the people here are already working security. You're not going to have enough to run the farm."

Mike knew there was no denying the validity of Erik's assessment. Though the addition of so many refugees over the last two years had provided more bodies for security, it also required more bodies for food and other necessities. A fine line had to be navigated to avoid a very secure but severely malnourished and exhausted population.

"I know. All right, for now start brainstorming ideas with the others and I'll see where we can scale back some of the work duty to free up people for security. Let's talk again tomorrow morning."

* * *

The following morning's meeting proved to be a wasted exercise. While several ideas had been generated to increase the farm's security—everything from reinforcing the fencing, to building a second fence, to even digging a moat—the fact remained that both labor and supplies were in short order. To actualize any of the suggestions would require diverting resources, human and material, from the current security and labor tasks. In the end it was decided that further security improvements would have to wait for warmer weather, at which time Mike could re-assign the refugees who spent their days providing firewood for the farmhouse. When spring came wood would only be needed for cooking, thus freeing up at least four people to work on other projects. He could only hope that spring would hasten to their need.

* * *

With a sharp breath, Mike's eyes jumped open. The night still clung heavily to the room, only the fading glow of embers in the fireplace provided illumination. A cheek-stretching yawn escaped from his lungs, and he rolled to his left as he allowed his eyes to close for his return to slumber.

POP. POP. POP.

Springing from the bed, Mike knew it was not a nightmare that had awoken him, but rather the familiar eruption of gunfire. Quickly donning his clothes and boots, he swung his holster harness over his shoulder, and bounded down the steps as other refugees began to react to the disturbance. Rushing out into the night, his breath thick in the chill air, he could see the beams of flashlights dancing in the distance. Muffled shouts were made unintelligible by the interruption of repeated gunshots. Mike could already sense the hysteria that was building behind him in the house.

"Get me a flashlight!" he shouted to one of the refugees who stood dumbstruck at the door. Before the man could even move, Derrick and Jenni followed quickly by Andrew, raced out of the house. The fourteen year old tossed Mike his flashlight before being pulled back by his mother. As he struggled to free himself from his mother's grasp and join the fight, Mike pointed down to Gazelle. The boy understood the message and scooped the dog up in his arms.

"Follow me," Mike called out to Jenni and Derrick.

The two followed him into the Jeep as Mike retrieved the keys from the car's visor. As soon as the engine roared to life, he engaged the high beams. Though still too distant to discern the situation, he could clearly see shapes running and firing in the direction of the farm's outer perimeter. The Jeep bounced along the uneven ground, slamming its passengers into the old vinyl seats.

In under a minute, they reached the center of the confusion. A large section of fencing had been completely ripped down, creating an opening a dozen feet wide. Several refugees knelt on the ground some yards from the breach and continued their punishing defense of the farm. At this range, even the loud, constant bursts of gun battle could not overcome the bloodthirsty sound of their attackers.

Infected bodies filled the ground in front of the opening, while more climbed across, and still others could be heard slamming into further sections of the fencing. It was clear to Mike the onslaught they faced rivaled any they had seen before that night. The number of Tils battering their entrance into the refugees' stronghold would soon overwhelm the defenses of the farm. Now that the hunt had been engaged, the enemy would not relent.

The front line—the *only* line—of defenders consisted of six men and women armed with a combination of hand and machine guns.

"Where are the others?" Mike shouted above the din as he, Derrick and Jenni joined the line.

A man's voice answered. "There were gunshots at the west side and we were heading there when the fencing came down here."

As he reloaded, Mike looked to his right and squinted into the darkness. Though the muzzle flashes and high beams severely damaged his night vision, he could still make out the faint sights of a second front waging along the western fence.

Two? Two attack points? he thought with dejection. *We'd*

be lucky to hold them back at one with all of our guns.

"Derrick, take the Jeep and tell the others to fall back to the house."

Without replying, Derrick quickly returned to the vehicle and sped off into the direction of the other battle. Issuing short orders, Mike instructed the men and women beside him to withdraw to the farmhouse. Before any objection to the retreat could be voiced, the ear-ringing squeal of breaking timber marked the collapse of another large section of the fencing. With the gap spreading to well over thirty feet wide, it was evident that defense of the barricade was over. Mike's goal now was to reach the house and determine some method of escape before the entire farm was overrun.

In unison, as the Tils swarmed through the destroyed fencing, the security line abandoned their defensive positions and began the retreat. Even with bullets streaking through the darkness, they were merciless in their advance.

Racing backwards, Mike could see the Jeep's headlights drawing closer to the homestead. Those that had been defending the western breach were piled into the small confines of the vehicle. Assured that the others would reach the farmhouse safely, Mike turned his attention back to the enemy bearing down on him. Unlike a typical foe, the infected were undeterred by the hail of gunfire raining down on them. He realized that any attempt to slow the Tils to cover the retreat would only result in losing precious ground and time. With quick shouts to his companions, he ordered a cease fire and instructed them to make a headlong dash to safety.

With no light by which to navigate the rough terrain, Mike and the others stumbled frequently as they sprinted towards the house. Despite the cold, his legs burned with the effort he demanded from his muscles. Still a half mile in the distance, he saw the Jeep reach the farmhouse. After a brief pause to unload its passengers, the Jeep joined the other vehicle now hurtling to rescue Mike and the security team. Men and machines met in seconds and he struggled to maintain his grasp on the roll-bar as the cars cut sharp turns to return to the house.

"I want a full retreat from the house!" he shouted above the roar of the engines. "Security will hold the line while the cars shuttle everyone else to the east gate."

The vehicles would cover the two mile stretch to the eastern gate quickly, but Mike knew that at least three trips would be needed to safely transport the refugees, with a fourth to rescue those that provided cover. *Fifteen minutes,* he told himself, *we just need to survive for fifteen minutes.*

Upon reaching the house, the security members dispersed with more exactness than he had expected. Forming a quarter-circle in front of the structure, they used the brief minute before the Tils were in range to reload their weapons. Derrick rushed up the porch and began ushering frightened refugees into the two waiting vehicles. Screams and tears of confusion echoed into the vacuous blackness of night. Sparing no time for collecting supplies or possessions, the cars lurched into motion, carrying the first group of refugees to safety. Without the headlights, Mike and the remaining survivors depended on the few flashlights they had to break through the dark. However it was the guttural sounds of the Tils that gave away their proximity.

To his rear, Mike heard Erik drop additional ammunition and weapons by each of the fighters. With relief, he reached back to grab the magazines he had not taken with him earlier. Fanned out in a Mafia-style hit formation, over a dozen men and women stood firm and fired into the ever-encroaching mass of Tils. Even with the overwhelming firepower, Tils still managed to break through the line. Mike could hear the screams of humans as infected descended and attempted to feast.

At his immediate left, Mike saw the yellow and red flashes of an M-16 arc into the dark sky above as one of the refugees fell to a Til. Turning, Mike drove two bullets into the infected, but he saw the damage had already been done.

"Kill me!" the man pleaded as the convulsions began to

shake his body, his blood already beginning to force the change. With a silent curse, Mike fired a shot into the man's head. Only in the brief flash of the muzzle did he see the face of Tyler Aaron.

Minutes passed with stubbornly slow speed before the headlights returned for the second, and then third, collection of refugees. As more Tils broke through the line, Mike thought he heard Andrew scream for his mother in the distance.

The bodies of fallen Tils created a short-lived impediment to the advance of the endless stream of attackers. While most climbed over the corpses, others began to shift around the obstacles, forcing the refugees to expand their range of defense.

"Into the house!" Mike commanded as he inched backwards up the porch steps. Even with a two mile head start, he knew the distance was short enough for the Tils to pursue their prey tirelessly. Though he hated the sacrifice, he knew his next actions could possibly turn the tide in favor of the refugees' safe escape.

The armed defenders fell back inside the house and quickly barricaded the front door. As Mike raced through several rooms, he could hear the crush of bodies slamming into the home's exterior. Windows smashed and the sounds of gunfire returned before he finally found the large, red plastic container in the basement. Climbing the stairs, the pungent liquid splashed through the nozzle and began to soak into the wood flooring.

The scene in the front rooms was one of horrifying chaos. Tils pressed through the broken windows, unaware of the glass shards that scored their flesh. Bloodied hands groped blindly and tore away at the window casings. The sheer weight of their number pressing on the outside walls caused the house to groan in dwindling defiance.

"Fall back to the kitchen!"

Hearing Mike's command, the men and women turned with surprise to see him standing with the gasoline container, its redness now glowing from the flashlights trained on it. Doubt passed through their eyes, followed by the inevitable sadness of comprehension. His own glare silenced all objections and without argument, they set their jaws and followed his order.

Once cleared, he began to splash walls, floors, and furniture in the front rooms. The angry snarls of the infected grew more persistent as he walked before them. Arms reached out for him from the window openings, but his mind refused to acknowledge their presence. From the kitchen, someone shouted that the vehicles had made their return. Passing within inches of the snapping teeth of a Til, Mike turned to exit the room. His hand dug into his pocket and withdrew a battered match book. With a swift strike, Mike let the match fall to the ground, and a soft orange-red glow flickered along the wet floors as the room roared to fiery life. The macabre faces of the Tils grew even more grotesque in the light and heat of the newly born inferno.

As the vehicles drove away, he did not take his eyes from the massive fire that engulfed the farmhouse. No Tils were seen following them. Instead, as he had hoped, the mindless infected continued to pour into the home. Two years of peace and safety had been the cost of the refugees' escape. Even from two miles away, one could see the funeral pyre of memory and flesh raging into the early hours of dawn.

* * *

The days that followed were marked by fatigue, hunger, and a thick depression that enveloped everyone. As the group continued their march in search of shelter, tears flowed unchecked down the faces of even the strongest souls. In all, six had fallen during the attack on the farmhouse. Mike had only a passing familiarity with most, but it was the loss of Andrew's mother Sarah that carved the deepest wound. He was told that she had been bitten while trying to protect her son. The boy, who had been the one to end her life, spent the last two days in silence, taking little water and no food.

Not that there was much food to be shared. With the suddenness of the attack, there had been no time to pack supplies for an extended journey. Stomachs growled painfully as the refugees, many still clad in bedclothes, walked steadily for the mountains in the east. Their route was through abandoned farms and small towns, and many voiced their desire to resettle at a farm, but Mike feared that another such location would soon only meet the same fate. If the food supply for the Tils was running low in the more developed areas, their dispersion into the rural communities was sure to continue. *No,* he thought, his eyes locking on the peaks miles ahead, *the mountains are all that's left to us.*

And so they trudged on, seeking shelter in the night and marching through the daylight, their vehicles out of fuel and abandoned miles back. Mike insisted on a brisk pace, driving the refugees to their limits. He understood their weariness but he was possessed of a dogged determination to reach the mountains with all possible speed. He blamed himself for the loss of lives and shelter, and was willing to endure any hardships the road might offer in order to avert future losses. Wrapped in his solitude, he urged the others to walk further than their bodies believed they could.

With Mike's unrelenting persistence, the refugees soon found themselves deep within the wooded protection of the Cherokee National Forest. Even with spring still some weeks off, the forest's evergreens stood tall and full, a welcome sign of life for the fatigued travelers. At the base of the Great Smoky Mountains, hundreds of thousands of acres reverberated with the sounds of birds and other wildlife.

A small collection of picnic tables and fire pits filled a clearing off one of the many trails. Though so close to their destination, Mike could feel his own body rejecting any further request for movement.

"Okay, let's stop here for the night," he instructed.

As the refugees slumped to the ground, a loud rustling of

branches and leaves was heard from the direction of a heavily wooded area. Exhaustion evaporated and immediately several refugees leapt up with guns at the ready. Mike signaled for a small group to begin to close in on the sound.

From the trees emerged a young man, Mike estimating the two shared a similar age, carrying the body of a buck across his shoulders. Heedless of the weapons drawn on him, the man walked towards one of the many fire pits at the camp site. The man moved with the casual grace of one well-experienced in the outdoors. Easing the animal's weight off his back and onto the ground, he then wiped his hands on his weathered jeans. Mike slowly lowered his gun as the man approached him with a hand extended in greeting.

"I saw you guys coming about an hour ago and from the looks of it y'all are in need of a good meal. This area is as safe as any. They haven't been coming into the woods, yet," he began. Then, with a glance to men around him, "Anytime you guys want to lower those guns would be great. I could use a few hands dressing the deer."

As Mike shook the man's hand in disbelief, his mouth worked to form some sort of reply, but words failed him. The man's affable, and apparently fearless nature, was stunning to Mike's current mood. He had spent the better part of the last seventy-two hours struggling to keep alive. Yet, here was this man, and his dead deer, strolling through the woods offering a shared meal. In the darkness of recent losses, Mike could almost feel the hope of a new beginning.

"Oh, I'm Paul, by the way," the man said. "Paul Jenson."

CHAPTER TWENTY-TWO

An endless cavalcade of bullets streamed through the air, showering Mike and Lisa with glass fragments from the windshield and passenger-side windows. Hugging the wide surface of the minivan, the two waited for a lull in the attack before risking exposure by peering over the vehicle's thick metal protection. Gazelle, though fearless of Tils, cowered next to Mike, the deafening sounds of gunfire forcing her tail and ears to slump. Several feet in front of them, the body of the man who only moments before had warned of being followed lay sprawled out on the cracked roadway. A large portion of his face was missing. Given the damage to the refugee, Mike knew whoever was attacking them was in possession of large, high-powered weapons capable of deadly force at a distance.

The projectiles continued to rip through the air forcing Mike and Lisa to stay pinned in their current location, though he left his crouched position and pressed himself to the surface of the road. Under the confusing maze of vehicles, he was able to see several other refugees likewise sheltering themselves from the ambush. There were a handful of unmoving bodies scattered along the road as well.

Resuming his crouch, Mike closed his eyes in an effort to

focus his hearing on the direction of the shots. Even with the poor acoustics of their environment, he believed the majority of their enemies' attack was centered ahead, with only a few gunmen hidden within the foliage along the highway's shoulders. As for their numbers, Mike knew he would not be able to get an accurate count unless he got closer.

Leaning closer to Lisa, he shouted over the gunfire, "We have to move up! Keep low and watch your flanks!"

Nodding her acknowledgement, she made a quick check of her weapons and angled herself to follow Mike's lead.

"Stay with me, girl," he said to the canine at his side. When she barked in reply, Mike found himself encouraged by the thought of the dog's incredible survival over the past several years. As she continued her barking, he recognized a slight change in tone. Previously sounding her obedience, Gazelle now called out in warning. Lisa followed the direction of her stare.

"Oh my God," she whispered into the air.

With a face suddenly ashen, mouth agape as muscles slackened, Lisa's demeanor forced Mike to seek the cause. Turning to their rear, his eyes widened as he understood that their situation had transitioned from dire to hopeless.

Behind them, and approaching with feral steadiness, a massive number of Tils slowly walked down the highway. If the refugees were unable to advance, they would soon be overtaken by the Tils at their rear flank.

"So close," Lisa said, her tone marked with abject resignation, "Damn it but we got so close!

"Lisa...*LISA!!*" Mike shouted at her to break the defeated trance that now gripped her. Slowly turning to him, she stared at him with pure vacancy in her eyes.

"Lisa, listen to me. We need to advance and take out those gunners. It's our only chance. Do you understand me? The gunners, that's your target."

"Gunners," she mumbled. Then, as if woken from a deep sleep, her eyes refocused, filling with understanding.

"You with me?"

"Yes, sir," she replied with her former conviction. Though relieved to see her emotions under control, Mike worried how the other refugees might react to the sight of the Tils if his head of security froze from the full awareness of their situation. Pushing the thought from his mind, Mike began a hurried crawl around the minivan. The Tils were still several dozen yards behind and not yet running. *Why aren't they running?* he thought as he wove his way through the maze of vehicles.

As man, woman, and dog rounded another car, they discovered both Erik and Dr. Marena huddled low behind the trunk of a black sedan. Just as Mike was about to speak, the gunfire, unrelenting since it began, came to a sudden and abrupt stop. Erik began to rise from behind the car, when Mike pulled him back down.

In answer to Erik's questioning look, Mike told him in a hushed voice, "They want us to give away our position." In confirmation of his assessment, a refugee hidden behind a truck several feet from them jumped into view and began firing towards the attackers. The man barely got off five rounds before his chest exploded from several shots of return fire.

"That's a fifty," Lisa said. Mike knew they were outgunned, but now wondered how many .50 caliber machine guns their hidden enemy possessed.

"We need to retreat," Marena said. His voice shook with fear. Rarely making any excursions from the mountain camp, the doctor had seen little field action and the current situation was clearly taking its toll.

"Can't," Mike said. "Tils."

As the doctor took to mumbling in despair, Mike scanned the wooded areas bordering the highway.

"So, what's the plan, Chief?" Erik asked.

"Lisa and I will swing around to their east and west flanks. You two stay low and keep moving forward and warn the others about the Tils," Mike said, trying to fill his words with authoritative certitude.

"How're you gonna reach the woods? That's at least a fifteen yard sprint in the open. You'll be cut down before you take your third step," Erik replied.

"That's where the diversion comes in," Mike said.

"What diversion?" asked Marena who had roused himself from his rumblings.

If the doctor had been anxious before, his blood pressure certainly sky-rocketed when he saw the mischievous smile Mike offered in reply while staring at the doctor's medical pack.

* * *

The cessation in firing was short-lived as refugees attempted to strike back, only to be met with the overwhelming force of the enemies' weapons. Through the bursts of gunfire, Mike could see the Tils closing the distance with the refugees. Though oddly still not rushing headlong in frenzy, the infected were now crouching and slinking between vehicles as if to avoid the flight of bullets in the air.

At the western edge of the highway, Mike hoped that Lisa had reached her eastern destination. Long seconds passed as he waited for Erik and the doctor to act. Finally, a thin stream of smoke wafted into the overcast sky. Soon other streams could be spotted, and then tongues of dancing fire grew large enough to mar the landscape with thick black smoke. Mike had doubted that any of the vehicles still had fuel, but their interiors would burn nicely, especially if doused with the doctor's supply of rubbing alcohol. Mike hoped that the fires would also consume some of the Tils. Over a dozen cars and trucks now burned furiously, filling the distance Mike had to cover to reach the safety of the tree line with cover.

With a breath and a prayer, he lunged forward and sprinted through the smoke. The flash of gray at his feet let him know that Gazelle raced alongside him. Mike mentally screamed at his legs to maintain their balance as they turned over wildly in his dash. The smoke shield was significantly thinner the closer he got to the woods. Several shots whizzed by his head before he reached the ground safely within the woods.

Out of breath and fighting smoke-induced coughs, Mike allowed himself to rest for a fraction of a second. "Get up," he commanded his body with a whisper.

As he rose from the undergrowth, he pressed his body against the rough exterior of a tall, green-needled tree. He was trusting that his six years of silent tracking and escaping would allow him to reach his targets without them drawing first blood.

Even though the sun had returned, the sky still possessed a grayish hue, which combined with the darkness from the thick evergreen canopy overhead and the smoke now creeping into the woods, provided excellent cover for his advance. Slipping silently from trunk to trunk, he moved as a candle-dancing shadow, a dark form seen briefly before melting away. Though big-city born, Mike had watched and learned from his companions through the years, and had grown to become a child of the forest. His feet moved mutely as he steadily closed in on the attackers. He heard the steady exchange of gunfire along the highway and followed the sound of the large caliber machine guns.

Pausing briefly in a thick bush at the base of a tree, Mike slowly scanned the woods before him. His heart pounded steadily, his lungs taking in deep, silent, controlled breaths. The mending bones of his ribcage strained with the expansion, but the pain was distant and mild. With each blast of the machine gun, he was able to narrow the area his eyes searched.

There! His mind shouted as his eyes took in a slight flicker of movement several yards ahead. Though it was well hidden among the trees, he could see leaves rustling as the recoil of the large weapon pushed the surrounding air. With his target close, Mike pressed forward. It had only been minutes since the attack had begun, but he knew that the refugees faced an even more deadly foe that would be undeterred by gunfire. *Then why were they crouching?* his mind asked.

As if sensing the need for stealth, Gazelle matched her master in both speed and silence as both glided forward towards the enemy. Whenever he paused to seek the next location of cover, she stood dutifully motionless by his side. Quickly, Mike had advanced enough that a line of fire opened up and he could see the man who controlled the machine gun.

Covered in ragged clothing of brown and green, the man lay prostrate behind the weapon, with his right eye pressed tightly against the gun's sight. Sparing a second to scan for cover once he took his shots, he slowly raised his firearms. To his right, he spied a thick congestion of entwined trees. Mike decided he would dive for their protection once he gave away his position by firing his guns.

His index fingers gently curled around the cool metal triggers. With long-established reflex, he could feel the series of muscles contract as he squeezed. Before the familiar click that would send forth the projectiles, Gazelle let out a wild series of barks. The distraction forced one of the rounds to go wide, while the other embedded itself into the prone man's lower back. The slow motion advance through the woods sped rapidly into flashes of action.

At the onset of the dog's barking, Mike had turned his head to his left as he blindly fired the guns pointed ahead of him. The bullets barely left their barrels before he felt the force of a collision. His weapons flew free from his hands once he hit the ground, followed by the crushing weight of a body smashing atop his own. His vision filled briefly with flashes of light while he screamed in pain as his mending ribs shattered once again. Hearing the growl from the figure crushing him, he managed to grab the Til's throat before its mouth reached his flesh.

Mike struggled to maintain his grip while the Til's jaws snapped wildly just inches from his face. The creature's face was covered in half-healed scars, and the skin beneath its nose was stained a deep red from the slow, constant hemorrhaging of the virus. Scabbed fingers, some cut off at the knuckle and mostly nail-less, wrapped tightly around Mike's wrist.

Turning his face away from the Til for fear of its saliva or blood reaching his eyes and mouth, he could feel the strength leaving his arm, and his elbow continued to give way. Reaching with his free hand, Mike grabbed the hunting knife sheathed at his waist. Armed with the blade, he still could not risk releasing the creature's blood while it was this close to his face. Marshalling the little flagging energy still within him, Mike let out a loud scream as he forced his arm to push the Til away from his body. As his tendons and muscles cried out, he moved the Til further and further back until his own arm was fully extended. He could feel his shoulder begin to buckle towards dislocation as he drove the six-inch blade through the Til's eye. When the guard reached the skeletal socket, he gave a quick twist of the handle. The Til jerked once, and then again, before its arms dropped from Mike's wrist. Shoving the dead weight to the side, he gasped raggedly to catch his breath, wincing as his lungs pressed into broken bones.

With great effort, he struggled to his feet and began to search the thick woodland carpet for his fallen weapons. The metal showed clearly in the murky browns of the undergrowth. In the collision, both weapons had come precariously close to going over a steep incline some forty feet in length. His eyes searched the trees for further Tils, as he reached down gingerly to retrieve the guns. As he rose back to his full height, he noticed the distinct booming of the .50 caliber machine guns was absent amid the sounds of small arms fire. Mike wondered if it was an indication of another lull in the attack or if Lisa had achieved her target on the eastern side.

Even if the heavy guns are out of commission, he told himself, *we still need to cut through the enemy line.* Moving more stiffly than during his previous stalking, he slid through the trees as best as his battered body could manage. He allowed his senses and instincts to direct his path, while his mind tried to determine how much time had elapsed. From his vantage point, he could still see the flames of the burning vehicles. Without a gasoline accelerant, Mike knew the interior of the cars and trucks would not burn for long. *Minutes,* he realized with surprise. If he was to judge by the beating his body had taken he would have assumed hours had slipped past.

Though the fires were visible, he had difficulty locating the refugees as they were hopefully making their way forward. The Tils advancing along the highway, however, were quite distinct, their numbers crowded closely together and appearing as a fleshed wave inching along a paved shore. The encroaching tide of infection had moved past the burning vehicles. Mike knew if the refugees did not break through soon, they would be crushed between bullets and disease.

Crouching low behind a heavily-leaved sapling, he identified two more targets. Closer to the road than their comrade had been, the two figures positioned themselves among the few remaining trees before the woods gave way to the highway's shoulder. Armed with semi-automatic machine guns, each would briefly spray the highway below with bullets before returning to safety behind the trunks. It had surely been luck that his attack on the .50 caliber had not been heard, but Mike understood that such lightning would not strike twice.

Past the two attackers closest to him, Mike could see several dozen others arrayed across the blockaded highway. A brief glance was all he needed to recognize how strong the enemies' position was. In his current state, he accepted his inability to enact a silent approach, let alone take on that large of a force with two handguns.

Mike forced his mind to process his options rapidly, fearing the seconds of delay that brought the refugees closer to a horrifying end. Before the idea was even concluded, Mike turned and retreated with as much haste as his body allowed. The needed immediacy of action allowed for a slight carelessness as he rushed through the trees. Sparing no time for subtlety or safety, he quickly returned to the site of the struggle with the Til. Grunting through the pain, Mike lifted the heavy machine gun and its metal case that overflowed with the belted cartridges. With a combined weight of well over one hundred pounds, he strained as he half-carried, half-dragged the weapon. What should have been crippling pain in his chest was masked by the adrenaline in his veins and the determination in his will.

Finally returning to the sapling and the enemy, Mike let the weapon drop to the ground, its tripod righting itself with ease. As the two figures heard the thundering crash, he slipped one of his guns from its holster and fired several rounds at them. His pained body hit the ground before their lifeless ones did. As expected his attempted sneak attack had easily been seen and he was now drawing fire from several of the enemies' number. Armed with the immense power of the .50 caliber, he thought the sacrifice of stealth was an even trade.

A slight rise in the landscape offered Mike an invaluable advantage over the enemies directing a substantial portion of their fire power up towards him. Depressing what he assumed to be the trigger of the weapon, his ears rang sharply as a steady stream of rounds exploded out the long barrel. Though the recoil was minimal, Mike still tightened his grip to better control his aiming. Spent shells began to form a pile on one side of the machine gun, while a seemingly endless belt of bullets were fed through the other. At this close range, the automobiles the enemy forces had been using as cover quickly became riddled with massive holes.

Without ceasing his barrage, Mike risked a glance to his left and was relieved to see Paul striding atop the hoods and roofs of cars. He held a medium-sized semi-automatic gun in each hand while he screamed words Mike could not hear over the din. The other refugees had begun to follow Paul's assault, and the tide of the battle soon shifted as the refugees made a daring push forward under the protection of Mike and the .50 caliber.

To their rear, however, the Tils closed the remaining gap of ground and had now reached the refugees at the rear of the assault. Every Til that was brought down by a refugee bullet was immediately replaced with three more of its kind. Now that Paul and the refugees at the front had reached the enemies' position, Mike swiveled the machine gun on its tripod while shifting his body. At his current angle, he could not risk directing the machine gun at the Tils for fear of hitting his own people. He could, however, thin the number of infected further down the highway.

The rhythmic booms of each round's release became almost hypnotic. With the vast number of Tils coalescing along the road, Mike no longer needed to use the weapon's sights, every bullet tore into infected flesh.

Mike could feel Gazelle's weight as she sat across the back of his calves. He had placed full trust in her senses to warn him of any danger that might be approaching in his blind spots. Only when he felt her tense up in alarm did he remove his focus from the targets below. A glance to his left showed only the tall trees of the woods. Turning to the right, he saw a figure jogging towards him through the foliage. From the shape and the gait, Mike quickly recognized the figure to be Lisa. When she reached him, he eased off the trigger-lever in order to hear her report.

"We've broken through the line," she said through gasps as she tried to catch her breath. Mike could see that he had not been the only one involved in a struggle. The skin above Lisa's right eye was deeply gashed and fresh blood streamed freely from the wound.

"I need you to scout ahead and find somewhere we can hole up and regroup," he shouted in reply, his ears still ringing.

"Sir," Lisa began.

"We need some place to figure a way out of this trap," Mike continued. "God knows how many we've lost."

"It wasn't a trap," she attempted to cut in again.

"Once we've secured a place, then we can plan our next move," he said. Though his engagement in battle was paused briefly, the adrenaline still flowed through him. His mind raced with plans and strategies. His resolve would not accept a defeat after so many years of survival.

"Mike! It wasn't a trap," she said. Her words finally managed to break through his warrior's fog.

"What…" he began, but trailed off with incomprehension.

"I mean it was, but not the way you think. Mike, I already scouted ahead. There's a ship, Mike. I don't know who these guys were," she said as she indicated towards the road. "But the message didn't come from them. There's a ship, and they were trying to stop us from reaching it. But there's a ship, and it's waiting for us."

"There's a ship?" he repeated in confusion. The words felt strange on his tongue as if he were a child speaking them for the first time.

With tears in her eyes, Lisa nodded.

"There's a ship." Mike said, voice cracking as his own tears traced his cheeks. Emotions he thought forever lost to him flooded through his body and his jaw trembled as he fought to keep control.

"Where?" he eventually managed.

"Half mile up," she replied. "It's docked but can't wait long with this many Tils following us."

Collecting himself once again, he said, "Okay, get the others there. I'll hold the Tils off for a few minutes before I follow."

Rising to her feet, she offered him a broad smile, which he returned. The nightmare was over, and it was difficult to hide their excitement. Breaking their emotion-filled stare, Mike returned his focus to the highway below, and Lisa set off to lead the refugees to the ship.

In the brief moments of his exchange with Lisa, the Tils had advanced further along the road than he expected. Mike placed his thumb on the lever and pressed down, filling the air once again with the deafening resonance of the heavy artillery. The armor-piercing rounds tore through the mass of infected, ripping limbs free of their bodies. Ticking off the seconds in his mind, he continued to pummel the crowd below. Before he reached the two minute mark, the belt feeding the machine gun ammunition delivered its last round. Abandoning the weapon and easing himself back to his feet, Mike looked down to his loyal canine companion.

"Well, girl, you up for a jog?" he asked with a smile. With a short bark in reply, Mike turned to follow the trail Lisa had come along to inform him of the waiting ship. As he took his first step, he heard the soft snap of a twig breaking behind him. Immediately, his left hand dragged one of his Glocks from its holster as he spun towards the direction of the sound.

As the landscape lurched across his vision, Mike saw the gunman he had shot earlier now desperately clinging to a tree for support with one hand, while the other leveled a small revolver at him. Barely completing his turn, Mike's finger found the trigger and a single shot sounded through the trees. The man lost his grip on the revolver and slumped to the ground.

He began to exhale in relief when his throat convulsed, forcing the air out in a cough. A warm, metallic liquid filled his mouth and dripped from his chin. With the back of his free hand, Mike wiped his face and stared at the deep red blood that covered his hand. Left arm still extended and holding his gun, he glanced down to find a small hole in his shirt. The hole was surrounded by an expanding ring of red saturation. A second cough ripped from his chest and blood splattered to the ground below.

The gun in his hand soon felt immensely heavy and he let it slip from him. With a numb thud, he crashed to a kneeling position as his legs gave out from beneath him. His right hand moved to the wound in his gut and the warmth of his blood flowed through his fingers. Gazelle sat in front of him, her head tilting with the same confusion that plagued him. She leaned forward to lick his left hand, dangling loosely at his side.

He tried to speak to her, but further coughing wracked his body, though now those coughs mixed with the gurgling rattle of approaching death. Intending to only fall back on his haunches, Mike slipped to the ground completely as his body no longer obeyed his commands.

The ground beneath his head was hard as his eyes stared into the canopy of green above. A nervous flash of gray fur danced back and forth in his peripheral vision. *Go to the boat, baby,* he thought silently, no longer able to speak. But Mike knew she would never leave his side. Instead, she nudged his head with her own, the cool wetness of her nose unnoticed by her master as icy numbness spread throughout his body.

Loss of feeling was soon followed by the inability to taste; though still expelling blood through his mouth, his tongue no longer recoiled from the harsh metallic tang. A consuming silence settled across the woods, real or imagined, Mike could no longer tell. The beating of his heart, slowly winding down, throbbed raucously in his head. The edges of his vision began to blur as he stared skyward. The branches and leaves were stirred by a gentle wind, though to Mike the motion was magnificently slow. Where some parts of his sight melded and hazed together, his eyes seemed to narrow their focus to a hawk-like perception. Dozens of feet above him, he could see the lingering drops of the earlier rain as they slid along the thinly veined leaves.

So beautiful, the voice in his mind spoke. *This is why we fought.*

A second sound made its way to his attention. Distant at first, but sounding closer the more he forced his thoughts towards it. Recognition finally reached him, and he heard the alarmed barking of the dog by his side. The miraculous and beautiful nature above him was then obscured by its converse monstrosity. His eyes stayed locked with the creature's own as their faces drew together. Like an animal determining the quality of its quarry, the Til sniffed loudly along the edges of Mike's face. It lingered for the briefest of moments at the flow of blood at his mouth. A blistered tongue slipped from the Til's lips and traced a short line down his chin. With what Mike thought was disgust, the creature pulled away from him.

It won't feed on the dead, Mike's voice echoed in his head. Laughter erupted in his thoughts. He had spent six years avoiding the bite of these monsters, and now, at his weakest and most vulnerable, the monster before him was dissatisfied with the meal.

The Til shifted its gaze from Mike to a spot over his shoulder. The infected man's thin lips drew back into a vile snarl as it growled antagonistically. A smaller, but no less vicious growl and bark was offered in return.

Gazelle, Mike shouted silently. *NO! You bastard…me…feed on me!!*

The arching branches returned to his view as the Til leapt towards its prey. A single tear escaped Mike's eye as the sky turned to black, the sounds about him faded, and he slipped into the emptiness of death.

* * *

"But, I don't want to."

"Then you're not coming with us."

The nine-year old watched his brother begin to pedal away down the block with his two friends. Indecision and fear gave way to pride, and the boy quickly mounted his own bicycle and spun his legs furiously to catch up to the trio. Though only a few years separated them, Jimmy was now at the age where he viewed his little brother tagging along as a burden. With a subtle glance over his shoulder,

Jimmy saw his brother breathing hard and he slowed his own pace out of pity.

Their destination that day was the quarry three miles across town. The northeast summer was at its peak, and the swimming hole offered not only a much needed break from the stifling heat, but also a local rite of passage. Many of the kids in Jimmy's grade had already made the jump off the quarry's high ledge. Jimmy and his friends had yet to set foot on the rocky outcropping. The plan had been to begin earlier than midday, but the boys' mother demanded that all their household chores be completed before disappearing for the day.

"It may be summer," she had said. "But you still have work to do."

The brothers rushed through their tasks with less than perfect efficiency. After an inspection of their efforts, the boys' mother frowned with a sigh and a shake of her head, but allowed the two to be on their way. She was of course unaware of the adventure that awaited them. Jimmy's brother was also kept in the dark about the journey, and when he found out his fear had caused him to balk at the trip. But now, drenched with sweat, the four found themselves carelessly dropping their bikes to the ground and walking up to the cliff face.

The real reason Jimmy wanted to go earlier was the hope that the quarry would be empty and if he chickened out none but his friends and brother would be the wiser. This late in the day, though, they found the place crowded with teens of varying ages. The older ones smoked cigarettes smuggled from the packs' of their parents, jumping to the blue water below after they flicked the butts from their hands. The younger teens milled about, mimicking the mannerism of their older counterparts as best they could in an effort to appear "cool." A couple of classmates greeted Jimmy and his friends, but the butterflies in his stomach made their words distant. His eyes flickered to the edge of the cliff.

His two friends made their running jumps into the open air, both shouting wildly as their bodies descended and crashed into the glassy water with a splash. Seconds later each boy's head crested the surface and triumphant exclamations echoed of the stone walls. Jimmy chewed the edges of his lip as he walked over to his brother.

"I'll jump first to show you it's okay, and then you can jump," he told him.

With paralyzing fear in his eyes, the younger sibling nodded his head. Jimmy wondered if his own face expressed the same dread he saw etched across his brother's face. With a deep breath, he began a long stride that quickly turned into a run. The edge of the cliff raced towards him until his body sprang into the air. Wind rushed over his body as gravity took control and pulled him down. Remembering the stories of pain told by older boys, Jimmy kept his legs tightly closed and his arms pinned to the sides of his chest.

Faster than it had begun, his body plunged into the sun-warmed water, and he found himself floating to the surface. Exhilaration raced through him as he looked back towards the heights from where he had jumped. The small shape of his brother was visible against the blinding sun.

"Come on!" Jimmy shouted to him, but the boy did not move. Finally, after numerous calls of encouragement, his brother backed away from the edge. Jimmy was unsure if the disappearance meant his brother would make the jump or if his fear had gotten the better of him.

It was only a moment's time before his question was answered. His brother's small body cleared the edge of the cliff and began its fall. Jimmy swam the short distance to where his brother had splashed down. When he returned to the surface, the boy's face was still a visage of panic.

"What's wrong?" Jimmy asked him.

"I hit a rock with my knee," the boy simpered as he fought back tears.

Jimmy took his brother's arm over his shoulder and helped him swim over to the rocky shore line of the bowl-shaped quarry. Once out of the water, Jimmy could see why his brother was close to crying. A large gash on his left knee dug close to the bone, while a sickening flap of skin, the size of a half-dollar, hung from the bloody wound.

One of the other people on the lower level of the quarry handed Jimmy a shirt that he then pressed against his brother's knee. The younger boy winced from the action.

"You have to keep pressure on it," Jimmy told the boy.

"I didn't want to do it," he replied through sniffles.

Jimmy smiled at his brother. "I know. I shouldn't have made you. But you did it, Mikey! You were afraid and you did it anyway! That's really brave."

"Yeah?" he asked, not sure if his older brother was being truthful.

"Yeah, it really was," Jimmy replied before reminding his brother, "Mikey, you have to keep pressure it."

* * *

"You have to keep pressure on it," a familiar voice spoke, not Jimmy's though. This one was older, more mature.

A second voice said something in response but the words jumbled together incoherently. Blurred shadows, black forms against white, danced across his vision. He was sure he was floating as the world rocked to and fro with soothing gentility.

"Come with us," the second voice said. The words clearer to him now.

"I can't," spoke the first. "Not now."

He could sense the owner of the first voice withdraw from his proximity, leaving only the one shadow which had grown more distinct.

"Mike, can you hear me? Look at me, Mike."

The shadow soon became detailed and he recognized Paul standing over him.

"There ya go, buddy. You're on the boat, Mike. The doc's

going to patch you up in a minute. Just hang in there. You're going to be fine and waking up in Cuba," Paul said to him.

"How...here?" Mike asked weakly.

"It was Derrick, Mike. He followed us, and found you. He brought you to the ship."

As he tried to speak again, the familiar lapping of his skin by a warm tongue followed by the nuzzling of a wet nose brought a smile to his weary face. Derrick had saved them both it seemed.

Around him, Mike began to hear feet scurrying purposefully. Men shouted orders across the ship's deck, and the low rumble of the engine reverberated as a soft breeze against his skin told him the ship was beginning its journey.

"Let's get him down there. Their infirmary is pretty well stocked, so I have everything I need," came Dr. Marena's voice.

"Okay, Mike, the doc's ready," Paul informed him. "It's going to be okay now, Mike. We're going to Cuba. It's over, Mike. We're safe."

"Safe," Mike said, as hands lifted him from the deck and gently carried him below deck.

THE END.

The story continues in:
The Tilian Effect:
Book Two of The Pandemic Sequence

PERMUTED PRESS

AMONG THE LIVING
BY TIMOTHY W. LONG

The dead walk. Now the real battle for Seattle has begun. Lester has a new clientele, the kind that requires him to deal lead instead of drugs. Mike suspects a conspiracy lies behind the chaos. Kate has a dark secret: she's a budding young serial killer. These survivors, along with others, are drawn together in their quest to find the truth behind the spreading apocalypse.

PERMUTEDPRESS.COM

AMONG THE DEAD
BY TIMOTHY W. LONG

Seattle is under siege by masses of living dead, and the military struggles to prevent the virus from spreading outside the city. Kate is tired of sitting around. When she learns that a rescue mission is heading back into the chaos, she jumps at the chance to tag along and put her unique skill set and, more importantly, swords to use.

PERMUTED PRESS

PERMUTED PRESS

ROADS LESS TRAVELED: THE PLAN
BY C. DULANEY

Ask yourself this: If the dead rise tomorrow, are you ready? Do you have a plan? Kasey, a strong-willed loner, has something she calls The Zombie Plan. But every plan has its weaknesses, and a freight train of tragedy is bearing down on Kasey and her friends. In the darkness that follows, Kasey's Plan slowly unravels: friends lost, family taken, their stronghold reduced to ashes.

PERMUTEDPRESS.COM

MURPHY'S LAW (ROADS LESS TRAVELED BOOK 2)
BY C. DULANEY

Kasey and the gang were held together by a set of rules, their Zombie Plan. It kept them alive through the beginning of the End. But when the chaos faded, they became careless, and Murphy's Law decided to pay a long-overdue visit. Now the group is broken and scattered with no refuge in sight. Those remaining must make their way across West Virginia in search of those who were stolen from them.

PERMUTEDPRESS.COM

SHADES OF GRAY (ROADS LESS TRAVELED BOOK 3)
BY C. DULANEY

Kasey and the gang have come full circle through the crumbling world. Working for the National Guard, they realize old friends and fellow survivors are disappearing. When the missing start to reappear as walking corpses, the group sets out on another journey to discover the truth. Their answers wait in the West Virginia Command Center.

PERMUTED PRESS

PERMUTED PRESS

INFECTION:
ALASKAN UNDEAD APOCALYPSE
BY SEAN SCHUBERT

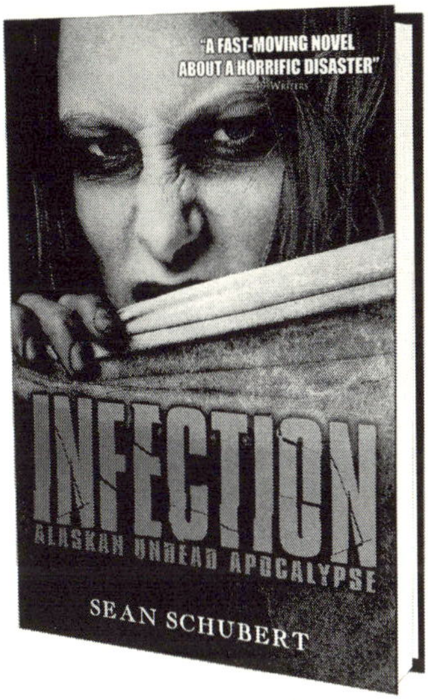

Anchorage, Alaska: gateway to serene wilderness of The Last Frontier. No stranger to struggle, the city on the edge of the world is about to become even more isolated. When a plague strikes, Anchorage becomes a deadly trap for its citizens. The only two land routes out of the city are cut, forcing people to fight or die as the infection spreads.

PERMUTEDPRESS.COM

CONTAINMENT
(ALASKAN UNDEAD APOCALYPSE BOOK 2)
BY SEAN SCHUBERT

Running. Hiding. Surviving. Anchorage, once Alaska's largest city, has fallen. Now a threatening maze of death, the city is firmly in the cold grip of a growing zombie horde. Neil Jordan and Dr. Caldwell lead a small band of desperate survivors through the maelstrom. The group has one last hope: that this nightmare has been contained, and there still exists a sane world free of infection.

PERMUTED PRESS

PERMUTED PRESS

MAD SWINE: THE BEGINNING

BY STEVEN PAJAK

People refer to the infected as "zombies," but that's not what they really are. Zombie implies the infected have died and reanimated. The thing is, they didn't die. They're just not human anymore. As the infection spreads and crazed hordes--dubbed "Mad Swine"--take over the cities, the residents of Randall Oaks find themselves locked in a desperate struggle to survive in the new world.

PERMUTEDPRESS.COM

MAD SWINE: DEAD WINTER

BY STEVEN PAJAK

Three months after the beginning of the Mad Swine outbreak, the residents of Randall Oaks have reached their breaking point. After surviving the initial outbreak and a war waged with their neighboring community, Providence, their supplies are severely close to depletion. With hostile neighbors at their flanks and hordes of infected outside their walls, they have become prisoners within their own community.

PERMUTED PRESS

PERMUTED PRESS

DEAD MEAT
BY PATRICK & CHRIS WILLIAMS

The city of River's Edge has been quarantined due to a rodent borne rabies outbreak. But it quickly becomes clear to the citizens that the infection is something much, much worse than rabies... The townsfolk are attacked and fed upon by packs of the living dead. Gavin and Benny attempt to survive the chaos in River's Edge while making their way north in search of sanctuary.

PERMUTEDPRESS.COM

ROTTER WORLD
BY SCOTT M. BAKER

Eight months ago vampires released the Revenant Virus on humanity. Both species were nearly wiped out. The creator of the virus claims there is a vaccine that will make humans and vampires immune to the virus, but it's located in a secure underground facility five hundred miles away. To retrieve the vaccine, a raiding party of humans and vampires must travel down the devastated East Coast.

PERMUTED PRESS

PERMUTED PRESS

THE BECOMING
BY JESSICA MEIGS

The Michaluk Virus has escaped the CDC, and its effects are widespread and devastating. Most of the population of the southeastern United States have become homicidal cannibals. As society rapidly crumbles under the hordes of infected, three people--Ethan, a Memphis police officer; Cade, his best friend; and Brandt, a lieutenant in the US Marines--band together against the oncoming crush of death.

PERMUTEDPRESS.COM

THE BECOMING: GROUND ZERO (BOOK 2)
BY JESSICA MEIGS

After the Michaluk Virus decimated the southeast, Ethan and his companions became like family. But the arrival of a mysterious woman forces them to flee from the infected, and the cohesion the group cultivated is shattered. As members of the group succumb to the escalating dangers on their path, new alliances form, new loves develop, and old friendships crumble.

PERMUTEDPRESS.COM

THE BECOMING: REVELATIONS (BOOK 3)
BY JESSICA MEIGS

In a world ruled by the dead, Brandt Evans is floundering. Leadership of their dysfunctional group wasn't something he asked for or wanted. Their problems are numerous: Remy Angellette is grief-stricken and suicidal, Gray Carter is distant and reclusive, and Cade Alton is near death. And things only get worse.

PERMUTED PRESS

PERMUTED PRESS

PAVLOV'S DOGS

BY D.L. SNELL & THOM BRANNAN

WEREWOLVES Dr. Crispin has engineered the saviors of mankind: soldiers capable of transforming into beasts. ZOMBIES Ken and Jorge get caught in a traffic jam on their way home from work. It's the first sign of a major outbreak. ARMAGEDDON Should Dr. Crisping send the Dogs out into the zombie apocalypse to rescue survivors? Or should they hoard their resources and post the Dogs as island guards?

PERMUTEDPRESS.COM

THE OMEGA DOG

BY D.L. SNELL & THOM BRANNAN

Twisting and turning through hordes of zombies, cartel territory, Mayan ruins, and the things that now inhabit them, a group of survivors must travel to save one man's family from a nightmarish third world gone to hell. But this time, even best friends have deadly secrets, and even allies can't be trusted - as a father's only hope of getting his kids out alive is the very thing that's hunting him down.

PERMUTED PRESS

11802298R00151

Made in the USA
San Bernardino, CA
28 May 2014